JOHN BANVILLE

The Infinities

PICADOR

First published 2009 by Picador

First published in paperback 2009 by Picador

This edition first published 2010 by Picador
an imprint of Pan Macmillan, a division of Macmillan Publishers Limited
Pan Macmillan, 20 New Wharf Road, London N1 9RR
Basingstoke and Oxford
Associated companies throughout the world
www.panmacmillan.com

ISBN 978-0-330-51391-3

Visit **www.picador.com** to read more about all our books
and to buy them. You will also find features, author interviews and
news of any author events, and you can sign up for e-newsletters
so that you're always first to hear about our new releases.

The Infinities

JOHN BANVILLE was born in Wexford, Ireland, in 1945.
He is the author of fourteen previous novels, including
The Sea, which won the 2005 Man Booker Prize.
He has received a literary award from the
Lannan Foundation. He lives in Dublin.

I

OF THE THINGS we fashioned for them that they might be comforted, dawn is the one that works. When darkness sifts from the air like fine soft soot and light spreads slowly out of the east then all but the most wretched of humankind rally. It is a spectacle we immortals enjoy, this minor daily resurrection, often we will gather at the ramparts of the clouds and gaze down upon them, our little ones, as they bestir themselves to welcome the new day. What a silence falls upon us then, the sad silence of our envy. Many of them sleep on, of course, careless of our cousin Aurora's charming matutinal trick, but there are always the insomniacs, the restless ill, the lovelorn tossing on their solitary beds, or just the early-risers, the busy ones, with their knee-bends and their cold showers and their fussy little cups of black ambrosia. Yes, all who witness it greet the dawn with joy, more or less, except of course the condemned man, for whom first light will be the last, on earth.

Here is one, standing at a window in his father's house,

watching the day's early glow suffuse the sky above the massed trees beyond the railway line. He is condemned not to death, not yet, but to a life into which he feels he does not properly fit. He is barefoot, and wearing pyjamas that his mother on his arrival last night found for him somewhere in the house, threadbare cotton, pale blue with a bluer stripe—whose are they, whose were they? Could they be his, from long ago? If so, it is from very long ago, for he is big now and they are far too small, and pinch him at the armpits and the fork. But that is the way with everything in this house, everything pinches and chafes and makes him feel as if he were a child again. He is reminded of how when he was a little boy here his grandmother would dress him up for Christmas, or his birthday, or some other festival, tugging him this way and that and spitting on a finger to plaster down a stubborn curl, and how he would feel exposed, worse than naked, in those already outmoded scratchy short-trousered tweed suits the colour of porridge that the old woman made him wear, and the white shirts with starched collars and, worst of all, the tartan dicky bows that it afforded him a wan, vindictive pleasure to pull out to the limit of their elastic and let snap back with a pleasingly loud smack when someone was making a speech or singing a song or the priest was holding up the communion wafer like, he always thought, the nurse on the Hospital Sweepstakes tickets brandishing aloft the winning number. That is how it is: life, tight-buttoned life, fits him ill, making him too much aware of himself and what he glumly takes to be his unalterable littleness of spirit.

He hears from somewhere unseen the faint, muffled clopping of small hoofs; it will be the early postman on his pony, in Thurn und Taxis livery, with his tricorn cap and his post-horn looped on his shoulder.

The man at the window is called Adam. He is not yet thirty, the young son of an elderly father, 'product', as he once overheard that twice-married father say with a sardonic laugh, 'of my second coming.' Idly he admires the dense, mud-purple shadows under the trees. A kind of smoke hovers ankle-deep on the grey-seeming grass. Everything is different at this hour. An early blackbird flies across at a slant swiftly from somewhere to somewhere else, its lacquered wing catching an angled glint of sunlight, and he cannot but think with a pang of the early worm. He fancies he can hear faintly the fleet-winged creature's piping panic note.

Gradually now he is becoming aware of something he cannot identify, a tremor that is all around, as if the air itself were quaking. It grows more intense. Alarmed, he takes a soft step backwards into the protective dimness of the room. Clearly he can hear the sluggish thudding of his heart. A part of his mind knows what is happening but it is not the part that thinks. Everything is atremble now. Some small mechanism behind him in the room— he does not look, but it must be a clock—sets up in its innards an urgent, silvery tinkling. The floorboards creak in trepidation. Then from the left the thing appears, huge, blunt-headed, nudging its way blindly forward, and rolls to a shuddering halt and stands there in front of the trees, gasping clouds of steam. The lights are still on in the carriages; they make the dawn draw back a little. There are bent heads in the long windows, like the heads of seals—are they all asleep?—and the conductor with his ticket thing is going up an aisle, clambering along hand over hand from seat-back to seat-back as if he were scaling a steep incline. The silence round about is large and somehow aggrieved. The engine gives a testy snort, seeming to paw the earth. Why it should stop at this spot every morning no one in the house can say. There is not another dwelling for miles, the line is clear in both directions, yet just here is where it halts. His mother has complained repeatedly to the railway company, and once even was moved to write to someone in the government, but got no reply, for all the renown of her husband's name. 'I would not mind,' she will say in a tone of mild sorrow, 'what noise it made going past—after all, your father in his wisdom insisted on us setting up home practically on the railway line—but the stopping is what wakes me.'

A dream that he dreamt in the night returns to him, a fragment of it. He was dashing through the dust of immemorial battle bearing something in his arms, large but not heavy, a precious but burdensome cargo—what was it?—and all about him were the mass of warriors bellowing and the ringing clash of swords and spears, the swish of arrows, the creak and crunch of chariot wheels. A venerable site, an antique war.

Thinking of his mother, he listens for her step above him, for he knows she is awake. Though the house is large and rambling the floors are mostly of polished bare boards and sounds travel easily and far. He does not want to deal with his mother, just now. Indeed, he finds it always awkward to deal with her. It is not that he hates or even resents her, as so many mortal sons are said to resent and hate their mothers—they should try dealing with our frenzied and vindictive dams, up here on misty Mount Olympus—only he does not think she is like a mother at all. She is absurdly young, hardly twenty years older than he is, and seems all the time to be getting younger, or at least not older, so that he has the worrying sensation of steadily catching up on her. She too appears to be aware of this phenomenon, and to find it not at all strange. In fact, since he was old enough to notice how young she is he has detected now and then, or imagines he has detected, a certain tight-lipped briskness in her manner towards him, as if she were impatient for him to attain some impossible majority so that, coevals at last, they might turn arm in arm and set out together into a future that would be—what? Fatherless, now, for him, and, for her, husbandless. For his father is dying. That is why he is here, foolish in these too-small pyjamas, watching the dawn break on this midsummer day.

Shaken by thoughts of death and dying he forces himself to fix his attention on the train again. One of the seal-heads has turned and he is being regarded across the smoky expanse of lawn by a small boy with a pale, pinched face and enormous eyes. How intensely the child is staring at the house, how hungry his scrutiny— what is it he is seeking, what secret knowledge, what revelation? The young man is convinced the young boy

7

can see him, standing here, yet surely it cannot be—surely the window from outside is a black blank or, the other extreme, blindingly aflame with the white-gold glare of the sun that seemed to take such a long time to rise but now is swarming strongly up the eastern sky. Apart from those avidly questing eyes the boy's features are unremarkable, or at least are so from what of them can be made out at this distance. But what is it he is looking for, to make him stare so? Now the engine bethinks itself and gives a sort of shake, and a repeated loud metallic clank runs along the carriages from coupling to coupling, and with a groan the brutish thing begins to move off, and as it moves the risen sun strikes through each set of carriage windows in turn, taking its revenge on the still-burning light bulbs, putting them to shame with its irresistible harsh fire. The boy, craning, stares to the last.

Adam is cold, and the soles of his bare feet are sticking unpleasantly to the chill, tacky floorboards. He is not yet fully awake but in a state between sleep and waking in which everything appears unreally real. When he turns from the window he sees the early light falling in unaccustomed corners, at odd angles, and a bookshelf edge is sharp as the blade of a guillotine. From the depths of the room the convex glass cover of the clock on the mantelpiece, reflecting the window's light, regards him with a monocular, blank glare. He thinks again of the child on the train and is struck as so often by the mystery of otherness. How can he be a self and others others since the others too are selves, to themselves? He knows, of course, that it is no mystery but a matter merely of perspective. The eye, he tells himself, the eye makes the horizon. It is a thing he has often heard his father say, cribbed from someone else, he supposes. The child on the train was a sort of horizon to him and he a sort of horizon to the child only because each considered himself to be at the centre of something—to be, indeed, that centre itself—and that is the simple solution to the so-called mystery. And yet.

He pads across the floor—at his passing that busy clock on the mantel gives a single soft admonitory chime —and opens the door into the hall and stops short with a grunt of fright, his heart setting up again its slurred clamour, like an excited dog pawing to be let out.

He quickly sees that the figure in the hall is only his sister. She is squatting on her haunches at one of the little slanted doors in the white-painted panelling that closes off the space under the stairs. 'For God's sake!' he says. 'What are you doing?'

She turns up to him her miniature white face and yet again he sees in his mind the child's face at the train window. 'Mice,' she says.

He sighs. She is in one of her states. 'For God's sake,' he repeats, wearily this time.

She goes back to rummaging in the cupboard and he folds his arms and leans one shoulder against the wall and watches her, shaking his head. She is nineteen and so much younger than her years, and yet possessed too of an awful ancientness—'That one,' Granny Godley used to say of her darkly, 'that one has been here before.' He asks how she knows there are mice in the cupboard and she laughs dismissively. 'Not the cupboard, you fool,' she says, the sleek dark back of her head—another seal!—aquiver with contempt. 'In my room.'

She rises, wiping her hands on her skinny flanks. She does not meet his eye but bites her lip and frowns off to the side; she does not meet anyone's eye, if she can help it.

'What is that you're wearing?' he asks.

It is another pair of ill-fitting pyjamas, these in faded blue silk, hanging limp on her meagre frame, the sleeves and legs absurdly too long; hers are too long, his too short, as if to mark something sadly comical about them both. 'They're Pa's,' she says sulkily.

He sighs again. 'Oh, Pete.' Yet who is he to talk?—whose cast-offs is he wearing?

His sister's name is Petra, he calls her Pete. She is tiny and thin with a heart-shaped face and haunted eyes. For a long time she had her head shaved bare but now the hair is beginning to grow back, a bulrush-brown nap that covers her skull evenly all over. Her hands are the scrabbly pink claws of a rodent. The mice, her brother thinks, must recognise one of their own.

'How do you know?' he asks.

'How do I know what?'—a petulant whine.

'About the mice.'

'I see them. They run around the floor in the dark.'

'In the dark. And you see them.'

She blinks slowly and swallows, as if she might be about to cry, but it is only a tic, one among the many that afflict her. 'Leave me alone,' she mutters.

He is so much larger than she is.

As a child she used to sleepwalk, appearing at the top of the stairs with her eyes rolled up into her head and her mouse-claws lifted in front of her chest. At the memory the small hairs stir at the back of Adam's neck. His loony sister, hearing voices, seeing things.

With a cocked big toe he pushes shut the cupboard door. She makes a gesture towards it, her left arm jerking out stiffly from her side and a finger childishly pointing and then the arm falling weakly back. 'I thought there were traps,' she says. 'There used to be traps kept in there.'

When she did that with her arm he caught a whiff of her, a musty, greyish smell, like the smell in the bedroom of an invalid. She does not bathe enough. Her mother says she despairs of her. As if they had not all done that, long ago, except for Pa, of course, who claims she is his inspiration, his muse made flesh, the invariable quantity in all his equations. But Pa claims many things. Or claimed: for Pa is in the past tense, now.

The light here in the hall is still dim but the sun is burning gaudily in the front door's stained-glass panes as if, Adam thinks, he and his sister were confined indoors while outside a gay party is in full swing. In their clownishly ill-fitting pairs of pyjamas they stand before each other in silence, the large young man and the diminutive girl, at a loss, each thinking and yet not thinking of what it is that constrains them so: the fact of their dying father, whose sleeplessly sleeping presence fills the house like a fog. In these latter days no one in the house dares speak above a murmur, though the doctors blandly insist that nothing any longer passes beyond the portals of Pa's hearing—but how can they be so certain, Adam would like to know, where do they get such assurance? His father is in another kingdom now, far-off to be sure, but may it not be that news from the old realm reaches him still?

'Why are you up so early?' Petra asks accusingly. 'You never get up this early.'

'The time of year,' Adam says, 'these short nights—I can't sleep.'

This answer she receives in silence, sullenly. It is she who is supposed to be the sleepless one. Her unsleep-ingness, like their father's gradual dying, is a pervasive pressure that makes the atmosphere in the house feel as dense as the air inside a balloon.

'Is the Dead Horse coming down today?' he asks her.

She gives a shrug that is more a twitch. 'He said he would. I suppose he will.'

They can get no more from this topic and are silent again. He has that feeling of helpless exasperation his sister so often provokes in him. She stands as she always does, half turned away, at once expectant and cowering, as if longing to be embraced and at the same time in dread of it. When she was little she had no tickles and would squirm away from him with a scowl but then would lean back again, droopingly, unable to help herself, her sharp, narrow shoulders indrawn like folded wings and her head held to one side, seeming miserably to invite him to try again to make her squeal. How thin she had been, how thin and bony, like a sack half filled with sticks, and still is. Now she lifts a hand and scratches her scalp vigorously, making a sandpapery sound.

Adam feels light-headed, weightless, seeming to float an inch above the floor. He supposes it is to do with the supply of oxygen to the brain, or lack of it. His sister is right, he is not used to being up at this hour—*everything is different*—when the world looks like an imitation of itself, cunningly crafted yet discrepant in small but essential details. He thinks of Helen his wife asleep up in the room that used to be his when he was a boy. Stretched beside her rigid and wakeful in the pre-dawn dusk he had wanted to rouse her but had not had the heart, so soundly was she sleeping. He might go up now and lie down again on the too-narrow bed and close her to him, but something that is a sort of shyness, a sort of fear, even, holds him back.

Good thing, by the way, that this young husband does not know what my doughty Dad, the godhead himself, was doing to his darling wife up in that bedroom not an hour since in what she will imagine is a dream.

On the subject of fathers: Adam has not seen his yet. When they arrived last night he pleaded his and Helen's weariness after the journey and said they would go straight to bed. He thought that to visit the old man then would have been gruesome; he would have felt like a body-snatcher measuring up a fresh specimen, or a vampire-hunter breaking into a crypt. Although he has not told her so he thinks his mother should not have insisted on taking Pa out of the hospital. Bringing him home to die is a throwback, something Granny Godley would have approved. Yet this morning he is sorry that he did not go at once and at least look at him, his fallen father, for with each hour that passes it will be so much the harder to force himself up those stairs and into that sickroom. He does not know how he will behave at the side of what everyone, without saying so, has acknowledged is his father's deathbed. He has never been at a death before and hopes not to have to be present for this one.

Petra is still scratching, but with decreasing momentum, absently, like a cat slowly losing interest in its itch. He wishes he could help her, could assuage even one of her sore, inflamed spots. Yet he resents her, too, has always resented her, since before she was born, even, his usurper. He has a sudden clear memory of her as a baby in her cot, wrapped tight in a blanket, like a mummified yet all too living infanta. 'Oho, my bucko, she'll make you hop,' Granny Godley would say with a cackle, '—you'll think your arse is haunted!'

'Come on,' he says now brusquely to the girl, 'come on, and we'll have our breakfast.'

And sister and brother, these waifs, shuffle off into the shadows.

It is shadowed too up in the Sky Room where Adam Godley at the centre of a vast stillness is going about his dying. Yes, he too is Adam, like his son. By the way, apropos names and the like, I suppose I should before going further give some small account of myself, this voice speaking out of the void. Men have made me variously keeper of the dawn, of twilight and the wind, have called me Argeiphantes, he who makes clear the sky, and Logios, the sweet-tongued one, have dubbed me trickster, the patron of gamblers and all manner of mountebanks, have appointed me the guardian of crossroads, protector of travellers, have conferred on me the grave title Psychopompos, usher of the freed souls of men to Pluto's netherworld. For I am Hermes, son of old Zeus and Maia the cavewoman.

You don't say, you say.

I understand your scepticism. Why in such times as these would the gods come back to be among men? But the fact is we never left—you only stopped entertaining us. For how should we leave, we who cannot but be everywhere? We merely made it seem that we had withdrawn, for a decent interval, as if to say we know when we are not wanted. All the same, we cannot resist revealing ourselves to you once in a while, out of our incurable boredom, or love of mischief, or that lingering nostalgia we harbour for this rough world of our making—I mean this particular one, for of course there is an infinity of others just like it that we made and must keep ever vigilantly in our care. When on a summer's day a sudden gale tears through the treetops, or when out of the blue a soft rain falls like the fall of grace upon a painted saint, there one of us is passing by; when the earth buckles and opens its maw to eat cities whole, when the sea rises up and swallows an entire archipelago with its palms and straw huts and a myriad ululating natives, be assured that one of our number is seriously annoyed.

But what attention we lavished on the making of this poor place! The lengths we went to, the pains we took, that it should be plausible in every detail—planting in the rocks the fossils of outlandish creatures that never existed, distributing fake dark matter throughout the universe, even setting up in the cosmos the faintest of faint hums to mimic the reverberations of the initiating shot that is supposed to have set the whole shooting-match going. And to what end was all this craft, this labour, this scrupulous dissembling—to what end? So that the mud men that Prometheus and Athene between them made might think themselves the lords of creation. We have been good to you, giving you what you thought you wanted—yes, and look what you have done with it.

All this, of course, I cast in the language of humankind, necessarily. Were I to speak in my own voice, that is, the voice of a divinity, you would be baffled at the sound—in fact, you would not be able to hear me at all, so rarefied is our heavenly speech, compared to your barely articulate gruntings. Why, the music of the spheres has nothing on us. And these names—Zeus, Prometheus, grey-eyed Athene, Hermes, even—these are your constructions. We address each other, as it were, only as air, as light, as something like the quality of that deep, transparent blue you see when you peer into the highest vault of the empyrean. And Heaven—what is that? For us, the deathless ones, there is no Heaven, or Hell, either, no up, no down, only the infinite here, which is a kind of not-here. Think of that.

This moment past, in the blinking of your eye, I

girdled the earth's full compass thrice. Why these aerial acrobatics? For diversion, and to cool my heels. And because I could and you cannot. Oh, yes, we too are petty and vindictive, just like you, when we are put to it.

Adam, this Adam, has suffered a stroke. By the way, I pause to remark how oddly innocuous, even pretty, a term this is for something so unpleasant and, in this case, surely final—as if one of us had absent-mindedly laid a too-heavy hand upon his brow. Which is perfectly possible, since we are notorious for not knowing our own strength. Anyway, for some time prior to this stroke that he suffered old Adam had been subject, all unbeknownst, to a steady softening of the brain due to a gradual extravasation of blood in the area of the parietal lobe—yes, yes, I have also some expertise in matters medical, to meliorate the more obstreperous of my attributes—which means in other words he was already a goner before that catastrophic moment when, enthroned at morning within the necessary place—to put it as delicately as I may—he crouched too low and strained too strenuously in the effort of extruding a stool as hard as mahogany, and felt, actually felt, a blood vessel bursting in his brain, and toppled forward on to the floor, his face to the tiles and his scrawny bare bum in the air, and passed at once, with what in happier circumstances would have been a delicious smoothness, into death's vast and vaulted antechamber, where still he bides, in a state of conscious but incommunicate ataraxia, poised upon the point of oblivion.

He is not alone—as one of your most darkly glowing

luminants has observed, the living being is only a species of the dead, and a rare species at that. He senses the multitude of his fellows all about, uneasy and murmurous in their state of life-in-death. And I am here as well, of course. When our time comes we shall go together, he and I, into what is next, which I may not speak of.

His wife has entered the room, making hardly a sound, as is increasingly her wont these days. She feels she is becoming more and more a wraith, as if Adam in his last illness were siphoning something vital from her, drop by glistening drop. She closes the bedroom door softly behind her and stands motionless a moment, letting her eyes adjust to the dimness. A teeming sword of early sunlight is falling through a parting in the heavy curtains of the middle window, breaking its blade across the foot of the bed. The Sky Room is a most capricious touch added on to the house by the man who built it, the famously eccentric St John Blount, a timber eyrie set into the north-west—or is it south-east?—corner of the main edifice, glazed on three sides and surmounted by a conical roof with a metal weathervane in the shape of a fleeting, short-cloaked figure, wearing a pudding hat with a circular brim and bearing a staff, who can only be—well, me, I suppose. How disconcerting. I did not expect to encounter myself here, in such surroundings, at this elevation, especially in the form of a two-dimensional tin representation of a godling. My staff must double as a lightning rod—that is something, I suppose, flash and fire and the reek of brimstone; that will liven things up.

Ursula with a qualm acknowledges to herself how

restful she finds it being here. There is a dense, intent quality to the silence in the sickroom; it is like the silence that reigns deep down inside her and soothes her heart, even in the midst of so much inward tumult. She can make out his form now, supine in the big bed, but although she listens breathlessly she cannot hear him breathing. Perhaps—? At the unthought thought something stirs in her, a yearning something that she tries to deny but cannot. Yet why should she reprove herself? Everyone says the end will be a blessèd release. Those are the words they use, *a blessèd release*. Yes, she reflects bitterly, a release—but for whom? All except, perhaps, the one being released. For who can know but that Adam in some part of his mind might not be awake in a way and experiencing wonders? People who are deeply asleep seem unconscious but still may be dreaming the most fantastic things. Anyway, even if she cannot hear him she knows he has not gone. The elastic link between them has not been broken yet: she can feel still the old twanging tug. She is sure he is thinking, thinking away, she is sure of it.

She closes the chink in the curtains and at once the dark seems total, as if the world had been suddenly switched off. Feeling her way through the black and therefore somehow heavier air she advances to the bed soundlessly on slippered feet. In their early days together he used to call her his geisha girl for her pattering, rapidly stepping gait. She recalls the antique kimono he brought back for her from one of his trips—'A kimono from Kyoto for my geisha!'—cut from heavy, jade-green silk, a garment so exquisite she could not bring herself to wear it but folded it away in tissue paper in a drawer, from where subsequently it somehow disappeared. He had threatened to take the thing back—perhaps he did?—and give it to one of his girls, all those girls he said he was well aware she imagined that he had, hidden away. Then he looked at her, with his head back, fiercely smiling and showing his teeth, daring her to call his bluff. For it was a bluff, about the girls, about there not being any, she knew it, and he knew she knew it. That was a way of lying that amused him, saying a version of the truth in tones of high, mocking irony so that to challenge him would be to seem a hapless dolt.

Her eyes are growing used to the blinded dimness. She can see more than she wants to see. Uncanny, to enter this room each morning and find him just as she left him the night before, the blanket moulded smoothly to his form, the sheet uncreased, the cockscomb of silky hair—still black!—rising unruffled above the high, white dome of his forehead. His beard too is dark still, the spade-shaped, pointed beard that gives him the look of a faintly diabolical saint. She has always loved his skin, the moist cool translucent paleness of it that the years have not sullied. She hates, knowing how he would hate them, the plastic tubes that are threaded into his nostrils and held in place with strips of clear sticking-plaster. There are other tubes, farther down, hidden from sight by the bedclothes. What a trouble there was settling him here, Dr Fortune fidgeting and the nurses cross. But she insisted, and so determinedly it surprised everyone, herself included. 'He must be at home,' she kept on saying, ignoring all their objections. 'If he is to die he must die here.' She hated the cottage hospital he had been rushed to, a caricature off the lid of a chocolate box, grotesquely pretty with ivy and rambling roses and a glassed-in porch; imagine if Adam died there and along with her grief she had to put up with all that flummery. Old Fortune, who looks like Albert Schweitzer and has been the family's physician since Granny Godley's day, squeezed her hand and mumbled a mollifying word through the yellowed fringes of his moustache, but the two young nurses narrowed their eyes at her and stalked off, their backsides wagging professional disapproval.

By now her ears have become accustomed to the acoustics of the sickroom and she can hear her husband breathing, the faint rustle of air in the passages of his throat and chest. At the end of each indrawn breath comes a tiny flutter, like an impatient twiddling of fingers. She realises what it is that is familiar about this sound. It is just how he used to sigh when she did something that exasperated him, with just that same little fluttering flourish. She misses him, as though he were already gone. She feels a pain such as she thought only those who are still young can feel, new and sharply surprising, enough to take her breath away.

Something brushes past her in the air, less than a draught, more than a thought. She has sensed it before, in recent days. Whatever it is she is convinced it is not benign; she has the impression of haughtiness and a bridling resentment, as if something were bent on jostling her out of position. There are other strange phenomena too, other haunting effects. She has glimpses of figures that cease to be there when she tries to look at them directly, like floaters in the eye. She wakes in the night with a start, her heart pounding, as if there had been a tremendous noise, an explosion or a clap of thunder, which shook her out of sleep but of which there is not even an echo remaining. When she speaks to people on the telephone she is convinced there is a third party on the line, listening intently. She wonders fancifully if perhaps this angry revenant might not be the ghost of Adam's first wife, or of his long-dead mother, Granny Godley the old hag, come back to claim her son and carry him off with her to the land of the shades. You see?—they think it is the dead that haunt them, while the simple fact is, as her husband could tell her and has often tried to, they live amidst interpenetrant worlds and are themselves the sprites that throng the commingling air. For all she knows it might be one of her countless selves that she is meeting, drifting from another plane into this one all unawares.

Or perhaps it is merely my ever-attentive presence that she senses, the whirring of dainty wings on my hat and at my heels that she almost hears. But I ask—am I haughty? Do I bridle? A little, I suppose. A little.

She dislikes her name. Adam was able to tell her of St Ursula of Dumnonia, martyred at Cologne along with her eleven thousand virgins—'What a day that must have been, eh,' he said teasingly, lifting an eyebrow, *'im alten Köln?'*—although this Ursula was recently removed from the calendar of saints, in a fit of anti-German pique, by one of the more reform-minded English pontiffs. When the children were small they called her La, and still do. Adam is Pa and she is La. She wonders if there is ill-intent in their keeping on with these pet-names. She fears she has not been a good mother. She did her best with Adam but poor Petra was too much for her. Having Petra was the start of all her troubles. For nine months she was sick, vomiting all day and not able to keep anything down, until in the end she could not swallow even her own spit; with a shudder she recalls the nurse taking the glinting nickel dish of slime and floating froth out of her trembling hands and emptying it into the washbasin. Then at last the pallid little fish that was her daughter slithered out of her and lay gasping on her breast, so wearied already that no one expected she would live. But live she did, and was called Petra, another stone dropped into Ursula's already heavy heart.

She touches her husband's hand where it lies on the blanket. It has an unsettling feel, the skin brittle as greaseproof paper and the flesh pulpy underneath; it is like a package of scrap meat from the butcher's, chill and sinewy; it is not the hand that she remembers, so delicate and fine. That invisible presence barges past her again, or through her, rather, and she feels it is she that is without substance, as if she and not this other were the ghost. Her husband's eyelids spring open and his eyes after a moment of agitated searching find her face. She smiles with an effort and speaks his name softly. It is hard to make out his features in the dimness but she is loath to switch on the light. Dr Fortune assures her that it is her loving care that is keeping her husband alive and nothing else—why then does he look at her now with such seeming fury?

Her head is very bad today, very bad, she must take something soon to soothe it.

In the well of the kitchen the morning light has a sharply metallic sheen and the square of sunlit garden in the window behind the sink is garish and implausible, like a primitive painting of a jungle scene. Adam and his sister are seated at one end of the long deal table, hunched over cereal bowls. When their mother appears at the top of the three wooden steps that lead up to or down from the rest of the house they sense rather than hear her—Rex the elderly labrador, lying on his blanket in the corner, gives a few listless thumps of his tail but makes no effort to get up—and they stop eating and lift their faces and look at her. She sees again with a faint start how alike they are, despite Adam's great size and Petra's diminutiveness, each with the same broad brow and little sharp chin and ash-blue eyes so pale they are almost colourless. Perhaps because she had no siblings herself she finds family resemblance always a little eerie, even in her own offspring. Both of them take after her, for it was from her they inherited the wide forehead and sharp chin and azury eyes.

'How is he, today?' her son asks. His skin is mottled from the sun and he has a scorched, raw look. For some reason just now she finds well-nigh intolerable his palely candid gaze. 'Much the same,' she says, answering him, and Petra laughs, who knows why, making a nasty sound. Yes, sometimes she thinks her children dislike and resent her, as if she were not their mother at all but a person brought in to be in intimate charge of them, a heartless guardian, say, or a bitterly resented stepmother. But surely she is mistaken. These are the creatures she carried inside her and gave birth to and fed from her own breast, phoenix-like. She recalls Adam just now glaring at her with that vengeful fire in his eyes. 'He seems peaceful,' she says.

Her son considers her as she hovers on the stair at the far end of the long, high-ceilinged room. He seems unable to focus on her properly. She has a new quality, of being not entirely present, of seeming to hesitate on an invisible threshold that is there under her feet wherever she steps. She has become blurred, as if under a fine layer of dust. This must be the effect on her of the catastrophe that has befallen old Adam; she has lost the sense of herself. She is wearing a cotton dress like a smock and a baggy grey cardigan the hem of which sags below the level of her hips. Her hair, the colour of a knife-blade, is pulled back in two flattened wings and pinned at the nape of her neck. She descends the steps and comes forward and stands by the table, absently kneading the worn wood with the fingertips of one hand, as if to test its solidity. 'You're up early,' she says to both of them. 'Did the train wake you?'

Neither will answer. 'Roddy will be here later,' Petra says, looking aside frowningly. Her tone is truculent, as if to forestall disparaging comment. Roddy Wagstaff, dubbed the Dead Horse by her brother, is Petra's young man, or so convention has it, although everybody knows it is not she but her famous father that Roddy comes to visit.

'Oh,' her mother murmurs, and a pained frown passes over her already frowning face, 'then there'll have to be lunch!' Since Adam fell ill the household has been content to shift for itself, but a visitor must be fed a proper, sit-down meal; Adam would insist on it, for in such small matters he is a strict observer of the conventions.

'We could take him into town,' her son says, without conviction. 'Doesn't that place what's-it-called serve lunches?'

'Oh, yes,' Petra says archly, with a sneer, 'let us all go into town and have a lovely time—we can bring Pa and prop him up at the head of the table and feed him soup through his tubes.'

She glares at her cereal bowl. Under the table her left leg is going like a sewing-machine. Adam and his mother exchange an expressionless look. Her father's collapse has been for Petra a great excitement, being at last a calamity commensurate with the calamitous state of her mind. The question of lunch is let hang. In the corner Rex the dog gives a contented, shivery sigh. He can see me plainly, lolling at my ease in mid-air, with folded arms, in the midst of these sad souls, but it is nothing to him, whose world is already rife with harmless spectres.

Petra has her subject now and will not let go of it. In a thick, tense voice, goitrous with sarcasm, she embroiders upon the notion of a family lunch in town to which her father would be brought—'in a hammock maybe or a sling slung between us or one of those things with two poles that red indians drag the wounded along behind them in'—and at which they would all celebrate his achievements and make speeches and raise toasts to him as man, as father and as savant. When she gets going like this she has a way of speaking not directly to the others in the room but to the air beside her, as if there were present an invisible twin version of herself off whom she is bouncing her taunts and who will give to them, thus relayed, an added extension of sarcasm. Adam and her mother say nothing, for they know there will be no stopping her until she has exhausted herself. The dog, lying with his muzzle between his paws, eyes her with wary speculation. The table-top vibrates rapidly along with the girl's bobbing knee. Adam tries to eat his cereal, which has gone gluey; he sees himself yet again as a boy, sitting at this table, listening to his father talking, in that coolly vehement, uninterruptible way that he did, and recalls how he would feel his throat thicken and his eyes scald with inexplicable tears he dare not shed, shaming tears, heavy and unmanageable like big drops of mercury. He glances sidelong at his sister now and sees the dab of sallow light shaking in the spoon-shaped hollow above her clavicle as she tries not to choke on the torrent of words that wells up out of her unstaunchably.

Their mother, standing by the table, regards her son and daughter with a troubled gaze. They seem to her still so young, hardly more than children, really, even Adam—especially Adam—with that babyishly fat overlip that trembles so when he is excited or upset. She notices the bowls the two of them have been eating from. Why does it irritate her that they are unmatched? Latterly so many things irritate her. She tries not to feel resentful of her son for so far not having set foot in the room where his father lies dying. She supposes it is simply the fear of death, its awful presence, that prevents him. But after all he is not a child, however he may seem. She crosses to the sink and looks out through the big, many-paned window above it at the sunlit day, a hand lifted vaguely to her face.

She thinks of Adam growing up in the humid conspiracy that was his Granny Godley. The old woman had seized on him early, a hostage against all the slights she imagined herself the victim of. Then Petra was born and her brother was at once usurped. A blundering, blond fellow he was, with a huge, round head, baffled at being so unceremoniously thrust aside in favour of this tiny, watchful creature clasped jealously in his grandmother's bony embrace. For the coming of Petra had brought on a grisly transformation in the old woman: she turned tender and clumsily solicitous, reminding Ursula of those shaggy clambering rust-coloured primates in the zoo, all hooped arms and peeled-back lips and baleful starings, that her husband was so fascinated by and would make her come with him to see on Sunday afternoons when Adam was a baby. Granny Godley was dying of a damaged heart and grimly turned over each new day like a playing card from a steadily diminishing deck, anticipating of each one that it would be the ace of spades, while what had come instead was this solemn-eyed coat card, this miniature queen of diamonds, swaddled and uncannily still and always looking at something off to the side that only she it seemed could see, clutching in her white-knuckled fist the wilting flower of the future.

'And and and,' Petra is saying now, her voice ashake on the sliding crest of its arc, 'and and and *and*—'

—And I it is who have contrived these things: this house, the train, the boy at the train window, that slanting blackbird, the dawn itself, and this mother musing on love and her losses, and her troubled daughter at the table gabbling out her woe, and the wife asleep in her husband's boyhood bed, and her husband, young Adam here, who presently will make up his mind and rise reluctantly from the table and ascend those three short steps and be borne upwards on my invisible wings into the presence of his earthly father.

AND LOOK, here he is, old Adam, the dying progenitor himself. Dying, yet he cannot conceive of a world from which he will have departed. No, that is not right. He could conceive of it. He can conceive of anything. Conception of impossible things is what he does best. He was ever pregnable by the world. I note the shifting of tenses. What I should have said is that he does not wish to conceive of a world from which, et cetera. Of course, he knows that after him everything will continue on much as before, except that there will be a minuscule absence, a barely detectable gap in the so-called grand scheme, one unit fewer now. Or not even that, not even an empty space where he once was, for all will rush immediately to fill that vacuum. Pft. Gone. Recollections of him will remain in the minds of others for a while, but presently those others too will die and his few relics with them. And then all will be dark.

What of his work? What of his work. He cares

nothing for their so-called immortality if he is not to be here to savour its vaunted consolations.

Me.

Me.

Me.

As to his immediate condition, he has been pronounced vegetate. And so he is, if we take this word in the old, not to say archaic, sense of being endowed with vegetable life. His heart beats, his blood circulates, his lymph courses, even his digestive system goes on mumbling and munching, making the best of the insipid wheys and saps that are fed to him through his tubes day and night without pause. But does a vegetable see, does a vegetable hear, does a vegetable—and this surely is the clincher—does a vegetable cogitate?

The doctors have not witnessed him opening his eyes and do not believe his wife when she says that he does. That he looks at her. That he sees her. They put on a stolidly blank expression and say nothing but she knows that inwardly they scoff, even Dr Schweitzer I mean Fortune, Dr Ferdinand Fortune, old Ferdie. Pah, doctors, what do they know?

He fears premature burial.

There is no pain. In the pain department he feels nothing. Or not nothing, exactly. He has an awareness of something, a dinning and hammering deep inside him, the surely agonising effects of which register only as a distant rumour. He is trapped in the celestial dentist's chair.

Yet why is he not content with this state? Is it not the apotheosis he always hankered after, to be pure mind,

mind unalloyed? Whirling and whirling his thoughts go, like the so many grains of grit swept up in a dust-devil. Pure mind, aye, pure thought.

He might have stipulated a little bell to be set on a stick above his plot with a string going down into the hole and tied to one of his fingers. But to what avail? Not even a digit is he capable of stirring. He has thought of a telephone, too, in the coffin, but how would he dial?

An hour ago, when his wife was here—or was it before she came? or after?—he heard the early train grinding past, making the window-panes buzz. When he was a child his mother took him once on that same train to the city for a Christmas treat and bought him a ten-shilling watch, which soon broke. Even in those days the train used to stop here for no reason, in the middle of nowhere, and he would press his face to the window and look longingly at this house standing in a shroud of frost-smoke —this very house, if he is not mistaken and he believes he is not—and dream of living here, of being what his disparaging mother would have called a big fellow, with money and a motor car and a camel-hair overcoat. A big fellow, now felled.

His mind wanders. There are gaps, short and sometimes longer periods of absence, when he is lost to himself, or no, not lost, but as if astray on some far, flat shore, at nightfall, with no moon, and the sea a fringe of soiled white foam off on the horizon, and the sea birds high up, calling and crying in the brumous air.

By the way, tenses: he is stuck in the present, though his preference would be for the preterite. As for the future, he avoids it as the plague. He wishes he had the powers of that emperor of old Cathay who on his deathbed forbade the use of the future tense throughout his vast realm, saying that since he was going to die there would be no future to speak of.

He wonders what time of day it is. If what he heard a while past was indeed the early train it means the sun will be well risen by now. He searches the ceiling for a sign of it but all up there is greyly indistinct, thanks to the curtains his wife insists on keeping pulled day and night. He is reminded of Venice—why? Surely a Venetian ceiling would be awash with lozenges of water-light, a shimmering, amoebic pulsing, and not, as here, soft-grey and crumbly-seeming, like mould. Yet it is definitely the city on the lagoon this memoryless memory is of. Venice! *La Serenissima*, as they call it, her. Whereas I think of a sea-captain's frowsty old relict, *una vecchia carampana*, in tide-stained billows of watered silk, squatting on her piles. To the picturesque I have always had a healthy aversion. I consider it healthy.

But why do I say *an hour ago*? I have—*he* has, *he*, I must stick to the third person—he has lost track of time, he who once was one of time's masters and a keeper of its keys. Now the things that happen merge and flow through each other unresisted, a hopeless mishmash.

Yet there must have been a ceiling like this some-where, in a waterside villa or hotel room in some southern sea port, where he lay love-sated and let his gaze bathe in bundles of mould-grey shadow above a bed—where? when? with what woman? So much he has forgotten because it meant nothing at the time or if not nothing then not nearly enough. This it is that torments him now, among his many torments, the thought of all that he had and did not prize as he should have when he had it. A trove of experience spurned as it was happening because it was simply that, something that was happening and not a thing anticipated or recollected. Now: that is a word he never appreciated the meaning of, until now.

Inside his head the numbers swarm in a vast grid, a matrix without limit, flickering, in stellar silence.

For diversion he sets himself to thinking of his daughter-in-law, slumbering somewhere in the house, like Mélisande, if that is who he means. In the night he heard them arriving, she and his son, heard their voices down on the landing, urgent-sounding because hushed, and imagined he was dreaming. But he knows it was no dream, and now at morning Helen is in that room down there, he senses her, yes; his senses extend their feelers and feel her sensate presence. Is she sleeping? He tries to grasp with his mind the reality of her, asleep or waking, being there where he is not. Before the autonomous existence of others he shares his son's doubt and wonderment—shares? shares? it is his doubt, his wonder, passed on second-hand to the next and lesser generation. He asks, how can people go on being fully real when they are elsewhere, out of his ken? He is not such a solipsist—he is a solipsist but not such a one—that he imagines it is proximity to him that confers their essential realness on people. Of course others exist beyond his presence, billions of others, but they are not part of the mystery proper since he knows nothing of them, cares nothing for them. The truly mysterious ones are the ones who are most familiar to him, his sad wife, his neglected offspring, his desired daughter-in-law. That they should have an existence independent of him, and, indeed, of each other, too, is an affront to the laws of—of what? He speculates sometimes if his early espousal of the theory that posits our existing in the midst of multiple, intertwined worlds was prompted by nothing more than the necessity for somewhere for people to be when they are not with him—I said he was a solipsist—but even there, shoved in sideways with their noses pressed against the glass of those countless crystalline fissures, what would there be to prevent them getting up to things that he cannot imagine or, if he can imagine them, cannot be certain of? Look at him now, unable even to know if his daughter-in-law, like Schrösteinberg's anxiously anticipant cat, is conscious or not, down there in her sealed chamber. He pictures her naked under a single sheet, the linen, softly aglow in the morning light, moulded to the shape of her lovely limbs. Aah. I wonder if his loins are any longer capable of stirring. Something could have come up down there the size and rigidity of an indian club and he would not know it. In younger days his scrotum was as firm and tightly furred as a tennis ball, but by now the testes have probably shrunk back up into wherever it is they dropped from all those years ago. Maybe there is nothing much there at all any longer, since he seems to have bypassed his second childhood and re-entered the embryonic state. Yes, that is how it seems to him, that he is being born in reverse, so that this garrulous dying he is doing will bring him not to the next world but back to a state of suspended pre-existence, ready to start all over again from before the beginning. It is a nice conceit, is it not? I shall let him entertain it for the nonce.

Down in the kitchen Petra in mid-rant pauses for breath and her mother seizes the moment to say on a falling sigh, 'Oh, I have such a headache today.' At this the girl goes furiously silent and shoves her spoon with violent force into a lumpy wodge of stirabout in the baby-bowl before her on the table. The back door opens, making its usual bang and rattle, and Ivy Blount appears, in her old brown mackintosh and her cut-off green wellingtons. She has a basket of eggs on her arm and is bearing by the neck a recently throttled chicken. She pauses on the threshold and looks at the three people in the room with an expression of distracted startlement. The dog thumps his tail in welcome. Miss Blount is unofficial cook, housekeeper and, as Duffy the cowman darkly asserts, taken-for-granted skivvy here at Arden House.

'Good morning, Ivy!' Ursula says, too loudly, for she persists in the mistaken conviction that Miss Blount is hard of hearing. Seeing the ill-plucked chicken she wonders if she might broach the subject of lunch. She really cannot think why she should have to feed that fellow Wagstaff yet knows she must. And how he will sneer, as always. Suddenly and with a shock she recognises the chicken. It is, or used to be, the speckled brown one with the orange feet; she saw it from the window of her room not an hour ago, unsuspectingly scratching for worms between the cobbles down in the yard. She was fond of that one. She used to have names for all the hens, though Adam laughed at her.

Something in her head is pounding; it is like a hammer hitting a block of soft metal, over and over. What if she, too, were to have a stroke? The sudden idea of it almost delights her. She pictures herself lying with Adam up there in the dark, the two of them motionless on their backs and blankly staring, their hands folded identically over their breasts, like a pair of statues laid out side by side on a tomb.

Ivy advances and sets the chicken and the basket of eggs on the table and takes off her mac. She is wearing a heavy tweed skirt and a man's old-fashioned striped shirt with the sleeves rolled. The wings of her finely aristocratic nose are translucent. She gives off a faint odour of roses and dishwater. The dog gets up with an effort and waddles forward and snuffles at her knees. Adam notes the chicken's glazing eyeball and tries to think of a word—obsidian? agate? Its head is still attached above a ruff of burnished umber feathers. He can smell the poor dead thing, its blood-warm reek. Petra is peering at the bird in smouldering alarm as if she fears it might suddenly struggle back to life and come flapping and squawking at her across the table.

The secret of survival is a defective imagination. The inability of mortals to imagine things as they truly are is what allows them to live, since one momentary, unresisted glimpse of the world's totality of suffering would annihilate them on the spot, like a whiff of the most lethal sewer gas. We have stronger stomachs, stouter lungs, we see it all in all its awfulness at every moment and are not daunted; that is the difference; that is what makes us divine.

Young Adam rises from the table and crosses the room and climbs the three steps to the door with the stricken mien of a man mounting the gallows. He pauses and glances back at no one in particular and then goes out, shutting the door behind him so softly it seems a rebuke. His departure leaves an unsettled silence. Ursula has drifted again to her place at the sink with her face lifted to the window. She is glad Petra has shut up and does not care that the child is furious at her for breaking in on her flow of nonsense. Everybody is on edge, everybody's nerves are stretched to the limit. This waiting is unbearable. It is as if Adam had toppled from an immensely high place and were falling, falling, with dreamlike slowness, and they were all looking up, in awe and anguish, at this plummeting speck that presently will lie sprawled at their feet, smashed, bloodied, dead. Dead. The word is another thud of the hammer, achingly soft and dull.

Ivy Blount takes down her stained old apron from its hook on the back of the door. This morning she is even more bemused than usual. She has had a shock, poor soul, though none here knows of it save she and I. It is said she is a direct descendant of Charles Blount, eighth Lord Mountjoy and first Earl of Devonshire, that eccentric soldier whom Mary, Queen of Scots, great Gloriana, on her accession to the English throne after the beheading of her cousin, the upstart and treasonous Elizabeth Tudor, sent over at the dawn of the seventeenth century to pacify this most distressful country. Ivy has the face of a Virgin in an icon, tapering sharply to the chin and touched with indeterminate sorrow. It was from her, last of the Blounts and so sadly come down in the world, that Adam Godley purchased this house, at a knock-down price, twenty years ago. She clings on in a two-storey cottage at the corner of a crooked field where the gates to the property once stood. Duffy, who minds what is left of the farmyard and the few scrawny cattle old Adam insists I mean insisted —tenses, tenses!—on keeping, is known to have a great notion of her.

'Petra's boyfriend is coming down today,' Ursula says, addressing Ivy without turning from the window. 'Perhaps we might have lunch in the conservatory?' She thinks she hears Petra snort but still she will not turn. It is, she supposes, her way of putting things—antiquated, no doubt, arch-sounding—that makes her daughter laugh. She wishes Ivy Blount would say something; Ivy's accent, her decayed-patrician intonations are far more laughable than hers; at least Ursula believes they are and takes a spiteful comfort from it. But Ivy has transferred the chicken to the draining-board and is doing something to it with a bone-handled knife and will say nothing. The blade of the knife is worn to a gleaming spur. A few feathers drift seesawing to the floor. Petra's leg is jigging under the table again.

What shall I do, Ursula thinks, what shall I *do*?

Adam on the landing upstairs comes to a narrow door set flush into the wall and taps on it softly three times with a knuckle. He stands intently still, leaning forward a little with his ear cocked, in the attitude of a domestic spy. He feels foolish but the old interdiction is unbreachable—no one would ever dare climb to his father's room without knocking first. But today, of course, there can be no response, so what is he waiting for? The porcelain door-knob is suavely cold and unwelcoming to his palm. He opens the door. From here a cramped flight of seven steps leads up to the Sky Room. He sets his foot on the first step with a twinge of reluctance. In his earliest memories the Sky Room was the forbidden place where his father worked, impervious it seemed to the discomforts of the place, the winter winds and the summer stiflings. How often when he was little he used to stand like this at doors, listening in vain for the faintest sound of his father at work. That was what fascinated him always, the silence from the study. In fact, it was not silence, not a mere absence of sound, but was a force, a field, like the fields his father once tried to explain to him, abstract spaces humming with the play of fantastically small and forever invisible particles. 'Imagine,' his father said, 'the little bits of everything in the universe all pulling against each other'—making claws of his long, pale hands and hook-

ing them together at the fingertips to demonstrate—
'keeping each other in place.' The boy thought of the
safety net in the circus, the way it was stretched there
with nobody noticing it until at the end of the trapeze act
the last one of the troupe, disdaining the rope the others
had already shimmied down, would let himself plummet
into its springy mesh and bounce on his back in leisurely
fashion, once, twice, three times, like a big baby, before
scrambling to his feet and wading off into the powdery
darkness on rubber legs, looking smug and brandishing a
triumphantly clenched fist. His father sighed—'Yes, yes,
something like that'—and turned away. They were living
then in the old stone house on Haggard Head and his
father worked in the room with the big curved window—
Adam had thought it was called a bay window because it
overlooked the bay—from where the sea seemed an oval
sheet of pockmarked steel and the waves broke in slow
motion on the rocks far below. He liked that house, and
cried when his father moved them here, to the empty
middle of the country.

Still he hesitates, unwilling to climb. It was not just
his father's presence at the top of it that made this unlit
narrow stairway so alarming a prospect to him as a
child. Something definite seemed to lurk here, where the
darkness was darker than anywhere else in the house,
something unseen yet clammily palpable, of which even
yet, in broadest of broad daylight, he seems to detect a
lingering, cobwebby wisp. He recalls his dream again, the
cries of battle, the bronze helmets flashing, the bloodied
dust. And what was it he was bearing in his arms, what?

—a wounded comrade, a corpse, perhaps? He shuts his eyes, opens them again.

He cannot recall his father ever addressing him by his name. He does not resent this or think it a spurning, only he wonders at it. Did his father find it awkward that they were both called Adam? Hardly. Anyway, his father rarely addresses anyone by name; names are something he does not think it necessary to take regard of or remember.

He takes a breath and ascends the stairs as he always does, at a soft run, head down, knees working like elbows. The stairs groan under him as if in outrage.

In the room he wonders why the curtains are shut. At first he can make out nothing but a jumble of standing shapes, vague, dust-coloured, which give the impression of hooded sentinels keeping silent vigil. After a purblind moment he locates the bed. It is the ugly four-poster from his parents' room that his mother had Duffy take apart and haul up here and reassemble when his father was being brought back from the hospital. No one knows why she moved him out of their bedroom; perhaps she does not know herself. The bed is not exactly too big for the room, but disproportionate, somehow, out of place, with its suggestion of the world of drowsy intimacies, sleep, and dream, that world into which his parents would withdraw to spend together their mysterious married nights. His father would not have a couch, not even an armchair, in the room where he worked. A plain steel desk and a bentwood chair, a block of graph paper in loose sheets, and a plentiful supply of pencils, of course, his famous Ticonderogas No. 4, extra hard, yellow with a green band

and pink eraser, specially imported by the boxful; these are, were, the tools of his trade, the implements of the arcanum. When he was famous first, caricaturists pictured him as a monk in a windowless bare cell, wild-eyed and hydrocephalic, hunched with his pencil over a gridded page of parchment; also as a spaceman in a globular helmet popping out of a hole in the sky, as a mad professor with electrified hair meeting and merging with himself in a mirror, as an entire crew of identical sailors marooned each one in solitude on his own earth-shaped island afloat in a sea of inky darkness. Young Adam was proud of his father and secretly clipped these cartoons out of newspapers and magazines and hid them in a cigar box at the back of the top shelf of the wardrobe in his room. Perhaps they are still there, mouldering now.

He makes himself draw nearer to the bed, and after some fumbling, finds the lamp switch and turns on the bedside light. At first he cannot bring himself to look directly at his father. The surface of the bed is another field, smooth and grainily grey and uniform except where his father's form makes a neat, elongated mound down the middle of it. The general arrangement reminds Adam of something though for the moment he cannot think what it is. Standing here like this he feels faintly ridiculous, as he did just now outside the door, and he has the notion that there are people in hiding, behind the curtains and under the bed, with their hands clapped over their mouths, getting ready to spring out at him, whooping and jeering and laughing. He does not know how to behave here. It is strange being in a room with someone who is present and at the same time not. His father's arms are on top of the sheet, stretched stiff at his sides; it is an oddly hieratic arrangement, as if he had been making a large blessing with arms outstretched over the heads of a kneeling multitude and now had stepped back to conceal himself in the shadows. The hands at the ends of the pyjama sleeves are long and bony and crisscrossed with swollen, greenish-blue veins, the kind of hands pianists are supposed to have, and nothing like young Adam's, which are short-fingered and blunt.

All at once he remembers what it is that the bed with his father in it reminds him of. One day, at the beach, when they were children, Petra let him bury her in the sand. It was his idea; he was bored, and thought it would pass the time. But no, that was not it, or not all of it. He had seen the look of alarm in his sister's eyes when he told her what he was going to do and got her to lie down in the sand, and it had excited him. Otherwise he would have tired of the project as soon as he started, for it was not easy: the sand was heavy and sluggish after a morning of rain and the spade that he had to use was Petra's, a toy plastic thing that was much too small and flimsy for the task. But he kept on until she was covered right up to the neck and all that was left of her was her face, as white as pipeclay, as she lay there in a cocoon of wet sand, with her eyes fixed on him anxiously, trapped and motionless like his father, here, now.

He grins to himself, joylessly, guiltily, leaning in the gloom.

But how shrunken his father seems, so much shorter

than in life and pitifully thin—in life, yes, for as he is now he is surely as good as dead; that seems evident. By the time he was twelve young Adam was already impossibly big, with a prizefighter's rolling shoulders and a weight-lifter's legs, half a head taller than his tall and sinuously articulated father. The disproportion only made him feel all the more clumsy and slow, and somehow the smaller of the two, a pygmy at the knee of the great, white man. He used to divert himself by fancying that he was not his father's son at all but the outcome of a desperate adventure entered into by his mother to pay his father back for the many affairs he was said to carry on; it cheered him to think of having been conceived in a flurry of anger and avenging lust. Sometimes he thinks he would like to be like that himself, unforgiving, coldly passionate, a dealer-out of retribution and just deserts. Perhaps, to buck him up, I should plant in his mind the idea that my father Zeus—? But no. Not the most loyal and loving of sons could imagine that Adam's mother, even in the flower of virginal youth, would have been my heavenly father's type.

Who else was on the beach that day? Adam tries to recall the wider scene, the tawny dunes behind and the flat slope of sand down to the water's edge shining like newly poured cement, and people in the water bobbing and squealing, and a sailboat out on the water, and, closer by, someone sitting on a blanket dispensing tea from a Thermos flask and querulously calling his name. The three of them, of course: him, his sister, his mother; always these three, never four, unless Granny Godley came with them, which she seldom did, for she had an aversion to outdoors, and deplored especially the sea and its shore. He thinks of his grandmother with rueful fondness, this fierce old loving woman unable to show her love to anyone.

At last he brings himself to look full at his father's face, or at his head, rather, that high-domed, ascetic head with its bony brow and axe-head nose and pointed beard and broad-lipped, prehensile mouth. What does he look most like? A high priest at rest after the throes and transports of a religious ritual. A dead pharaoh, mummified and shrunken. Or just Petra, buried to her neck in the sand.

Now he rouses himself from his musings and leans over the bed determined to do he does not know what, and immediately falters. Should he kiss his father? Is that what is expected of him? But if so, does it matter whether he does or not, since there is no one here to see him doing or not doing it, and his father cannot know either way? And when did he kiss his father? When did his father kiss him? If either ever did, it is long beyond remembering. He feels constrained and ill at ease in this crepuscular atmosphere, these dim and somehow churchly surrounds. Does he wish his father gone? The thought comes to him unbidden; he is shocked not to be shocked. He looks at those hands resting motionless on the sheet and all at once, without warning, something gapes open inside him, a vertiginous hollow into which at once he pitches forward helplessly. For a second he cannot make out what is the matter; then he realises that he is weeping. This is more than anything a surprise, for it is a long time since he last wept. He does not know the source of these tears, brimming unstoppably over his scalding lids, so copious and heavy they seem unreal, the fat, hot tears of childhood that in childhood he so furiously forbade himself to shed except when he was alone. But it is simple, surely—he is weeping for his dying father. Why would he not? Yet he is so much taken aback that it seems he might begin to laugh, even as he weeps. The only sound he hears himself produce, however, is a series of little gulps, or gasps, little soft hiccups. Altogether it is a not disagreeable sensation, this sudden extravaganza of grief, if grief is what it is, and he is pleased with himself, proud, almost, as if his tears were a demonstration of something, some task or proof that for long has been required of him without his knowing. And when after a minute or two he regains control of himself he feels almost invigorated, as if he had undergone a religious drenching. Shriven, he thinks—is that the word? Yes, shriven. But also he feels as he felt when he was a child after wetting the bed in his sleep, guilty and gleeful at the same time, and obscurely, shamefully avenged, though on whom, or what, he does not know.

He mashes his wet eyes with the heels of his hands, and having no handkerchief he wipes his nose on his sleeve, and is conscious again of his absurd get-up, the too-small pair of pyjamas he has squeezed himself into, and his big bare feet glimmering down there far below him in the gloom. He lets fall a heavy sigh, which in the shrouded silence sounds exaggerated and almost comical, a stage version of a sigh. He feels sheepish—everything he does is overdone. He tries to touch his father's stirless form but cannot, and that act too, that non-act, seems histrionic and false. He is not used to feeling like this. He thinks of himself, when he thinks of himself, as a simple being. Helen is the complicated one; he stands before the intricacy of her in awed amazement, like an indian watching from the shore the unheard-of, marvellous ships with shining masts bounding towards him out of dream-blue distances.

He lumbers down the narrow stairs and once outside he shuts the door behind him, easing the doorknob on its spring so as to make no sound. When he turns he is surprised to find how bright the day is already, how rich the morning sunlight streaming down upon the landing. The house is built on four sides around a big, square space two storeys deep, at the bottom of which is the black-and-white tiled floor of the central hallway; the roof is made of rectangular sheets of rippled, greenish glass grimed with moss and bird droppings and plastered with last year's blown and blackened leaves, and by some trick of light the well below it seems always filled to the brim with impossibly still, impossibly clear water. The walls, clad in slotted wooden laths, were painted immemorially with buff distemper that has turned an unpleasantly sulphurous shade, and with the sun on them, as now, give off a dry, not unpleasant, wood-and-paint smell, the smell of family hotels and rickety seaside chalets, though the sea is a good twenty miles off, and who would think of holidaying here at Arden House, except perhaps Roddy Wagstaff, and he does not count? What caprice led Ivy Blount's great-grandfather, the whimsical St John Blount, to have half the house's wall-space covered with this cheap wood battening? The wonder of it is the place has survived so long and not been set fire to by lightning bolt or rebel torch. 'Tinder,' his mother says, 'this great gazebo —nothing but tinder.'

Adam walks round two sides of the balconied landing, moving under the leaded glass roof through sharp-edged flickers of light and shadow, hearing his bare feet paddling softly, moistly, on the uncarpeted boards. He comes to another door and again stands listening; he fancies he hears from within his sleeping wife softly breathing, and the faint, diaphanous sound stirs his senses.

'What are you doing?' Helen blurredly demands, sitting up quickly. Something in him always vibrates anew to the sound of her voice, its dark, true note, as on an oboe. She looks at the empty place in the bed beside her, feels the cold pillow with her hand. She frowns. 'Where did you go?'

As always his wife's beauty strikes him as if for the first time—strikes him, yes, for he feels the effect of it like a soft blow to the heart. Why was it he that she chose to marry when so many others had pled with her in vain? The question gnaws at him, he broods on it, but finds no answer. Strangely, though, it warms him, too, affords him a bodeful, warming thrill, which he cannot account for. He toys repeatedly with the possibility of losing her; he is like one afflicted with a fear of falling who drags himself back again and again to the very brink of the precipice. Life without her is unimaginable for him. He wonders if this will change, if one day, old and tired and disenchanted, he will look back and ask himself how he could ever have been held in such helpless thrall by her. She is only human, after all, a human being, like himself. But no, no, she is not like him. The beautiful ones, the rare ones as beautiful as she, are different, he is convinced of it: they carry their beauty like a burden that does not weigh down but magically lightens. Theirs is another way of being human, if they are human at all.

Hear my old Dad licking his chops in the background?—she is no goddess of loveliness, but a human girl, all right. If she were not he would not pine after her as achingly as he does. It is their very humanness he covets, the salacious old rip.

Neither of them brought nightwear, and Helen, excitingly to Adam, has on Adam's shirt that he wore yesterday, pale blue, like his undersized pyjamas, with a faint white stripe. She is still looking at him strangely, with a strange surmise. The small, square room is shoddily furnished with things that over the years since it ceased to be his have migrated to here from elsewhere in the house. There is the old-fashioned high bed, two bedside lockers painted a sickly shade of chocolate brown, a spindle-legged table, ditto, bearing a china basin with matching jug and a speckled oval shaving mirror on a wooden stand; there is a straw-bottomed chair and, on the floor at the foot of the bed, a brass-bound mahogany chest with SS *Esmerelda* inscribed in neat poker-work on the lid. Some old things of his remain, too, a glue-encrusted model aeroplane on a stand, a faded poster of a football team pinned to the wall, a hurley stick standing in a corner like the long leg-bone of some fleet creature. The floor is of rough-hewn pitchpine beams that have driven a splinter into many an unprotected toe. The window opposite the bed is shaded with a muslin blind, and the room is filled with a powdery white effulgence that seems to slow everything down a beat; there is the musty smell of sleep.

'I was awake,' Adam says. 'I went downstairs. Did you hear the train?'

Helen's frown deepens and she tilts her head to one side and looks at him hard, as if she thinks he is teasing her and is cautioning him to stop. What colour are her eyes? They must be blue, yes, dark blue and deep as the Grecian sea itself. Her head is an exquisite, cream-and-gold inverted egg that sits on its pale length of neck as on a plinth of polished stone. She has cut her hair in a new fashion, close to the skull in countless imbricated layers like flakes of gold leaf; he is not sure he likes it in this style but would not dare to say so. In the matter of his wife and the things she does or does not do he feels he is standing astride the hub of a great steel disc that is spinning at an immense speed and that at the tiniest ill-judged action on his part will begin to wobble wildly and a second later fly off its spindle with terrible shrieks and clangs and send him flailing into darkness and irreparable damage. 'You were here, not downstairs,' she says, more in puzzlement than contradiction. 'You were here, with me.'

'I couldn't sleep.'

She gives an odd, dry laugh. 'Is that so?' Her tone too

puzzles him; she must still be half in a dream. One naked foot has kicked free the hem of the sheet; he notes the heel's callused rim and his already smitten chest seems to open and let something fly out, like a bird out of a clock, love's desperate cuckoo. 'I have to go to the bathroom,' she says. 'I'm sopping.'

When she steps from the bed the tails of the blue shirt open briefly in front and he catches a glimpse of her russet fleece. He wants to touch her, to detain and hold her. There is a grain of sleep at the canthus of her left eye, the one that has a slight and captivating droop. She brushes past him and as she goes to the door he is treated to a brief view under the shirt-tails of two pale half-moons of pendent, glimmering flesh. He imagines licking that fleck of hardened gleet from the corner of her eye with just the very tip of his tongue.

Sopping?

He kneels on the side of the bed and leans deeply forward on his hands as if prostrating himself in prayer and buries his face in the still-warm nest in the bedclothes where until a moment ago his wife was sitting.

The tiny bathroom is wedge-shaped, narrowing from the door to where the handbasin and the single small window are, which makes the place feel all the more cramped. Half the space is taken up by an enamel bath the size of a sarcophagus with a chipped rim and brown and yellowish-green streaks running down from the taps. Over the bath there is a giant geyser, also enamel-plated, also chipped, which long ago ceased to function but which no one has thought to have removed. The first time Helen came to stay at Arden and was unwise enough to take a bath here she stood up and cut her head on the sharp edge of the brass spigot that sticks out under the hole where the pilot light used to be. That was before she was married to Adam. Married. The word stops her, as it always does. It has to her ears an antiquated and faintly indecent ring, like one of those innocent-sounding words in the old plays, *swive*, or *fig*, or *mutuality*.

The window looks down on a field of thistles and, farther on, a circular dark wood that seems to huddle around itself in fear of something, and over which now the morning sun is pouring in vain its somehow heartless cheer. When she is outside she can never seem to locate that field, or that wood—how is that?—not that she would spend much time searching for them. It is just another of the place's many small but exasperating mysteries. She is a city girl and finds the countryside either dull or worrying, or both.

She hikes up the shirt she is wearing by grasping a handful of it at the front and lowers herself on to the lavatory like, she thinks, a big white soft hen getting ready to lay an egg. The antique lavatory seat is a mighty frame of varnished, maroon-coloured wood that reminds her of the collar of a work-horse—but where would she ever have seen such a thing?—and feels cold and sticky at first and then warm and stickier still. She listens in mild dismay to the splashings and ploppings going on underneath her. She is sure she can be heard all over the house.

She plants her hands on her bare knees and gazes straight ahead of her at nothing. White light glows on the patch of pale-yellow wall in front of her. She hears from below scraps of the life of the house going on, people talking, a door opening and shutting, a dull thud that could be anything; the dog barks, three unemphatic woofs; that door again, banging this time; light steps on the stairs; a brusque, back-and-forth rattling as someone riddles the cinders in a grate. Why is it that people heard from afar like this, in distant rooms on other floors, always sound as if they are doing things—confiding, fighting, striking loud deals—far more interesting than the mundane things that they are really engaged in?

It seems old Adam is going to die, the doctors say so, and everyone except Ursula has given up hope. It is strange to think of him not being here any more, at Arden; strange to think of him not being anywhere. What is it like to die, she wonders, what is it like to be dead? Is it like anything? Like being under an anaesthetic, perhaps, with the forgetful anaesthetist gone home and all the lights in the operating theatre turned off and the doors locked and the last squeaky footsteps fallen silent down all the long corridors. She is not sure what she is meant to feel about this coming death. She knows the old man lusts after her—lusted, now—she has seen him eyeing her when he thought she was not noticing, has seen how he puts his head back, running his nails through the underneath of his beard, and how that white patch of skin between his eyebrows creases as if he were in faint pain. It gives her the shivers to think of it now. Yet he must have been handsome, once, beautiful, even, with that narrow brow and those deeply indented temples, the sharp nose and the large, slightly slanted, glistening black eyes. He is nothing like his son—how can the two of them be so different? But she would not have wanted to be married to old Adam, and not just because he is dying. Why, then? Something uncanny in him; something cold.

She reaches out to the roller and tears off a length of tissue. The parched, leaf-mould smell of the paper reminds her of something from the past—trees, summer, a boy—but it is gone before she can fix it. The flush is operated by a chain with a wooden handle polished and worn thin from use.

> *—oh, such a dream!*
> *We were upon some golden mountain top,*
> *The two of us, just we, and all around*
> *The air was blue, and endless, and so soft!*

She wonders at herself and how she fairly fled just now from the bedroom and her husband in a confusion of unwonted shyness, of shame, almost, that was more pleasurable than not, and now—could it be?—there is already a heat beginning to glow again in her lap. What came over her? And, more amazingly, what came over him? She puts a hand between her thighs and probes inside herself with squeamish fingers. She expects to find all raw and sore there but does not. She lifts her fingertips to her nostrils and sniffs. There are only her own familiar pungencies. Was it a dream? Surely not. Surely something so intensely felt must have been real.

She thinks again of the dying old man.

Loosened, released, she rises from the cascading bowl and walks to the window and peers at what she can see of her face in the cracked looking-glass in its worm-eaten wooden frame. Who if not her husband was that monstrous man who made such love to her in the dimness of the dawning bedroom? And if her husband, how transfigured! Her limbs are shaking still from the awful weight of him. The things he did to her, the things he had her do! Never, never in all her life—! In the glass with its diagonal crack her face is slashed into two ill-fitting halves and a lopsided eye looks back at her quizzically, with a sceptical cast. The morning beats around her like a pulse, the cistern gurgles. The warmish afterglow of her own spicy stink lingers on the air. Through the little window the glare of daylight startles anew, making her squint. The light out here in the country, the hue of headaches, is different than in the city, brighter, more intense, as if there is shining behind it another light, mysterious, unvarying, with an acid cast. The water, coiling from the tap like running metal, shatters on her knuckles in silvery streels. She seems to herself gathered up, somehow, enfolded and gathered up. The burning in her belly is growing more intense, a sullen fire. She lowers her head with eyes shut fast and braces her hands on the sides of the handbasin and leans forward heavily on locked elbows, trembling in remembered pleasure that seems a part of pain. She would swoon if I were not there to hold her up with arms of air. This is how it always is when Dad has done what he does with a girl, the old lecher. I am remembering Tyndareus's wife, and, later, that trollop her daughter—another Helen!—who caused all the trouble at Troy and brought great Ilium low. Not to mention the nameless ones, countless in number, before and since, betrayed, spurned, forgotten.

Adam is waiting for her in the bedroom. He has dressed. He wears a white shirt and a preposterous pair of rough tweed trousers, of a rusty colour, much too tight for him, that she has never seen before—they cannot be his, he must have found them somewhere in the room. He always does strange things at Arden. Coming here he still speaks of coming home. He is sitting sideways on the bed. This bed—it is wider than a single but far too narrow for the two of them; last night she said she was afraid he would turn in his sleep and squash her against the wall and kill her, as it is said babies are sometimes suffocated when their sleeping mothers roll on top of them. At the mention of babies they both went silent, and he looked away though she made herself stare at him, her eyes narrowed, daring him to say something, but he would not, of course. She looks now at the things of his in the room, that aeroplane, the hurley stick, and in her mind she curls a lip. He is propped on an arm and smiling up at her as if in entreaty. What does he want? She wishes he had gone downstairs. She would like to be alone. She does not want to dress in front of him. She feels still a vestige of excited shame, recalling the dream of their love-making. For she has decided it was a dream, after all. What else could it have been, her seeming to wake and find him looming over her arrayed in light, unspeaking, urgent, his arms outstretched and his hands on her breasts—what else?

When you return, who will you be but you?
What other you is there that I might love?

Again now he moves a hand towards her, the hand he had been leaning on, its fingers scurrying crablike playfully over the sheet. She likes his hands, foursquare and always warm, but now she does not want to be touched and draws back an almost imperceptible inch from the edge of the bed. He makes a smiling frown. 'What's wrong?' he asks. 'Did Duffy spot you in my shirt?'

She considers this. She has had cause before now to remark the cowman's seeming freedom of the house, his way of popping up at inappropriate moments in unexpected places, with his beetling brow and his bold, undeflectable stare. What if he did see her, scampering out of the bathroom and up the steps with her backside on show? Well, let him see, she does not care.

'Did you go in yet to see your father?' she asks. Her overnight bag is open on the floor, things spilling out of it as if stalled in a desperate scramble to escape. 'How is he?'

He stops smiling but continues to frown, his upper lip protruding over the lower. As always when he dips his head a wing of hair falls forward on his brow and he lifts a hand impatiently to brush it back. His hair is soft and pale. His eyes are pale too, a limpid blue, like her own, but uncanny, somehow, uncanny, that word again. In her dream he was himself and yet not, a figure of cold fire, burning her; his mouth was gold.

'I don't know how he is,' he says. 'He's just there, not

doing anything. I hope he is not suffering but how am I supposed to know?' He pauses, and picks at something on the sheet. 'I burst into tears at the bedside.'

'Did you?' is all she says, as if she were thinking of something else. He wonders if she will ask to see him, the dying man.

She walks to the window and pulls up the muslin blind and secures its string by winding it on a hook screwed into the sill and stands looking out. It is supposed to be possible to see the sea from here but she never can. 'Poor thing,' she says, and neither of them is sure whom she means, Adam's father or Adam. Below, there is a different field from the one the bathroom window looks down on, or maybe, she thinks, it is the same one but from another angle. Beyond it there is no wood, though, only a long, lush slope—surely even grass should not be that unreally bright shade of green—behind which rise the roof and single chimney of Ivy Blount's cottage. Three black-and-white cows are desultorily at graze. A tiny bird flits down from a bough as if not flying but falling, a quick, brown leaf, and then can be seen no more. There is something less than real about the look of this place, especially in summer; it all seems got up, to her. Everything is too flat, somehow, the distances especially but the nearer hills, too, and all laid over with a weak lavender wash, like a badly done backdrop.

She has played Hedda, and Miss Julie. She has swept on in a matt-black gown and seduced and scorned. In the farthest back row they saw the flash of her azure eyes. She had the whip and the whip-hand. Now she will play

Alcmene, the soldier's wife, sweet and baffled and beleaguered. How to pitch it?

'What?' She looks back.

When you return, who will you be but you?—

Tee-tum tee-tum tee-tum tee-tum tee-*tum*. Like Duffy in his big boots.

'I said nothing,' her husband says.

She glances, frowning, about the room. 'She even kept your toys,' she says, wonderingly.

'Who?'

'Your mother—who else?'

She recalls again the gold man in her dream, the looming weight of him. She strides quickly to the bed—a maenad! look!—and clambers over the steamer trunk on to the mattress and wades along it on her knees and with an impassioned violence takes her husband's head between her hands and presses his face to her breast. He wriggles, and says something that is too muffled for her to make out. She feels his breath on her skin and a shirt button that his chin is pressing into her. Although she is slight compared to him she seems to herself a giantess, towering over him, voracious and commanding. He reaches around and lifts the tail of his shirt that she is wearing and puts his hands on her bare behind and they both feel the blood-heat of her flesh. He is trying to speak again but she will not let him, and grinds his face against her, rolling it from side to side. He makes muffled, laughing noises. His nails dig into her behind, stingingly. She throws back her head with a savage sigh.

My father in his lethargy groans, off dreaming in some other place, of some other lass, I hope. But come, Daddums, come put on your horns and take a gander at what these your little ones are up to.

OLD ADAM PLUNGES, a pearl-diver, into the past, going down deeper with each dive. There is a lost world there, he sees the sunken roofs and spires, the streets where currents glide, the people phosphorescent as fish, drifting in and out of houses, through half-familiar rooms, their seahorse eyes wide open. He is frightened; he does not want to drown, as they have drowned; he knows that he soon will. He feels the tide drawing him on, drawing him on. He grasps at tendrils but they slip through his hands, slimy and cold. There is a gleam, a glint, but when he scrabbles in the sand he finds nothing, only shells and jagged coral and bits of bone, and all around him is soon obscured. His breath is running out. He feels his heart beat, hears the blood in his veins, a hollow, rushing roar. He struggles. The water coils around him, heavy as chains and ungraspable. A great bubble bursts from his mouth. *Mother!*—

He wakes, but what he wakes to is not waking.

He is once again in the humpbacked town above the

estuary, with its church, its ruined tower, its steep-roofed, jostling houses. He sees it in raw April weather, a rinsed blue sky with smudges of cloud, ice-white, bruise-grey, fawn. From all the chimneys flaws of smoke fly back, as if a close-packed flotilla were putting out to sea from here. The wind ruffles the widening river, pricking up white-caps. It is all there, compact and tiny, like a toy town in a snow-globe. He is a child, trudging up a hill beside a high, grey-stone wall. He wears a tweed coat with a half-belt at the back, and a peaked cap, and thick woollen stockings the tops of which are turned down to hide homemade, soiled white elastic garters. He has his satchel on his back. It is four o'clock. There are houses on the other side of the sharply tilted street, each one set a step higher up than the other. On the front door of one a black crape bow is tied to the knocker with a pasteboard card attached with a name on it, and dates, written in black ink. The door is ajar. Someone has died and anyone may go in to view the corpse. The town drunks are always there first, for a free drink in which to toast the dead man on his way. He stops and stands for a moment, looking at the house. He could go in. He could just push open the door and walk straight into the parlour. There would be someone there, a woman wearing black, standing with her hands folded in front of her, her eyes pink-rimmed and her nostrils inflamed along the edges. He would shake her thin, chilly hand and murmur something; it need not even be words. He would cross the room, his school shoes squeaking, and gaze down stonily at the dead person laid out in the coffin in his unreal-looking suit, his waxen knuckles wound round with a rosary. There would be that smell, of lilies and ashes, which the recently dead give off, or which at least is always there when someone has died. The woman would offer him cake on a plate and a tumbler of tepid lemonade. There would be others there before him, sitting in the gloom on straight chairs ranged against the walls, gripping whiskey glasses in red fists or balancing cups and saucers on their knees, sighing and shifting, murmuring pious complacencies that set his teeth on edge.

But he does not cross the road. Instead he turns and walks on up the long hill towards home.

Spring winds flow through the streets like weightless water. The blued air of April. The trees tremble, their wet black branches powdered with puffs of green. The tarmac shines. A strong gust pummels the window-panes, making them shiver and throw off lances of light. The priest's car passes, its tyres fizzing on the wet road. The boy salutes dutifully and in return is gravely blessed, as a reflected cloud slides smoothly, fish-like, over the windscreen.

A fellow in an old black coat and corduroy trousers that are bald on the knees comes out of the church gate with a spade over his shoulder. Without stopping he leans sideways and shuts one nostril with a finger pressed along the side of it and from the other expertly ejects a bolus of snot.

O lost, raw world!

The house stands in a crooked street, wedged narrowly between its taller neighbours as if it had sidled in there one day and stayed put. He slides his hand through the letter box—it gives him a shiver of terror every time—and fishes up the key that hangs inside on a string. In the hall the familiar smells meet him: floor polish, blacklead, soap, gas from the kitchen stove. He hangs his coat and cap on a hook, throws his satchel on the floor. His mother, in her apron, a strand of hair come loose from its bun, wipes the back of a hand across her cheek; she gives him the look that she always does, suspicious, sceptical, faintly desperate. He walks his fingers along the table edge. His father is in the back room, propped against pillows on a makeshift bed made up for him on the brown leather sofa in the corner, his big hands spread out flat in front of him on the blanket. The boy thinks of the crape bow on the door-knocker, and of himself standing in the parlour here, in his Sunday suit, amid the smell of ashes and lilies. His father stirs, sighs, and makes a slithering sound in his throat. The banked fire in the grate has a frightening glare at its heart, and the coke gives off a hot reek of cat. Low in the window there is a patch of late-afternoon sky, milk-blue, and a bit of the mossed wall on top of which his mother's hens make illicit nests and hide their eggs. Gooseberry bushes out there, potato drills, cabbages gone to seed and grown as tall as paschal candles. Then the fields, and behind them the rocky hills, and then, beyond that again, elsewhere.

The first present that he can remember getting is a clay pipe. It must have been his birthday. His sister took him to the tobacconist's shop and bought it for him with money their mother had given her. It came with a waxed-cardboard pot of soapy stuff for blowing bubbles. In the garden by the hen-house he tried it out. At first he could not get the hang of it then suddenly did. The bubbles hesitated on the rim of the pipe-bowl, wobbling flabbily, then broke free and floated sedately away. They seemed to be rotating inside themselves, as if the top was always too heavy, and the iridescent surplus kept cascading down the sides. Sometimes two of them stuck together and formed a fat, trembling shape something like an hourglass only squatter. They were made of an unearthly substance, a transparent quicksilver, impossibly fine and volatile, rainbow-hued. They popped against his skin like wet, cold kisses. They were another kind of elsewhere.

His father died at Christmastime. In the back room the bed in the corner was dismantled, leaving the stripped sofa standing in what seemed a gaping hole in the air, and no more fires were lit and as the December days went on the light in the room congealed and grew steadily dimmer. At the end the dying man had suddenly lifted himself up from the pillows with starting eyes and called out something in a voice so strong and deep it shocked everyone. It was not his voice, but as if someone else had spoken through him, and Adam's sister burst into tears and ran from the room, and his two brothers with their greyish bloated damp-looking faces glanced at each other quickly and their eyes seemed to swell. What their father had shouted had seemed a name but no one had been able to make it out. He had kept on glaring upwards, his head shaking and his lips thrust out like a trumpet player's, and then he had fallen back and there was a noise as if he were drowning.

His mother said they must have Christmas as usual. She said his father would want it so, that Christmas was his favourite time of all the year.

She baked a cake. Adam helped her, measuring out the ingredients on the black iron weighing-scales with the brass weights that were cool and heavy as he imagined doubloons would be. It was night, all outside a frozen stillness, the leaning roofs purplish-grey with hoarfrost and the jagged stars glittering like splintered ice and the moon high up in the middle of a glistening, blue-black sky and small as if shrunken by the cold. His mother stood at the table with her sleeves rolled, mixing in a brown bowl the dry ingredients he had weighed out for her. Her head was bent and he did not realise she was crying until he saw the tears fall into the bowl, first one and then quickly two more, making three tiny grey craters in the white mixture. Without a word she handed him the wooden spoon and went and sat down by the fireplace with her face turned away from him, making no sound. He held the bowl by the rim, encircling it with his fore-arm in the way that he had seen her do. When he swirled the spoon in the flour mixture the tears became three grey pellets but they were quickly absorbed. He did not think he had ever seen his mother cry before—even beside his father's grave she had stood dry-eyed—and now he felt embarrassed and uneasy and wished she would stop. Neither spoke. They were alone in the house. He wondered how long it would take before everything in the bowl was completely mixed. But what did that mean, *completely mixed*? Every grain of the ingredients would have to be distributed perfectly, the particles of salt and baking soda spaced just so throughout the flour, each one a fixed distance from all the rest. He tried to picture it, a solid, three-dimensional white field supporting a dense and uniform lattice of particles of other shades of white. And what about the flour itself, no two grains of which were alike—how could that be *completely mixed*, even if there were no other ingredients present in it, making their own pattern? And how would he know when that moment of perfect distribution had been achieved?—how would he know the instant to stop mixing in order not to upset the equilibrium and throw everything back into disorder? He watched the spoon going round and round, making troughs and peaks and crumbling cliffs in the soft pale powdery mixture. Where were those three tears now? How well into the mixture were they mixed? Was everything in the world so intricately linked and yet resistantly disparate? His mother stood up and blew her nose on her apron and without a word took back the bowl and the wooden spoon and began mixing again.

His aunt came down from the city for the funeral and stayed on for Christmas. She took over the house, directed the putting up of the decorations and the trimming of the tree, ordered in a crate of stout and bottles of port-wine and whiskey, oversaw the distribution of presents, even carved the turkey, while his mother hung back, tight-lipped and watchful, saying nothing. His aunt was not married, and worked in the city for a solicitor. She wore a dove-grey coat with a fox-fur collar and fox-fur trim on the hem, and a black toque with a pearl pin and a piece of stiff black veil at the front, and big shoes with chunky high heels. She had an air about her always of angry sorrow. She was lavishly ugly, with a long horse-face and a mouthful of outsized teeth the front ones of which were always flecked with lipstick. Her Christmas present to him was a box of puzzles made from lengths of shiny steel bent into intricate shapes and linked together seemingly inextricably, though it took him only a moment of motionless concentration to see the trick of each pair and to separate them, which caused his aunt to sniff and frown and make a humming sound. It was voluptuously satisfying the way the two gleaming skeins of metal slid apart so smoothly, with what seemed an oiled ease, and his mind would become for a moment a limitless blue space, calmly radiant, through which transparent forms moved and met and locked and unlocked and passed on through each other in a vast silence, endlessly.

His mother, not to be outdone by his aunt, gave him a little clothbound book of curious and amusing facts about numbers. Here he first encountered the magic square. How strange it was, to add up the numbers in the boxes along each side and down each diagonal and come out every time with the same result, the same and yet, for him, always somehow new. This impression of novelty among identical values he could not account for. How could fifteen be different from fifteen? And yet the difference was there, a sort of aura, unseen but felt, like air, like warmth—yes, yes, we gods were there with him even then—like the breath he breathed, the breath that sometimes caught and swelled suffocatingly in his lungs, so avid was he for more facts, more conundrums, more solutions. He borrowed books from the library, by people with letters after their unpronounceable names. He tried to devise puzzles and problems of his own. The terms eluded him, they squirmed and writhed, slipping through the mesh of his mind. He would close his eyes and seem to be seeing into clear depths, where the figures glinted, but when he reached down he would grasp nothing but shards, shards and surds, and all would become clouded and thick with murk.

He counts. How many steps it takes him to walk to school. How many times in the course of a class the teacher will say a certain word. On the way home he counts how many cracks there are in the pavement, how many men he will meet and how many women, how many counted beats it will take to get from one telegraph pole to the next, how often that bird on that bough will chirp before he has passed underneath the tree. At night in bed he counts his heartbeats. The impossibility of accuracy torments him. So many this, so many that, but what before anything is the unit?

And then there is the question of time. What for instance is an instant? Hours, minutes, seconds, even, these are comprehensible, since they can be measured on a clock, but what is meant when people speak of a moment, a while—a tick—a jiffy? They are only words, of course, yet they hang above soundless depths. Does time flow or is it a succession of stillnesses—instants—

moving so swiftly they seem to us to join in an unbreaking wave? Or is there only one great stillness, stretching everywhere, in all directions, through which we move like swimmers breasting an infinite, listless sea? And why does it vary? Why is toothache time so different from the time when he is eating a sweet, one of the many sweets that in time will cause another cavity? There are lights now in the sky that set out from their sources a billion years ago. But are there lights? No, only light, flowing endlessly, moving, every instant.

Everything blurs around its edges, everything seeps into everything else. Nothing is separate.

Has the early train gone by yet? Has his wife paid her morning visit?

The waters of time muddy, the figures flicker in silence.

THE FATHER OF the gods is in a sulk. It is always thus when one of his girls, all unknowing, goes back to her true, that is, her rightful, mate, as she must. What does he expect? He comes to them in disguise, tricks himself out as a bull, an eagle, a swan, or, as in the present case, a husband, and thinks to make them love him—him, that is, and not what or who he is pretending to be, as if he were a mortal just like them. Ah, yes, love, what they call love, it drives him to distraction, for it is one of that pair of things our kind may not experience, the other being, obviously, death. He is convinced the two are intimately linked, to the point, in his case, at least, that one conduces to the other. In this I grant he may be somewhat in the right. Certainly their love takes it out of him. I do not mean the act itself, which gives no pleasure to us since aeons ago, when the world was young and fecund still and required our constant generative attentions—remember those herds of mares all standing with their hindquarters turned to the north in hope of an inseminating breath

72

from Boreas the amber-winged? Nor is it the effort, the vain effort, of compelling a passionate response from them that drains his strength and leaves him limp and languishing, no, but something in the exchange itself, in the needful shuttling to and fro between her humanness and his divinity, this is what debilitates him so, even as it delights him. Hence he keeps coming back for more. Each time he dips his beak into the essence of a girl he takes, so he believes, another enchanting sip of death, pure and precious. For of course he wants to die, as do all of us immortals, that is well known.

This love, this mortal love, is of their own making, the thing we did not intend, foresee or sanction. How then should it not fascinate us? We gave them that irresistible compulsion in the loins—Eros and Ananke working hand in hand—only so they might overcome their disgust of each other's flesh and join willingly, more than willingly, in the act of procreation, for having started them up we were loath to let them die out, they being our handiwork, after all, for better or, as so often, worse. But lo! see what they made of this mess of frottage. It is as if a fractious child had been handed a few timber shavings and a bucket of mud to keep him quiet only for him promptly to erect a cathedral, complete with baptistry, steeple, weathercock and all. Within the precincts of this consecrated house they afford each other sanctuary, excuse each other their failings, their sweats and smells, their lies and subterfuges, above all their ineradicable self-obsession. This is what baffles us, how they wriggled out of our grasp and somehow became free to forgive each other for all that they are not.

And all the time the entire thing is a self-induced fantasy. What my Dad, lusting after their love, does not see and will not hear said is that that which love loves is precisely representation, for representation is all it knows. Or not even that much. Show me a pair of them at it and I will show you two mirrors, rose-tinted, flatteringly distorted, locked in an embrace of mutual incomprehension. They love so they may see their pirouetting selves marvellously reflected in the loved one's eyes. It is immortality they are after—yes, what we would be shot of they long for, or at least the illusion of it, to seem to live forever in an instant of passion. Hence their ceremonies of surrender and engorgement. *Agape?* —aye, at that feast they eat each other, gobble each other up. And this, this it is that great Zeus covets, their little manufactured transports from which he is excluded.

Those troubadours and their lays have a lot to answer for.

Maddened by prurience, like an old dog by his fleas, my divine father scratches and scratches, until he has exhausted himself. No bull or bird but a mangy old dog, yes, that is what he is. Or, if you prefer, a hapless boy, a shepherd lad, say, hunched in hiding in some Attic grove, spying on a bevy of nymphs at their bath and frantically rubbing himself and stifling yelps of anguished ecstasy. What else can he do, my poor old man? They will not love him—they do not even know it is he, seeing only whatever outlandish disguise it is he presents himself in and lacking the imagination to conceive of a god. And yet he goes on pressing them for a word, a pledge, a plight. It is pathetic.

This morning, with young Adam's wife, he was more abject in his entreaties than I think I have ever known him. It was shaming, and I would have absented myself from the scene were there not in me, too, sometimes, a panting Daphnis spying on a world of pleasures and passions beyond his savouring.

Besides, I had been working hard and had earned a little diversion. Not only did my Dad set me to monitor the house and ensure he was not disturbed at his illicit amours but I also had to render the lady Helen's husband sleepless so he would go night-wandering and vacate the bed. Then—and wait till you hear this—then I was commanded to hold back the dawn for fully an hour, to give the old boy extra time in which to work his wiles on the unsuspecting girl. Imagine what effort that little feat of prestidigitation involved: the stars stopped in their courses, the rolling world restrained, all chanticleers choked. And then the readjustments afterwards! You try telling that hotspur Phaeton why he was reined in, or rosy-fingered Aurora why I had to shove her in the face. But an hour of suspended day there must be, and was.

Consider the scene.

Their passion all used up at last, they lie in bed together naked, Dad and his girl, reclining on a strew of pillows in the morning's plum-blue twilight. Or, rather, Dad reclines, leaning on an elbow and cradling the girl's gold head and burnished shoulders in his lap. Her left arm is raised behind her and draped with negligent ease about his mighty neck. He gazes before him, seeing nothing. In his ancient eyes there is that look, of weariness, dashed hope, tormented melancholy, which I have seen in them so often—too often—at moments such as this. He is rehearsing in his head the age-old inquisition. When he speaks she hears not his but her husband's voice, and feels her husband's familiar breath waft over her breasts, a lapsing zephyr. Familiar but, it must be mundanely said, unfamiliarly sweet, for this early, sleep-encrusted hour. For, oh dear, they do tend to pong in the mornings.

'Can people who are married be in love?' he asks, in young Adam's very voice. 'I mean, can they still care as deeply, as desperately, for each other as they did when they were lovers?'

Always at the start like this his heart races, as he thinks, Perhaps, this time—?

'Mmm,' she says, and squirms, snuggling closer against him, making the tangle of dry old hair at his lap crackle under her like a nest of thorns. 'You ask such things, and at such times.'

His arm is across her belly, his great, rough hand caresses her warm thigh. 'You know,' he says, 'it is not your husband who is here now.'

She smiles. He sees upside down her mouth, with lips pressed shut, flex like a myrmidon's small-bow being drawn; her eyes are lightly closed under fluttering lids. 'Who, then?' she asks.

He waits a weighty moment. 'Why, your lover, of course.'

'Oh, yes,' she says, with a contented, feathery sigh, squirming closer still, 'him, too.'

Such far silence, not a sound, in this suspended world.

She opens her eyes and vainly seeks for focus in the depthless shadows above her. A blissful ease suffuses her veins. She thinks of the baby she lost last year, not with the all too familiar breath-catching stab of woe, but calmly, remotely, even; it is like looking back across a plain and seeing only a smudge of dust where a moment before had been fire and ruin and loud lamentation. The baby died inside her after some weeks of a sort of life. Not a baby at all, then, really. She pictures it as a little soft limpet clinging to the wall of the womb, blind and bewildered, washed at by amniotic tides, assailed by the muffled sounds of her innards at work, a frail failing impossible thing.

'But which would you rather,' he persists, and she feels his fingers tensing on her thigh, 'the lover, or the husband?'

She might be exasperated but instead is amused. She is accustomed to her husband's finicking way, his insistence on tracing all lines of enquiry to their logical end, as if things had an end, as if they were logical. He wants to be his father, reducing life to a set of sums. But Adam is softer than his father, and younger than the old man ever could have been, and love, not logic, is his weakness. What need has she of a baby when she has him? This is one of her secretest thoughts, one of the ones she must never utter.

'Husband or lover,' she says, 'what is the difference— a ring?'

'A vow.' She puts back her head quickly to squinny up at him. His voice had sounded so strange, so deep and strange, as if it were he, now, who was making a solemn pledge. 'Don't you see,' he goes on in that same, thickened tone, in earnest haste, '—what I feel for you exceeds infinitely what a mere husband could ever be capable of feeling? Didn't you sense that, here, with me? Have you ever been loved like this before?'

'Oh,' she says, laughing, 'it was divine, surely!' She is looking up lazily again into the somehow luminous dark. She feels him nodding.

'Yes,' he says. 'And you won't forget this night, will you? When the sun rises and your husband returns you'll remember me—won't you?'

'But you'll be him!'

'I shall be in him, yes, but he will not be me.'

'Well, whichever. You're making my head swim.' With the arm that is about his neck she pulls his head forward and kisses him on the mouth the wrong side up. 'Oh,' she says with a little shiver, 'you feel like you have a beard.'

'Promise,' he whispers, his face suspended featureless above hers, 'promise you'll remember me.'

She grasps his head by the ears as if it were a jug and tries to waggle it. 'How could I forget you, you dope?'

When she releases him he leans back on the pillows and she sees that the window behind its thin curtain is engreyed, and there is a gleam on a curtain rail, and the outline of Adam's football poster appears on the wall, and when she looks along herself she can see her toes. It is all too quick, too much. Her eyelids droop. *'Promise!'*— the whisper comes again but as if from far off now. She tries to say yes, tries to give her pledge, though to what,

78

exactly, she does not know, but sighs instead and draws up the sheet to cover herself and turns on her side and sleeps.

He too is sleeping now, my foolish father, having ranted his fill on the fickleness of girls—he, *he* complains of fickleness!—and their interfering husbands, the poor boobies, who do not even know themselves cuckolded. Young Adam is lucky not to have got a thunderbolt between the shoulder-blades as he blithely ploughed his wife there on that bed my Dad had so lately vacated, in the light of this day I was at last allowed to let break. And now the great god, all ardency spent, is stretched upon a cloud-bank with his thumb in his mouth, dreaming of who knows what. He is heart-sore, or would be if he had a heart. Do not mistake me, I feel a certain compassion for him. I too have found myself in his predicament, or ones very like it. I am thinking of Acacallis, Minos's daughter, and fair Chione, mother of my boy Autolycus—oh, yes, Dad is not the only one: I have had my dalliances among the mortals, and afterwards, like him, have gnawed my knuckles in rage and pain when I had to give this or that girl back to the bonehead she was shackled to. But I do not think I suffer the same weakening effects, these droops and desponds, as Dad does from his adventures in the flesh. It seems worse for him each time, which is supposed to be impossible since nothing may change in our changeless world, either for good or ill. Perhaps he really is dying, perhaps the pursuit of love is killing him, and this is why he so fiercely persists, because he longs for it to kill him. A dying god! And the god of gods, at that! Ah, mortals, have a care and look to your souls, for if he goes, everything goes with him, bang, crash and done with at last, his Liebestod become a Götterdämmerung.

I have a confession. I indulged in a little adventure of my own this morning, after I tired of spying on my father at his pleasures with the supposedly dreaming Mrs Adam and had fixed the clocks and set the morn to rights. Hotly restless, I ranged the house in search of diversion, and chancing on nothing to suit me there—the lady Helen was asleep and anyway off-limits, and the poor child Petra would hardly have been a fit candidate for my purposes— I swooped outside and in a twinkling found myself before Ivy Blount's cottage. It is a grim, two-storeyed edifice with a steep-pitched slate roof and narrow, arched window-frames painted a shiny and peculiarly unpleasant, even sinister, shade of blackish green. Ivy when she saw me gave a little bat-squeak—even Ivy's frights are tentative—and put a hand to her mouth, as maidens are meant to do, even elderly ones.

'God almighty,' she said, 'how did you get in?'

'Down the chimney,' I answered, rather overdoing the gruffness, I suspect—it takes a moment to slip fully into character, even for a god. But Duffy the cowman is a fine big chap and his frame fits me well. He is called Adrian, unlikely as it may seem. I note that Ivy does not address him by this name, or by any other, for that matter, out of a reserve natural to her class and vintage—

she is a daughter of the demure 'fifties—along with an inability to take as genuine the attentions he persists in pressing upon her. Mind, she is not indifferent to his rough charms, not at all, only she cannot make herself believe that such a strapping fellow could possibly be romantically drawn to the dry old maid she has reconciled herself to being—he must be a good ten years younger than she is. She darkly suspects it is the house, her little house, that he is after.

Anyway, there I was, incorrigible prankster that I am, got up as a horny-handed son of the soil, Gabriel Oak to the life, in an old torn tweed jacket and corduroy trews, a calico shirt *sans* collar and a red kerchief knotted carelessly at my throat. I fancy a pair of leather gaiters would have rounded off the picture nicely, but at that, prudently, I drew the line, though with regret.

Those green window-frames are still troubling me, I wonder why.

Ivy was sitting on a kitchen chair in the sunlight in the open back-doorway. She held a freshly killed chicken in her lap—yes, the speckled brown one, with the orange feet—which she was plucking. When she turned, startled by the sound of my step behind her, the legs of her chair shrieked on the slate doorstep. The early sun was shining full in the doorway and there was a mingled smell of poultry and stewed tea-leaves and damp grass, and that particular sharp, gooseberryish something that the countryside exhales on summer mornings. I had put on the look—earnest, awkward, annoyed—that Duffy seems always to adopt in Miss Blount's presence. The annoyance springs from that resentment all mortal men feel towards those to whom they are attracted; I imagine even the brow of Peleus's son Achilles must on occasion have darkened when lover-boy Patroclus came clanking into his tent for the umpteenth time. Ivy's face is long and sharp and her unruly brown hair resembles a rook's nest, yet for all this, and the fact that the first blush of youth has long ago faded from her cheeks, she is possessed of a peculiar, subtle beauty. Her smile, rare and radiant, flips open a charming little fan of crow's-feet at either temple, and when she smiles she dips her head quickly in shyness, and for a second seems a girl again.

'I wanted to talk to you,' I said.

She had turned back to her grisly task—is not the skin of a plucked chicken horribly reminiscent of what I imagine is the look and texture of the back parts of an old man?—and gave a laughing sniff. 'Oh, do you now? And what about, may I ask?' Ivy has a sweet voice, too, light and mellow; in it, she used to speak three or four languages, thanks to her time at a Swiss finishing school, whence she was bundled without notice in the middle of a spring term when the family's fortunes went wallop.

'The future,' I said.

'Well, that is a big enough topic.'

I went and stood in the doorway with my hands in the pockets of my trousers, looking down on her. I noticed that her nest of hair, so abundant elsewhere, is thinning at the crown, and the white skin shines through, as if mother rook had laid an egg there.

'Are you not going to offer me a cup of tea?' I said.

She did not look up from her work. 'I'm busy, as you see.' How deft she is, the feathers fairly flew. 'Anyway, you're out early.'

'They're all business up at the house, too,' I said, 'just like yourself.'

'You came that way?'

'I did.'

'No news?'

'No news.'

Which is their coded way of conferring together on the question of old Adam's expected demise.

I went to the dresser that stands against the wall opposite the back door and took a big brown mug down from its hook. There was a pitcher of milk on the table. I filled the mug and drank deep. The milk was barely cool and noticeably soured; one of the incidental interests of taking on temporary mortal form is the opportunity it affords of sampling new sensations. I had never tasted sour milk before; I shall not taste it again. I went back to the doorway. Ivy looked askance at me from under a straggle of that hair. 'You have a white moustache,' she said. I flew a finger to my upper lip, fearing I had made a blunder when getting into my disguise, but of course it was only a moustache of milk. I speculated afresh as to the extent of the freedoms Duffy enjoys here. I had helped myself to the milk with an almost proprietorial bravado and had met with not a peep of protest. It was a modest liberty, I admit, but in this area the small things can be the greatest giveaways.

'What I'm saying,' I said, squinting off into the

sunlight, 'is that the upkeep of a house of your own these days is no joke.' Ivy's vegetable garden, modest but scrupulously tended, is bordered at its far end by a fuchsia hedge hung with a profusion of intense red blossoms. It made a pretty picture, the scarlet bells and the dark hedge and then the green beyond, of bank and field and tree, in all its shades. Ivy had made no response to my gambit, but was waiting to hear how I would proceed, and waiting with pricked-up interest, as I could sense. Yet I paused. I would have been glad of a helping word from her. You must understand, a god is not a gentleman and likes nothing better than to trifle with a lady's affections, but there are rules that apply even to a divinity, and it was incumbent on me to proceed with caution and deference, if the niceties of the game were to be preserved. Nevertheless, I did not have all day. 'That place of mine,' I said, 'is beggaring me.' Duffy too has a cottage, not unlike this one, crooked, stark, stone-faced, on the other side of the hill, in which he has lived all his life, until recently in uneasy cohabitation with his widowed mother, a rough-edged baggage generally considered to have been a witch, who died at a great age only last year.

'Beggaring you!' Ivy said in false wonderment, mildly mocking me. 'That's terrible.'

Ivy's cat appeared, slinking out of the grass on the far side of the cobbled yard. He is a ragged old tom called Tom, mottled in grey-brown shades that make me think of slugs; he has a great star-burst of spiked fur surrounding his face, like a tilted, horrent ruff, as if at some time in the uncertain past he had been given a great fright and had not yet recovered his composure. Seeing me he stopped and stared, his green eyes narrowed and a paw lifted. Baffling for him, I suppose, a Duffy who seemed Duffy in all particulars and yet was not Duffy.

'The roof on my place is gone,' I said, 'or going, anyway.'

I brought out a tin box of tobacco from the partly ripped left pocket of my jacket and a packet of papers from the right and rolled a cigarette, one-handed. Not easy. What skills they acquire, in their little span of life!

'Well, yes, a new roof would be an expense,' Ivy said, in a studiedly neutral tone. She was meant to admire my trick with the fag but refused to be impressed. She knows that Duffy's mother left a wad of banknotes stuffed in a nylon stocking under the mattress of her bed, but guesses the stash cannot have amounted to much. Oh, yes, she thinks, oh, yes, it is the house he has his eye on.

By the way, I am glad to say this is the last we shall hear of the tedious and hexish Ma Duffy.

'I'd sell up tomorrow,' I said, 'if I thought I'd get a decent price.'

The chicken was plucked but still Ivy did not raise her head to look at me. The backs of her hands are liver-spotted and her fingers are like bunches of fine, dry twigs. Across the yard, Tom the cat abruptly lost interest in me and sat down on his hunkers and lifted high a straightened hind leg and began nonchalantly licking the puckered grey eyelet under his tail. I listened to the medleyed buzz that summer makes, and thought how tentative these humans are, how they grope and fumble among their motives, hiding their desires, their hopes and trepidations from each other and themselves, perennial children that they are.

'And what,' Ivy asked in a faraway, muffled voice, still leaning forward and away from me, 'what would you do then?'

She lifted her feet out of the wellingtons and set them on the sun-warmed slate. Her arthritic toes are all knobbled and crooked. She waggled them slowly. Feet: how strange they are, tuberous and pulpy, like things growing under water. I looked away, embarrassed; strange that the littlest intimacies, such as a pair of bared feet, can make a mortal flinch, even one as stoutly bucolic as Mr Duffy. Above the hollow where the house is set the sky was a deep, packed blue, with here and there small clouds stuck to it like dabs of cotton wool—what a make-believe world it seems sometimes, no more than a child's bright daub. The cat came stalking across the cobbles and, ignoring me—obviously he had decided I must be a phantom—rubbed his flank against Ivy's bony bare shins that are diamonded all over with the marks of old chilblains.

'You mean,' I said, 'where would I live?' I ran a hand through my hair. Duffy is vain of this hair, so black, so glossy, so extravagantly waved. He never washes it, but lets it maintain itself, as an animal its pelt. He does not take care of his teeth, either, it seems, for when I sucked on them just now at the side I got a most unpleasant bitter taste, like wormwood. 'That's the question, though, isn't it?' I said.

As can be seen, in the matter of wooing I am not my father's son. What I lack in intensity, however, I make up for in cunning. You shall see.

Suddenly, violently, almost, Ivy rose from the chair and pushed past me into the room carrying the chicken cradled in her arms, where now it suggested not an oldster's backside but a fat, grey baby. Her damp soles had left wonderfully slim, stylised outlines of themselves on the blue step—odd, that such ugly extremities should make such lovely prints. The cat scampered nimbly after her without a sound. I did not quit the doorway but continued leaning against the jamb and turned my head and followed Ivy with my eye. What have I done with my cigarette? She set the chicken on its back on the table with its neck dangling over the edge and its claws retracting on themselves slowly in a gruesome and unnerving fashion.

'If you have something to say to me,' she said, in a voice that had a noticeable shake to it, 'come out and say it, then.'

What a striking tableau we must have made, a genre scene by one of the minor Dutch masters, me in the bright doorway and she in the smouldering dimness of the room and the still-life chicken on the table; look at the cat, the crockery on the dresser, delph, they call it—from Delft!—the red and black floor-tiles, and that glimpse of the sunlit day behind me in the door, mute and calm as money. Poor Ivy braced a hand on the table to support herself and looked at me with a look so needy and defenceless even I experienced a qualm. Something to say? I had nothing to say. I was just amusing myself, toying with one of my creatures, as so often is the way.

Turning to go, I nodded in the direction of the jug. 'That milk,' I said, 'is gone sour.'

ADAM FEELS LIKE Adam on the first day in the Garden. He is bowling along, yes, bowling along a country lane in his father's ancient station-wagon with his elbow set in the rolled-down window, whistling 'Lillibullero', the only tune he knows. The car is one of the original Salsol models, fitted with a prototype salt-water converter, which makes such a racket, housed in a big black box set lengthways under the front seats. The passenger window also is wide open and in the straight stretches where he puts his foot down there is a wild green rushing and thrashing on either side of him that makes his heart pound with a childish excitement. The mid-morning sun is shining strongly and the air flowing in from outside is redolent of fragrant dust and grass and a myriad growing things too faint and jumbled together to identify or name, even if he knew the names. At one time, when he was young, he had thought of becoming a professional gardener, not that he had a great feeling for husbandry or a great knowledge of what it entails, but he had believed it would be a pleasant and productive way of making a living. His interest had been sparked by the recent over-turning of Wallace's theory of evolution and the resulting to-do in the natural sciences that everyone was talking about; however, nothing came of his plan—another false start. Through gaps in the hedge he catches glimpses of gorse bushes yellowly aflame on the low hillsides, and in the hollows there are lingering blurs of morning mist. He is absurdly happy, perilously so—as is well known, human happiness is a great provocation to us. Under the flaccid worm in his lap he harbours still a warm, sticky smear of juices, his and Helen's mingled. At the thought of his golden wife he stops whistling and closes his eyes for a moment, remembering her this morning in the bedroom, in his shirt, advancing on him bare-legged along the length of the bed. The wind seizes his hair and shakes it. Yes, we gods do sometimes smile on our creation, but only sometimes, and never for long.

Is it not affecting to see him so pleased with himself, when we think of all that occurred earlier up there in his old room, while he was prowling the house unsuspect-ingly in that delayed hour before dawn? Mind you, it is a nice question whether he was betrayed by Helen and my Dad, in the technical sense, I mean. After all, Helen did not know the true identity of her divine lover, and thought he was her Adam, as why would she not? Then she decided it was all a dream and proceeded to re-enact as best she could what had happened in it, this time with her true, that is, her real, husband. And so passionate was she, fired with the godhead's inspiration, so wanton, indeed, to her husband's surprise and somewhat scandalised delight—after all, they were in the very bedroom where his hottest boyhood dreams were dreamt—that it could be said my father did nothing but prepare the way for the young man, this fellow whistling for happiness now as he steers the rattly old Salsol one-handed along these green lanes, bathed in remembering bliss.

He has a secret, one he will tell to no one, not even his wife, for fear of ridicule. He believes unshakeably in the possibility of the good. Not the transcendent piety of the saints, not the abstract entity of the philosophers, but that unemphatic impulse which, he is convinced, is the source of countless humble and largely unregarded decencies, decencies that in turn feed and sustain the source of their inspiration. Now, this would be a harmless fancy, if he did not conceive of the good as a thing in itself, active and forceful, and independent of any agent. For him, good and evil are two species of virus competing against each other for hegemony in the heart of man, with good managing to hold the upper hand, though barely. It is a not uncommon delusion among many millions since the days when the pale Galilean walked amongst you, or from earlier still, from the dawn of that awful day when Moses came marching down the mount with the news inscribed in stone that there is but one God and thou shalt have no other. But thou shouldst have stuck with us. We offer you no salvation of the soul, but no damnation, either; no afterlife in which to be bored for all eternity; no parousia, no day of reckoning and divine retribution, no kingdom of heaven on earth; nothing, in fact, except stories, comforting or at least comfortingly reasonable accounts of how and why things are as they are and by what means they may be maintained or even, on occasion, rare occasion, altered. If the wise man suffers it is due to a hidden flaw in him that we deplore, if the tyrant prospers it is because we admire his overweening and irresistible will. Why plague?—because your king is cursed. How shall your armies be victorious in battle?— place oxen and the odd virgin before our graven images and slit their throats. Sometimes we ask terrible things of you—think of Iphigenia, think of Iphigenia's father— and often we give you nothing in return. It is our way of demonstrating to you the inscrutable action of Fate. Above all, we would have you acknowledge and accept that the nature of your lives is tragic, not because life is cruel or sad—what are sadness and cruelty to us?—but because it is as it is and Fate is unavoidable, and, above all, because you will die and be as though you had never been. That is the difference between us and your mealy-mouthed Saviour, so-called—we do not pretend to be benign, but are playful only, and endlessly diverted by the spectacle of your heart-searchings and travails of the spirit.

The little station when Adam arrives there is deserted, no station master, no porter, no waiting passengers. He is early, the train is not due for another fifteen minutes, and besides it is sure to be late, as it usually is. The station is by the river, miles from anywhere, not even attached to a village—why was it built here, at the desolate edge of a marsh? It must have been for the convenience of some grand house nearby that is now long gone. Adam thinks of the past piled up behind him, its countless overlapping layers, and of what will have been his own brief moment on this so tender, frail and suffering earth. He parks outside the ticket office and walks through to the platform unchallenged. The pair of tweed trousers he is wearing, which he found in the wardrobe in the Sky Room, have begun to chafe the inner sides of his thighs. What was he thinking, to put them on? It seemed the necessary thing, at the time. This is another mark of his inherent and humble piety, this sense he has of the sacramental in even the smallest, even the most absurd, of actions. Well, holy these trousers may be, but he suspects they are not clean: they have an unpleasant smell, at once stale and sharp. They are the wrong fit, being tight at the waist and short in the leg, like the pyjamas he wore last night. Still, small as they are on him they are too roomy to have been Pa's, so whose, again, can they have been? He experiences a flash of anger. Is the house itself set on making a fool of him, getting him up in these laughable outfits and sending him stumbling into the world like a village idiot? But he knows it is not the house's fault that he looks foolish: it is his own.

He stands on the platform in the shade. Why is it, he wonders, that railway tracks always give off a smell of kitchen gas? He looks about. Nothing has changed here since he was a child, so far as he can see. The metal canopy overhead is painted yellow and edged with a wrought-iron filigree and must have been put up a century ago or more. The station is lovingly kept. There are pots of geraniums on the window-sills of the waiting room, the benches set at intervals along the platform are freshly varnished, and on the wall a stylised hand pointing the way to the lavatories is painted in bright-red lacquer with a shiny, thick black outline. But where is the station master, where is the cross-eyed porter with the black hoop thing that porters carry on their shoulders, who used to be a fixture of the place? The emptiness is eerie. He paces for a while, then sits down on one of the benches; the new varnish with the sun on it is hot and gummy to the touch. Beyond the tracks the grass is sere and ticks faintly in the heat. Beyond that again the broad reach of the river is a whitish-blue drift throwing off fish-scales of platinum light. The silence buzzes. Down on the track a ragged grey crow hops jerkily from sleeper to sleeper, looking for something, does not find it, gives a disgruntled croak and flaps away. The surge of heedless happiness that rose in him as he drove along the lanes has all subsided now. He has shattered the sunlit surface of the day, like a clumsy gardener putting his foot through a vegetable frame to the humid tangle of things beneath. He gets up from the bench and paces anew, more agitatedly this time.

He is prey again to the fear that his marriage is failing. There is nothing definite he can point to, as that big red hand points towards the jakes, only over the past year he has been aware of an increasing vagueness, an increasing insubstantiality, in his life with Helen. Something is fading, becoming bleached and dry. Does she blame him for the miscarriage? He does not see how it could have been his fault but maybe in some way it was. He cannot be sure; he cannot be sure of anything. The fact of the lost baby, the non-fact of it, is a tiny, desolate presence always between them, getting in the way. Sometimes when Helen looks at him it is as if she does not know who he is. He feels he is retreating in her sight, like a man standing on a railway platform, being looked back at from a window as the train pulls out, slowly at first, then gradually gaining speed. He imagines her turning from the window and settling herself on the plush seat, smiling at the other passengers in that unfocused way that she does, and taking up a magazine, and him already growing distant in her mind—

Suddenly, as if the thought had conjured the thing, the real train comes shuffling into view down the line, one of the new-fangled models that run on steam, the big imperial-blue engine with the black cow-catcher and the carriages after it, scarlet with gold piping around the doors and windows, all shimmering in a silky veil of heat-haze rising from the track. On time, for once!

—And yet, an hour ago, when she came stumping comically on her knees over the bed to him and seized his face and pressed it against her breasts and laughed her tigerish laugh, surely he was wholly there, wholly himself, flesh and blood and solidly present in her arms?

What casuistries they are capable of, even the simplest-minded among them, what fine distinctions and discrim-inations they devise! This is what we never cease to marvel at, the mountains they make out of the molehills of their passions, while all the time their real, their savage, selves are crouched in hiding behind those outcrops, scanning the surrounds for danger or opportunity, for predators or prey.

When the train draws to a stop Roddy Wagstaff is the only passenger to get down. Tall and slender and slightly stooped, Roddy has the aspect of a film heart-throb of a former time. He wears narrow fawn slacks sharply pressed, and pale-tan, slip-on shoes, and a white shirt that fairly shines in the sunlight, the collar open over a loosely knotted yellow cravat. His caramel-coloured hair is parted at the side and carefully arranged in a casual sweep across his brow. He has green eyes and a phthisic pallor. A white linen jacket is folded over one arm, and he carries a slim pigskin suitcase, old but good, which for some reason adds a touch of the sinister to his appearance. When he sees who is there to meet him a delicate frown concentrates itself between his rather close-set eyes. He casts a dubious glance at Adam's rust-coloured trousers and the three inches of ankle showing below the turn-ups. 'Oh, hello,' he says without warmth. Like Adam's father, Roddy does not bother with proper names.

The two young men walk side by side along the plat-form. Adam spots on the wall outside the waiting room a faded tin advertisement for Player's Navy Cut—lifebuoy with rope, stout Jack Tar, and distantly behind him on the rolling main a pair of three-masters under full sail—that he has never noticed until now although it must have been there since before he was born. Time once again brushes him glancingly with its cold wing. As if prompted by the advertisement Roddy pauses to take out of the pocket of his linen jacket a flat silver cigarette case, flips it open and chooses a cigarette and lights it with a petrol lighter of the same antique vintage as the silver case. A waft of rich, exotic smoke reaches Adam's nostrils. They walk on.

'Your father,' Roddy says between puffs, 'how is he?' He does not look at Adam. Roddy affects always a distracted mien, distracted and faintly gloomy, as if he were in constant anticipation of something that he is certain will displease him. His hands betray a slight tremor.

'Much the same,' Adam says.

'The same as what?' Roddy almost snaps. 'You forget, I haven't seen him since he suffered the stroke.'

They come out on the station steps. Roddy's sour expression softens when he sees the familiar old Salsol with its lacquered, brown wooden trim waiting for them on the gravel in the sun. Moving forward they pass under a nondescript tree that stands in the heat with its head hanging, and for a second it seems to Adam that Roddy as he enters its shadow fades somehow, becoming a blur, almost transparent, almost vanishing. He blinks, and then Roddy has stepped through into the sunlight again, and is turning back to him, saying something. 'Yes,' Adam replies, 'yes,' not knowing what he is agreeing to, not listening. He is carrying Roddy's suitcase, which Roddy set down on the platform when he stopped to light his cigarette and did not bother to pick up again, and now he goes to stow it in the back seat of the station-wagon, and leaning in at the door he pauses and closes his eyes and breathes deep the car's familiar smells of crusted salt and mildewed leather and human sweat, and at once he catches again faintly a snatch of the melody of that happiness he felt only a little while ago, driving along, and he recalls again too his wife kneeling before him on the bed, her hot hands on his face, her glittering, avid eyes. When he clambers in behind the steering-wheel— even the big station-wagon is too confining for his bulk —he finds Roddy already settled in the passenger seat with his jacket on his lap. He has not finished smoking his cigarette and waves it now airily and says, 'You don't mind, do you?'

The heat of the latening morning has intensified and as they drive back along the narrow roads the scent of dry grass and baking earth is stronger than ever and stings their nostrils. Roddy has shut his window but the shuddering rush of air from Adam's side scatters burning specks of ash from the tip of his cigarette and forces him to stub out the last quarter of it in the ashtray under the dashboard.

'Pete is looking forward to seeing you,' Adam says. 'She has been up since dawn, talking about you.'

'Oh, God,' Roddy murmurs, and looks out at the high hedgerow streaming past. Roddy knows what Petra's day-long monologues are like. 'Is she still collecting diseases?'

'Still at it,' Adam answers with spiteful cheer. Roddy finds Petra's projects exasperating. Her latest is an almanac of ailments in which she aims to list, complete with clinical definitions, all the illnesses known to afflict mankind.

'How far has she got?'

'Astasia-abasia is the most recent one I heard her

mention.' Roddy turns to look at him. 'Losing the will to stand up and walk. Rare, but recorded, so she claims.'

'God,' Roddy moans again.

I, by the way, in case you have forgotten me, am perched in the middle of the back seat, leaning forward eagerly with my hands pressed between my knees—I have knees, I can perch—taking in everything, words, gestures, looks, noting it all, for this that is happening, or not happening, between these two is what they call life.

'You should take her out somewhere,' Adam says.

Roddy snickers. 'A hike, you mean, something like that? A tramp in the hills?'

'Why not? Or take her into town.'

'Into town?'

'Yes, take her out to lunch.'

Roddy is looking at him again. 'Take Petra, to town, for lunch?'

'Well, just for a walk, then—anything. She's lonely, Roddy. She's too much on her own. It is not good for her.'

To this Roddy makes no reply, only turns to the windscreen again with a deep, irritated sigh. Roddy's ways are older than his years would warrant. In his middle twenties, he has the manner, by turns prickly and jaded, of a much more elderly man. He leads a mysterious life, being of shadowy provenance and uncertain intent. It is hard to know exactly how he makes his living. Pieces by him appear occasionally in the pages of broadsheet newspapers and in the glossier magazines, on abstruse subjects —Byzantine ceramics, American vernacular furniture of the nineteenth century, contemporary monastic life on Mount Athos—but these can hardly provide an income sufficient to keep him in the Turkish cigarettes and silk foulards to which he is so partial. His people are said to have money, but his relatives, those numerous rich great-aunts and venerable landed cousins whom he makes frequent mention of, all seem to be distressingly long-lived. One night when he was staying for the weekend at Arden he drank a glass of wine too many and confessed to young Adam his plan to persuade young Adam's father to appoint him his official biographer. Adam laughed at this, to Roddy's hurt surprise. The following morning, crapulent and shaky, Roddy took Adam off into a corner and swore him to secrecy on the night's blurted indiscretion, and even yet Adam is aware of a certain restraint towards him, however grudging, on the part of an otherwise sharp-tongued Roddy.

They hurtle down the green lane and then come out on the Hunger Road, a long, straight stretch of smooth tarmac running beside the river. It dates from the famine times, a make-work project for the unemployed poor and starving of the county. Adam feels uneasy on this road. A sense of its desperate purposelessness weighs on him. All this area of marsh and slobland is uncanny. Everything seems to face away, looking stolidly elsewhere, and even when it is sunny the sunshine appears watered and weak. The river drifts into the estuary here, and the widening expanse of water, flatter somehow than even water should be, is featureless and forlorn. There are wide stands of sedge, dry and grey—why is it, Adam wonders, that one never sees green sedge?—and herons and an occasional egret, the latter seeming the smaller, pure-white ghosts of the former, and a black cormorant perched on a log with wings spread wide to dry, as though posing for its portrait as an imperial emblem. Forgotten jetties, their silvered planking smashed or crumbling, extend a yard or two into the water and abruptly halt. There are broad sheets of shiny, indigo-tinted mud arrowed all over with the prints of wading birds, and here and there a rowing boat or a duck-shooter's white-painted punt is stuck at a drunken angle in the sludge. At a point where the river narrows, a mysterious wooden footbridge with a rusted hand-rail crosses from one sodden bank to the other, going from nowhere to nowhere.

Adam is wondering idly where exactly it is that the river ends and the estuary begins. Beside him Roddy is trying to light another cigarette but the draught keeps snatching the flame of his lighter. Adam pretends not to notice, and will not roll up his window despite the sulphurous reek of mud and rotting seaweed being borne in from outside. 'How was the journey down?' he asks. Roddy, annoyedly fitting the unlit cigarette back into its case, looks askance with an exaggerated frown, pretending to find the question too baffling in its simple-mindedness for him to begin to comprehend it. 'The train,' Adam says, in a louder voice. 'How was it?'

Roddy shrugs. 'I don't know. Same as usual, I suppose —dirty, slow.'

Adam nods absently; he is used to Roddy's languid rudenesses. Of course, he is thinking, there would be no line or boundary at which the river stops being the river and the estuary starts being the estuary: they would flow into each other, necessarily, back and forth, according to the onward rush of the river and the more or less pressure of the alternating tides. Yet there must be some area of demarcation, surely, however broad or amorphous. He ponders the problem and, having pondered, comes to the conclusion that it is not a matter of the river being one thing and the estuary another; all that separates them, really, and it is not a real separation at all, is his having put the question in the first place. For the question is premised on two, man-made, terms—river, estuary—whereas in fact there is but one body of water, commingling here at the whim of unceasing flow on one side and of changing tides on the other; any separation is a separation made only by the action of his asking. This is strange.

'Does your father speak at all?' Roddy enquires. 'I mean, can he?' There is a tinge of umbrage to his tone. The world keeps putting hindrances in his way, of which Adam Godley's sudden collapse is the most recent and, for the moment, most serious example.

'Oh, no,' Adam says. 'He's in a coma.' Roddy nods. 'But of course,' Adam continues, 'no one can say how deep the coma is. He may be aware at some level, and able to think, and hear, for all we know. La says she's convinced he's conscious but just can't communicate—she says he opens his eyes, though no one else has seen him do it. You might talk to him. He always did like having a talk with you.'

Roddy glances at him sharply, suspecting irony.

A further thought has struck Adam. Salt—what about salt? The river is fresh water but the sea is saline. That is a definite distinction. He does not know why he did not think of it at once, especially since—thanks to the discovery of cold fusion, the science of it founded, to the surprise of all, on his father's notorious Brahma equations—the greater part of the world's energy nowadays is derived from brine. And there is motion, too. All very well to speak of whim, but when the river's outgoing flow meets the tide's incoming flood there are two forces in opposition, and two forces mean two separate things doing the forcing. Then after all it is not merely a matter of man—in this case Adam himself—proposing, but of fact disposing. River here, estuary there, not two names only but two discrete entities. Yet where do they merge, exactly? He sighs. He is back to where he started.

Now they turn off the straight road and leave behind the river and its wastes of water and climb into the low hills that were once a part of Arden demesne. As this little elevation is steadily gained Adam's spirits lift too. The going on this road is bumpy and the station-wagon yaws and rumbles and they hear the salt water sloshing in the tank under their seats. The hill to the left is a hedge-less upward sweep of close-cropped sward capped by a small stand of larches. Sheep are placidly grazing the hillside. A pied horse kicks up its hoofs as they pass by, gallops friskily a little way, stops and turns its head and looks back at them boldly, showing them its behind and flicking its tail from side to side. Rooks wheel in sunlight above the little wood. O Arcady! how I pine for thy brooks and glades.

'I have a great fondness for your father,' Roddy says. Adam has to make an effort not to smile—Roddy has a way of saying things as if they had been written down on prompt-cards and practised many times—but before he can reply Roddy speaks again, quickly, in a muted yet vexedly accusing tone. 'I know what you think of me.'

'Do you?' Adam, surprised, says. 'I'm not sure I know myself what I think of you, or of anyone else, for that matter.'

Adam waits, but Roddy, it appears, has nothing more to add. He sits with his head thrust forward, looking steadily out through the windscreen with a faint, pursed smile, of satisfaction, even of triumph, it might be, as if there had been a hash in need of settling and he had settled it with gratifying finality and dispatch. Adam has the unsettling sensation of having been engaged in a far more extensive, far more rancorous exchange, involving him but carried on somehow without his full participation.

I am admiring the gorse blossom: it is truly glorious, a froth of buttery gold over the hillsides and along the hedgerows. Aye, this world we gave them appears a pretty place, on occasion.

'Is this all your father's land?' Roddy asks.

'No, no. There's only the house and the acre or two it stands on, and the wood behind. The rest was sold off long before our time.' Roddy nods. He peers out at the passing spectacle of green and gold and wrinkles his brow as if faintly deploring all he sees. Adam glances down sideways at Roddy's tan slip-ons. His white linen jacket is folded on his knees as neatly as a parcel. 'Everyone is glad you've come, you know.' Roddy does not respond to this, but holds himself aloof, pretending he has not heard or is too preoccupied to pay heed. Adam presses on. 'It's strange, the house, since Pa got sick. We feel we're all'— he sadly smiles—'mourners-in-waiting.'

Roddy turns his head quickly to look at him. 'Is he going to die?' He sounds incredulous.

They round a bend and the house comes into view. Really it is, Adam sees, not for the first time, an impossible sort of folly, square and mad-looking, with its yellow-painted walls and pale-blue shutters and that winged tin figure—ahem!—atop the single turret. Viewed from this perspective the entire structure seems to lean slightly to one side, drunkenly. Two palm trees, dusty and dejected, stand one each before either pillar of the gate—palms, in this climate, and here, in the heart of the country!— brought from afar, perhaps on the SS *Esmerelda*, by a Blount forebear of missionary or, more likely, buccaneering bent. When he was a boy Adam used to play with their shed fronds, pretending they were scimitars, duelling two-handed with himself. As he turns the car from the road on to the drive the crunching sound the wheels make in the grit-filled ruts brings back for an instant a confusion of lost, sunstruck summers. Rex has heard their approach and in the distance sets up a deep-throated barking, each bark followed by a measured pause, as he waits in vain for echo or response. They wallow on soft tyres to the end of the avenue of limes and make a half turn around the no longer functioning fountain—a blank-eyed boy on a rampant dolphin, last year's dead leaves choking the dry basin—and pull up short on the gravel outside the front door and sit unmoving for a moment in the sudden, startled silence.

'Look, Roddy,' Adam says, and pauses. Roddy has taken out the flat silver case and is judiciously selecting a cigarette, as if they were not all perfectly alike. 'I want to ask something of you. I want to ask you to be nice to my sister.'

Roddy stops with the cigarette half-way to his lips and lifts his eyes and looks straight ahead. The sloping glass of the windscreen with the sun on it is greyly hazed and all beyond is indistinct. 'Nice?' he says, seeming to dangle the word aloft by one corner.

Adam's bare elbow is hot where it rests in the car's open window. Five ducks in a skein fly over fast, their wings making a whirring sound—*hurry-hurry-hurry*—and from far off, out on the slobland, there comes, insequentially with the seemingly fleeing ducks, the miniature muffled thud of an out-of-season shotgun-blast. The front door's blue paint is peeling; gnarled wisteria wreathes the lintel.

'Yes,' Adam says shortly, and puffs out his cheeks and lets them deflate again. 'Nice. It's not so much to ask, is it? Think of it as a gesture to Pa. Because he is dying, you know.'

Roddy, lighting his cigarette, seems about to laugh—at what?—when the front door opens and Rex shoots out, barking again. He dashes menacingly towards the station-wagon with stiff, arthritic gait, not so much running as bounding up and down from back legs to fore like a rocking-horse set jerkily in motion. When he sees Adam his bark breaks and he snaps his jaws shut and looks embarrassed. Adam gets out and Roddy on his side opens his door but holds it close and hangs back behind it until he judges the dog has done capering and the gravel-dust has begun to disperse. The harsh dry salt reek from the car's exhaust spreads thinly in the dusty air. Petra has appeared in the doorway, in baggy corduroy trousers and a long-sleeved blue shirt buttoned at the wrists, and stands with her left arm pressed stiffly against the peeling frame and frowning hard at a point on the ground half-way between her and the station-wagon, from behind the door of which now Roddy emerges, with his bag held protectively in front of him and his linen jacket folded over his arm, still keeping an eye on the dog, and advances towards her, queasily smiling.

Ursula in the Sky Room has heard Rex's barking and the sound of tyres on the gravel but goes on clipping her husband's fingernails. They do not really need to be clipped but she is doing it anyway, to be doing something. The curtains are still closed and the room is dark and she has switched on the reading lamp on the bedside table and angled it to light her task. She does not know why she keeps the curtains pulled against the summer day, or why, indeed, she set a reading lamp beside the bed. She cannot tell if her husband registers light or lack of it in those rare moments when he opens his eyes; she cannot be sure that he registers anything, but she makes herself believe that he does. His hands are cold as water, soft, and clammy. The nails are flattish and finely striated, and the skin beneath them is milky blue and the half-moons at their bases are a ghostly shade of grey. She started off with scissors but they were too fiddly and made her flesh crawl, and so she is using the clippers, which are easier though still it is a shivery business. She has never cut anyone's fingernails before, except her own, and she would not cut even those if there were someone who would do it for her. When Adam and Petra were small she was too squeamish to do theirs and left the job to their father or to his mother. She seems to remember that Granny Godley used to trim young Adam's nails with her teeth when he was a baby. Can that have been? Surely not—surely she is imagining it? Yet in her mind she clearly sees the old woman, lanky and white-skinned like her son, leaning over the cradle and baring her long, yellowish horse-teeth, exactly like the witch in a fairy-tale.

She knows it is not so yet she has the unnerving feeling that her husband, even though his eyes are closed, is watching her from the gloom outside the yellow circle of lamplight in which she leans, watching her along the blanket from under his eyelashes. It is how she often caught him looking at her, askance, smiling to himself, silently amused, especially in their early days together. She might have been his daughter rather than his wife, and even yet there are times when she feels like his child.

She is sure this is a terrible notion, and would never confide it to anyone.

Years ago, he shaved off his beard, without telling her, just appeared at the breakfast table one morning with half his face missing, or so it seemed to her in the first, shocked moment of seeing him. If she had met him in the street she would not have recognised him, except for his eyes. How strange he looked, grotesque, almost, with those indecently naked cheeks and the chin flat and square like the blunt edge of a stone axe. It was as if the top part of his head had been taken off and carved and trimmed and jammed down into the scooped-out jaws of a stranger. She almost wept, but he went on eating his toast as if nothing had happened. He had bought a cut-throat razor with an ivory handle, an antique thing from the last century; he showed it to her in its black velvet box lined with scarlet satin. She could not look at it without a shiver. He liked to show off his skill with it, and would leave the bathroom door open so she could admire the deft way he wielded the dangerous, gleaming thing, holding it at an elegant angle between fingertips and thumb, his little finger fastidiously crooked, and sweeping the blade raspingly through the snow-like foam. Harsh light above the bath and the steely shine of the mirror and one dark, humorously cocked eye glancing at her sideways from the glass. Where is it now, she wonders, that razor? In a week or two he got tired of using it and let his beard grow back.

Disturbing things, these little horny flanges at the ends of everyone's fingers and toes that never stop growing, even after death, or so she has heard said. What are they, were they, for? Killing, skinning, rending? Too weak and brittle for that. Perhaps they were stronger, long ago; perhaps they were claws. She thinks she read somewhere that they were originally tufts or pads of hair that became fused and hardened, in the same way that thorns on roses are supposed really to be leaves that over aeons coiled themselves tighter and tighter until they were sharp as needles. Yet it all seems highly improbable. She knows so little, and even the things she does know she doubts. Adam would be able to tell her about fingernails and how they came to be as they are. He would look it up for her. He liked looking things up. He would throw himself back on his chair, frowning deeply, his lips pursed as if to whistle, then sprint off to the bookshelves and return a minute later with a big book open on his hands, hurrying along as if on tiptoe, stooped and swift, reading even as he went.

Her mind has not allowed her yet to grasp the full extent of the calamity that has befallen them, not only Adam and she but the rest of the family, too. There is a saving numbness around her heart, she can almost feel it, like a film of insulating air between the walls of the beating muscle and the soft red pulp inside the rib-cage where it is suspended. For all that the doctors tell her, she will not, she simply will not be persuaded that he is entirely beyond consciousness and not merely asleep in some special, profound sense, and she keeps waiting for him to sit up and clear his throat and start asking for things, his clothes, food, a glass of wine, in that deceptively diffident manner he affects when he is at his most furious, looking aside and frowning, pretending to be thinking of something else. No, he is not unconscious, she is sure of it, only more deeply sunk than ever before in one of his impenetrable reveries. He always had the ability to withdraw from his surroundings, for days on end, wrapping himself up in himself and shutting out everything and everyone. When she sits here alone with him like this, in this peculiar daytime darkness, she seems to hear, or at least to feel, a distant low unwavering hum, which she is convinced is the sound of his mind still at work. When that sound ceases she will accept that he is gone, and not until then.

I approach and lean over her solicitously, folding my invisible wings about her sad, sloped shoulders. You see how, despite our callous ways, we keep you all in our care? She does not feel my presence, only its soothing effect.

She has finished trimming her husband's nails and holds his right hand now at rest on her left palm. Closer to the lamplight his skin loses its softness and takes on the look of marble, pale and moistly agleam. She hears voices outside on the stairs. Her son is showing Roddy Wagstaff to his room. She supposes Petra will be trailing behind them, going along by the wall, hunched and hangdog, as always.

Before Adam, she had thought herself content. Early on in her life, when she was still quite young, a child still, really, she had decided that the world was not for her. She had even thought of joining an order, entering a convent, but she stayed at home instead. She was the bird who builds its nest behind the waterfall and perches there quite placid, amid the constant crashing, the spume, the flashing iridescence. Adam was the one who drew her, briefly, into the heart of the cataract.

Water: it was always his element, his emblem, for her. The first time she saw him was on a bridge above a torrential river one winter day, under a scudding sky. She had come to witness the famous tidal bore, and someone had brought him to see it, too. She was anxious, for she was afraid of heights. She had a sensation of constantly falling forward, and kept feeling she was about to topple irresistibly over the rail and plummet down into the moiling river far below. He was standing a little way from her. He too was holding on to the rail, as if he too were afraid. The wind was blowing in his hair and his beard and to her he seemed to have a stricken, desperate look. Before they saw it they heard the sound of the bore, a low rumble that seemed to make the grey light around them shake and the metal of the bridge vibrate under their feet. Then it came surging round the river bend, a smooth, high, almost stately wall of water crumbling in slow-motion against the banks on either side. She was thinking how cold she was, despite her heavy coat and woollen hat. When the huge wave was about to pass under the bridge, for some reason she looked upwards instead of down, and the mass of low-slung, lead-coloured clouds sweeping overhead, like a confused reflection of the river raging below, made her feel dizzier still and for a moment it seemed, thrillingly, that she was going to faint. But she did not faint, and when she lowered her head, blinking, she saw that he was looking at her, and did not stop looking when she looked back at him. He smiled, though it seemed as if he were wincing in pain. She was nineteen.

They went to a pub set among trees on a grassy rise at the far end of the bridge. They sat in a tobacco-brown snug where the noise from below of the endless traffic rounding a broad bend in the road seemed an echo of her own blood sizzling in her veins. She could see the bridge through the trees, a pale-blue spectral web. When he asked her what she would like to drink the only thing she could think to say was gin, though she had never drunk gin before. And indeed it was like nothing she had ever tasted, cold and insidious and subtly discomposing. She liked the look of it, too, shinily metallic with the faintest tinct of paraffin-blue in its depths. He did not take off his overcoat but sat with one hand moving about inside the lapel, as if he were feeling for the source of an ache; he was always cold, he told her, could never warm up. With his plume of smooth black hair and great bony gleaming nose he looked like a bird of prey, sharp-eyed, distracted, brooding on some other place, some other solitary height. She sat opposite him very straight on the stool and sipped her drink. The mist from the river advanced up the hillside and pressed its flanks shyly against the bottle-glass windows behind them. The gin went straight to her head.

She cannot remember what they talked about. He was very cool and playful, teasing her a little and watching her with his head held to one side, smiling. She was not fooled. Despite the gin she saw through him straight away, saw through the hairline crack running athwart the carefully fashioned mask that he was holding up to her, saw right down to all the things that were coiled and curled inside him like those unimaginably tiny strings he told her people used to think the world was ultimately made of. She asked for another drink but he said he thought that two were enough. Then he started to tell her about his wife, about Dorothy, who had died. He stared before him intently as he spoke, frowning, as if it were all printed on the air and he had only to read it out to her. His tone was one of dull amazement; grief had amazed him.

He was older than her father. She did not care. When he asked her to marry him it seemed to her that she had already said yes, a long time ago.

She places her husband's hand back at his side on the blanket and watches it intently for the slightest twitch. She believes he would give her a sign if he could. Although she is convinced he is still there in his mind, present and conscious, it occurs to her that maybe it is not she that he is conscious of. Maybe it is not she that he is with, in there, as he was not quite with her that first day, in the pub, for all his teasing smiles and all his talk. Has he ever been a complete presence, for her? She feels a slow heave in the region of her diaphragm, as if some slothful and horribly distressed thing is trying to turn itself over on its back. What if he is with Dorothy? Who is to say he is not nearer to the dead wife than he is to the living one? There is a world of the living and a world of the dead and he is suspended in a place between the two. In that place, is it not likely the dead have more power than the living, are more distinctly present to the one who is already half-way along the way to join them? Maybe even now his lost wife is reaching out a hand to him, over the dark water, and calling to him softly to come to her.

She stands up quickly. When she switches off the reading lamp the darkness spreads itself instantly, and she imagines she can feel it against her face, on the backs of her hands, a softly clinging stuff. She moves away from the bedside, pressing a hand to the base of her spine, and softly groans.

From below she hears faintly the chiming of the clock in the drawing room, calling her back to the world and its wants.

The things that to Petra seem perfectly ordered are for others all jumbled and strewn. It is as if she were written in a primitive script of straight lines and diagonals, a form of Ogham that no scholar has yet learned how to decipher. Not even her father was able to crack that code. The others do not realise that this is what so tires and vexes her, the endless effort of interpreting herself for their benefit. Everything she thinks and intends must be translated into an approximation of their language before they can understand anything of what she is saying. She knows the world is not as she conceives it; she has known this for a long time, for as long as she can remember. Some parts of it are missing and some that are there are there only because she has put them there. This does not mean the parts that are missing are real and the ones that are present are not. It is a matter of fact.

It is, in fact, a matter of matter, as her father would tell her. For what is spirit in this world may be flesh in another. In an infinity of worlds all possibilities are fulfilled; that is one of the things that have been proved by what her father disparagingly calls his sums. Not that he would say it was proved, since all proofs, according to him, are provisional.

Time too is a difficulty. For her it has two modes. Either it drags itself painfully along like something dragging itself in its own slime over bits of twigs and dead leaves on a forest floor, or it speeds past, in jumps and flickers, like the scenes on a spool of film clattering madly through a broken projector. She is always either lagging behind or hopelessly far in front of everyone else, calling plaintively after them through cupped hands or gabbling back at them breathlessly over her shoulder. When she confessed this to her father, confessed how she never seemed to be in step with anyone else, he showed no surprise, and said she was quite right, that time is not uniform and only dull people imagine it is so. It was a summer evening, and they were in the wood behind the house, sitting beside the holy well in the little hollow of brambles and holly that has been here, her father says, since the Druids. She recalls the dampish light, the smells of moss and musty water, the sunlight a spiked glare of white gold and a swarm of tiny, translucent flies busily weaving an invisible design above the water of the well. They were sitting one at either end of the old school bench that someone long ago brought up there so that pilgrims to the place would have a seat to rest on—

there is a right of way through the fields to here and anyone is free to enter, and some still do, on holy days especially. She had her feet up on the seat and her arms around her legs and her chin resting on her knees. Time, her father was saying, looking upwards and scratching his chin through his beard, time has tiny flaws in it, tiny slippages, that in the very beginning hindered the flow of formlessness and created form. In the same way, he said, that your nails catch on something made of silk, with little hooks you did not know were there until they snagged. 'Do you see?' he asked. Flaws in the matrix, temporal discrepancies. So at the start, when there was still nothing, the world was, you could say, hindered into existence. The whole enormous thing—here he gestured towards all outside the dimness of the grotto where they sat—a vast grid of tiny accidents, infinitely tiny mishaps. He looked at her, smiling helplessly. 'Do you see?'

What would Roddy Wagstaff not have given to be there, listening to her father talking about time and its origins. She knows very well that Roddy only pretends to care about her so he can come down to Arden and see her father. Everyone, her brother, for instance, thinks she is hurt by this but it is not so—the contrary, in fact. It was Roddy's absorbed and single-minded sense of himself that so impressed her the first time he came to stay at the house. She had never known anyone like him before, except for her father, of course. Roddy seemed to her an entirely free spirit, weightless and airy and, unlike her father, unencumbered by labours, achievements, lavish renown. Roddy seemed to spend his life diligently and happily doing nothing. How she wished she could be even a little like that. All her life she had lived under the vast crag of her father's looming presence. When Roddy scrambled in and sat down beside her in the shadow of that rock, dusting off the knees of his slacks and nonchalantly lighting up a cigarette, he invited her to look, whether he meant to or not, at the grand vista that had been there before her all along, beyond the confines where for so long she had been crouching.

The word she thought of for Roddy, that first weekend when he came down to Arden, was debonair. It was not a word she had ever had occasion to use before, about anyone, even her father. She watched Roddy, in the conservatory after lunch, sitting on a straight chair with one slim ankle crossed on a knee and an elbow resting on the back of his chair and a hand tensely holding aloft his cigarette, vigilant, missing nothing, and all the while smiling tirelessly in her father's direction. She had never encountered anyone so smooth, so poised and yet so concentrated and determined, too. She even found the tiny rapid tremor in his hand a mark of distinction, the result no doubt of being watchful always of everything, himself in particular. He had fitted himself into the household like a knife into a sheath. It is his very lack of substance that she considers his most becoming quality. He is not earnest and dependable like her brother; he is not good, or nice; he is not anything, much, except ambitious, and acquisitive—he has a magpie's glittering alertness for small bright advantageous things, the useful trifles that others overlook. He has, besides, a fastidious sheen. She finds most people disconcertingly repellent, men especially. One of them will be standing in front of her, suited and belted, tie neatly knotted and a flower in his buttonhole, talking away and grandly gesturing as they all do, and suddenly she will picture him squatting on the lavatory, with his elbows on his knees and his drawers around his ankles, and underneath him all his awful puddingy things dangling over the steaming bowl. She thinks of puckered anuses, oniony armpits, disgusting tufts of curled-up, glistening hair—she cannot stop herself—of stuff under the flaps of their prepuces, up their nostrils, between their toes. Roddy, however, comes to her as bland and unblemished as a shop-window dummy. His skin has the dulled, waxen gleam of the slightly tarnished plaster of paris that manikins are made out of. She imagines him under his clothes all rounded and seamless save for the intricate joints at elbows, knees and ankles, and nothing between his thighs but a smooth, featureless bump. Unsleeping in her bed in these twilit nights she has fantasies of him being there with her, a beautiful plaster man lying motionless beside her, one knee flexed and one hand extended with an index finger raised as if to signal a waiter or flag a taxi, his perfect rosy lips curved in a pleasingly inane half-smile, his wide-eyed empty stare fixed on nothing, and she with her arms around him, feeling against her the soothing coolness of his shins, his flanks, his navelless belly.

Duffy the cowman is the opposite of Roddy. Only last night she thought of getting up and slipping out of the house just as she was, in Pa's oversized pyjamas, and running all the way down to Duffy's house behind the hill and throwing a handful of gravel at his window as people do in books, so that he would let her in and take her upstairs to his room and—and what? The thought of Duffy's rancid bachelor bed makes her tremble with revulsion, but with something else, too, something to which she cannot, will not, put a name. There is dirt embedded in the seams of the cowman's hands; the skin of his palms would be hard and rough and burning hot as all men's hands are hot, except her father's. She imagines that skin on her skin, the rasp of it, like a cow's tongue licking her.

Poor Petra, poor mooncalf, she is the one of all the household who is dearest to us. And because we love her so we shall soon take her to us, but not yet, not yet.

Now she trails along the hall behind Roddy Wagstaff and her brother, the one slim and vaguely beige, the other broad-bummed and big-shouldered. The heels of Roddy's narrow, neat shoes make a crisp tap-tapping on the black flagstones. In fact, when looked at closely the flags are not black, she has noticed it before, but an unpleasant, shiny deep brown, like the colour of burnt toffee or of the thick pelt of some large extinct animal. This hallway, which leads under a shadowy arch into the big square black-and-white central hall of the house, always stirs in Petra a memory, if memory is what it is, of something she cannot quite grasp, something out of a past too far for her to remember, too long ago indeed for her to have known, in the last century, it must have been, or in the one before or even the one before that again. It is to do with a man, heavy-set, scowling, though she does not see his features at all clearly, in old-fashioned clothes and high boots, standing here and not wanting to do something, to accede to some request or command, but knowing he will have to, will be forced to. That is all there is to this ghostly manifestation, the man looming here, bullishly sullen—does he wear something around his broad neck, a knotted scarf, or a stock?—on a summer day like this one, with the grandfather clock ponderously ticking and a splash of molten daylight from the open front doorway reflected in the mirror of the hall-stand. She is sure the man is one of Ivy Blount's forebears. She does not doubt that this memory of him, or vision, or whatever it is, though impossible, is real, too, in some way.

When she looks back to see what the phantom man would have seen—the front door open, the mirror shining—she notices Roddy Wagstaff's case standing on the doorstep, where her brother left it, having decided he had carried it far enough.

They pass under the archway into the chequered hall, the two young men going ahead, Roddy's heel-taps suddenly making a sharper sound in this taller space, and Petra behind them, she now with Roddy's pigskin case in her hand. The air in the hall has a faint sweetish fragrance —dry rot, Duffy suggests, with satisfaction—and the light coming down from the tall windows seems somehow bruised. Roddy has not said a word to her yet, not a real word. She will wait for him to look at her, to look at her properly, so that she is sure he is seeing her, and then she will smile, and not turn aside, but hold his gaze for as long as he holds hers. That is what she will do.

MEANWHILE, on a blast of divine afflatus, I am wafting Adam the elder across the seas to where together we shall invent Venice. Forty years ago, more. It is wintertime, and the city's vaunted charms are all crazed over by the cold. There are caps of snow on the bronze horses outside St Mark's and a freezing mist is suspended along the canals and under the quaint, toy bridges. He is sitting in a restaurant, upstairs, at a corner table, with a view across the canal to where the wedding-cake façade of a white church, which he knows he should know the name of, gleams phantasmally through the midday murk. In some corner of the low-slung sky a weak sun is shining and each wavelet of the leaden canal waters is tipped with a spur of sullen, silver-yellow light. He eats lamb chops and drinks a melony tokai from Friuli—today he can recall that wine as if he were tasting it again, the tawny flash and oily sway of it in the glass, the sour-sweet tang of the fat, late grape. He is grieving for his wife, newly dead. Grief is the shape of an enormous globe that has been thrust unceremoniously into his arms; he totters under the unmanageable, greasy weight of it. Thus burdened he has fled to the sinking city where he knows no one and there is no one who knows him.

And promptly a stranger approaches his table and introduces himself. He is a long-limbed fair smooth-faced person with a narrow head and high cheekbones and a somehow inappropriate ginger moustache which he keeps fingering as if he knows it is not quite the thing. He wears English tweeds, though he is no Englishman, and an unlikely canary-yellow waistcoat and a matching yellow silk handkerchief that droops negligently from the breast pocket of his houndstooth jacket. His name, presumably his surname, outlandishly to Adam's ears, is Zeno, and he claims to be a count, though from what line or by favour of which monarch he does not say. He makes polite and easy conversation—the weather, the outrageous prices in this restaurant, the slovenly ways of the Venetians—and presently, after three or four thimblefuls of grappa at the bar downstairs, the two of them are crossing the canal in a gondola. The winter afternoon is all salt and smoke and the harsh cries of seagulls. Adam sits in a huddle on the damp wooden seat with his thin raincoat pulled tight around him. He seems to himself a hollowed-out vessel with something rattling around inside it, the dried pea that his formerly solid self has shrunk to. At his back the gondolier, a gnarled old-timer wearing a short pea-coat over his regulation striped jersey, plies a long, amber-coloured oar and croons snatches of a barcarole. The boat wallows in the wash of a passing launch. Vague rain drifts out of the air.

The house, tall and shabby, is in a narrow lane behind the Salute. The ochre stucco of the front is missing in continent-shaped patches, which show the brick and clay-like mortar underneath. It is apparent from the dankness in the rooms and the silence hanging over everything like dust sheets that no one has lived here for a long time. In the windows of the living room there are views of the Giudecca and, beyond that, out over the lagoon to the great hydrogen-powered breakwater, recently erected to save the city from imminent inundation, that appears a low, dull silver beading strung along the curved horizon. On a squat table in the middle of the room there is set an enormous chipped marble head of Zeus—why, hello, Dad!—neckless, with a tight crown of curls and a pubic beard, seeming sunk to its chin in the wood and wearing an expression of puzzlement and slow-gathering indignation. In an armchair facing this irate godhead Adam sits, hapless and distracted, his hands resting limply in his lap with palms upturned, like one of the *commedia dell'arte*'s mournful clowns. The Count, who has not taken off his overcoat, produces a bottle of red wine and two goblets of purple Murano glass. He has the blandly unimpedable manner of a circus ringmaster. The wine is as cold as stone and so thick it makes Adam's gorge rise. Outside, the air has turned to the colour of inky water. In a window opposite him the parchment-brown dome of the Salute looms. He feels spongy and raw all over, he has felt like this for a fortnight, sodden with grief, flayed by guilt. He had always thought bereavement would be an inward process only, a malady of the soul, and is dismayed by its brute physical manifestations. His eyes scald, his lips are cracked, even the follicles of his hair seem to simmer and twitch. He is convinced he has developed a smell, too, a rank hot meaty odour, and there is a brackish taste in his mouth that nothing will shift. And yet, too, he is swept at intervals by a gust of what seems to be, of all things, euphoria, a trembling giddiness the like of which he has not known since he was a boy on the last afternoons at school before the summer holidays. How is this?—as if he had wanted his wife to die, as if he had longed all along to be rid of her. This is surely an appalling thought and yet, at the mercy of grief the inquisitor, he is compelled to think it.

The young woman when she arrives is called Alba. Her skin is of an impossibly delicate paleness—Adam thinks of ice, of breathed-on glass, of the cool hard creamy-silver sheen of a pearl. She perches on the arm of his chair. Her gaze moves here and there, settling with mothlike inconsequence on random objects, his wine glass on the table, the frayed edge of a floor rug, the god's outsized, glaring head. She has a look, at once dreamy and expectant, as if she were awaiting the imminent arrival of some as yet unguessed-at, marvellous thing. When she shifts her position on the chair-arm and puts a hand briefly on Adam's shoulder to steady herself he twitches as if a ghost had touched him. The Count beams upon them both and seems mentally to rub his hands.

The bedroom is bare of all furniture save a large low

square bed with a not entirely clean white cover and no pillows; above it on the whitewashed wall hangs an iron crucifix, which instead of a crucified Christ has four studs of ruby glass set one into each of its extremities. Adam savours the sudden candour of being with a stranger in a strange room, unclothed, in broad or at least broadish daylight; how cool the air feels against his skin, how poised the stillness, poised and somehow archaic. Alba has stepped out of her dress in one flowing, stylised movement, like a torero, the object of all eyes, trailing his cape in the dust before the baffled bull; underneath, she is naked. She looks to the side, downwards; her eyelids are so shinily pale and fine that Adam can see clearly all the tiny veins in them, blue as lapis. He takes a floating step forward until his chest is barely touching the tips of her nipples, behind which he senses all the gravid tremulousness of her breasts. She puts her hands flat against his chest and leans into him in the simulacrum of a swoon, making a mewling sound. Her hips are goosefleshed and he can feel all the tiny hairs erect on her forearms. When he kisses her hot, soft mouth, which is bruised a little at one corner, he knows at once that she has been with another man, and recently—faint as it is there is no mistaking that tang of fish-slime and sawdust—for he has no doubt that this is the mouth of a busy working girl. He does not mind.

They conduct there, on that white bed, under the rubied iron cross, a fair imitation of a passionate dalliance, a repeated toing and froing on the edge of a precipice beyond which can be glimpsed a dark-green distance in a reeking mist and something shining out at them, a pulsing point of light, peremptory and intense. His heart rattles in its cage, a vein beats at his temple like a slow tom-tom. When they are spent at last, and that beacon in the jungle has been turned low again, they lie together contentedly in a tangle of arms and legs and talk of this and that, in their own languages, each understanding hardly a word of what the other says. Alba, twisting a lock of her hair round and round a finger, pauses now and then to explore with the tip of an agile tongue the mauve bruise at the side of her mouth. She is from somewhere in the north—she waves towards the window behind her, showing him a damp, unkempt armpit—Bergamo, it sounds like, hence perhaps her pale skin and paler hair, for he imagines Bergamasks as blond, laughing types, he does not know why.

He tells her about Dorothy who has died. He marvels at how easy it is, suddenly, telling it all to her, out loud, with not a word of it understood.

In a little while he rises from the white bed and wanders off through the house until he finds himself in what appears to be the kitchen, an odd, elongated room, also white, that makes him think, disconcertedly, of a milking parlour, with a lofty ceiling and a row of frosted-glass windows high up along one wall. Zeno the Count is there, still in his overcoat, seated at a small round table on which stands, aptly enough, a glass of milk, partly drunk. The Count, who is taking his ease and smoking a cigarette, greets him with an open-handed gesture, in the papal manner, smiling. Adam is conscious of being shirtless and barefoot. He sees, in the stark light reflected from the walls, that the Count is older than he had seemed at first. His sideburns are grizzled and there are broken veins in his nose and in the pouches under his eyes. Adam senses a large weariness in him, the weariness of an old actor in the middle of a long run in a poor part. Yet perhaps he really is a count, last of a line as old as the Guelphs and the Ghibellines, reduced to pandering to bereft and needy travellers such as this one that he chanced upon today. He points to the glass of milk and then pats his belly and smiles wincingly and says, '*La solita ulcera.*' He goes on smiling; his expression is one of calm and not unkindly knowing. Adam sits down opposite him, suddenly exhausted, and folds his arms before him on the table and rests his forehead on them. He is cold. Shivers pass across his back in spasms like gusts of wind on the surface of the sea. Bells are tolling slowly all over Venice. He weeps, making no sound. The Count rises and taking off his overcoat comes and drapes it on his shaking shoulders. '*Poverino,*' the old man murmurs, 'you are cold.' Adam weeps on.

Dorothy, called Dottie, or Dot—even the diminutions of her name reducing her to next to nothing—a mere fortnight dead, is already, shockingly, this day in Venice, fading in his thought. It is as if she had not been sufficiently present, when alive, for her memory to flourish after death. She was a large woman, tall, that is, though not at all heavy. He recalls his surprise, the first time he held her in his arms, at the lightness of her; it was as if all her long bones, of which she seemed to have more than the normal quota, were hollow as reeds. He might have been embracing a tall, fragile bird, at once graceful and ungainly, a crane, perhaps, or an ibis. It strikes him how much in looks she resembled his mother, for they were the same type, pale, lean, angular.

She was secretive, was Dorothy, and led an endearingly furtive existence. The house where they lived for the years of their marriage was not extensive yet she could somehow manage to disappear in it for hours on end. An entire morning would pass without a sound from her, so that he would assume she had gone out—but where would she have gone out to?—then suddenly, padding from his study to the kitchen or the lavatory, he would chance upon her lurking in a passageway, or a doorway, or in the recesses of a room mysteriously made deeper and dimmer by her presence in it. She would start and turn towards him quickly, whipping her hands behind her back and widening her eyes in a panicked show of innocence, like a naughty child caught in the act. When he was with her he had always the impression that she was listening anxiously beyond him for something in the house, some small, telltale sound that would give her away. He wondered what she did all day long. She took up projects— gardening, exotic cooking, carpentry, even—but quickly tired of them. He could tell when a pastime had palled, for she had a particular way of laying a thing down out of her hands, a cookery book, a pair of secateurs, a ball of wool pierced heraldically with two crossed knitting needles, and turning vaguely away, with a vague sigh, trailing her fingers along a chair-back or the edge of a window-sill. The thing would stay there, where she had left it, until by a gradual process of transformation worked by time and neglect, its original identity would blur and it would become a mere object, inert and lifeless, its use almost forgotten, and as often as not he would be the one who in the end would put it away, discreetly, without comment. She had the guardedly distracted air of holding back some large revelation, or terrible confession. In the latter weeks of her life she grew increasingly remote, and he would catch her looking at him with a frowning surmise, as if she knew she knew him but could not for the moment recall just who exactly he was. He would say something then, softly, calmly, and yet would feel that he was calling out to her, more loudly than he had meant to, and she would start, and the light of recognition would dawn in her face and she would smile her radiant, helpless smile that seemed to start from a long way off and make its way to him over immense and difficult distances.

He wonders for how long she had been planning to go. Would she have made a plan, she who seemed to live as if each moment were discontinuous from all others? His mother was furious, at Dorothy and at him, insisting at first it must have been an accident, then accusing him and saying it was his fault, that by his neglect of her he had driven Dottie to her death.

When they took her body from the water there were stones in the pockets of her dress. How could she have thought a few stones would weigh her down and carry her to the bottom? Yet something had.

He accepted all his mother's charges, and blamed himself—they always do, as if they were the lords of life and death—and blames himself still, when he remembers to. The nights are especially hard. He tosses on his bed, sweating and moaning and muttering imprecations, like a martyr being roasted on a grid. He must not have loved her enough, that must be it. When he was young, the lesson he learned from his mother, as much by cuffs as caresses, was that love is action—what you do, not what you feel—but perhaps, he thinks now, it was a false lesson, and that love is something else altogether, something he knows nothing of. He sees it, this love, hovering like the Paraclete above the heads of a fig-leafed Cranach couple, streaming divine grace down upon them in burning rays. Where was his soul when this pentecostal fire was falling from the sky?

And the girl, now, the girl in Venice, Alba, was she Dottie's ghost, come back to comfort him? Perhaps she was. Sometimes a soul will be permitted a brief return from Pluto's domain by that taciturn gate-keeper and his polycephalic hound, but I do not know if she was one of them—I only conduct them thither not thence, for Pluto is a jealous god and fiercely guards his dread domain. Yes, yes, I know, I tried to do Orpheus a favour, he was so heartsore, but look at the consequences. Poor Eurydice, and poorer Orpheus, first losing his wife, then losing her a second time, then losing himself and ending up a severed head bobbing on Hebrus's little waves, singing still. I often think that for all our powers, or precisely because of them, we should not be allowed to meddle in mortal affairs, considering the catastrophes that our meddlings result in more often than not.

Once, many years later, Adam saw her again—Alba, I mean, not Dorothy, for he sees her every day, in a manner of speaking. This second sighting took place not in Venice but some small landlocked Italian city, he cannot remember which one. He was sure it was she, although it was the merest glimpse he had of her, in the street, in the midst of shuffling crowds. She looked no older than she had that afternoon in the house under the Salute, but she was changed, greatly changed. She was in a wheelchair, being pushed by another young woman, short and round and of a resentful aspect, with a frizz of red hair like so many filaments of copper wire bristling with electricity. This person also Adam was convinced he recognised. Was she not there, in the background, that day in Venice, when he was trying to leave and got into a wrangle over money with the Count? The Count, though firm about his fee, remained amusedly forbearing, showing the faintly rueful, patient smile of an adult being haggled with by a clamorous child over sweets, while, yes, there behind him this red-headed, fat young woman prowled the room in seeming anger, smoking a long cigarette and ejecting smoke in thin quick jets, like squirts of venom. How strange, the way they come and go, memory's figments. The wheelchair in which Alba sat, or better say was held fast, was of the old-fashioned kind, black, with a wooden hoop, worn smooth by long use, attached to the wheels on either side for the occupant to grasp and propel herself onwards, or backwards, for that matter, and two handles behind should she need to be pushed, which evidently, today, she did. She was clutching the padded arms of the chair and leaning forward urgently, her upper body twisted tensely off to one side, as if her helper had started off pushing her without warning while she was in the act of trying to pull herself up forcibly out of the seat. Her feet, with those slightly splayed, blunt toes that he surprised himself by remembering so clearly, were braced on the foot-rests, as if she might be about to make another desperate and doomed attempt at leaping up and effecting an escape. She wore a childish pair of transparent, cheap pink plastic sandals. The look of thrilled expectancy that he had remarked that afternoon in front of the god had become one of furious distraction; the marvellous thing she had been waiting for would not come, now. She was talking to herself, her lips moving in a slack, rapid mumbling, like a penitent in the confessional gabbling out a litany of sins and urgently demanding forgiveness. He might have hailed her, might have followed after the two of them and accosted them, but what would he have said, what done? Instead, he went on standing there in the lemony sunlight of the Italian noon, and saw again Venice in winter, the grimy air and the wheeling gulls, and gnarled old Charon the boatman crooning for his coin.

II

REX the dog is the first to spy the stranger toiling over the crest of the hill from the direction of the railway line. It's long past noon and a hazy stillness has settled over the fields. The trees stand seething in the heat. The air is grey-blue and lax. Everything shimmers. The man is short and fat and rather than walk he seems to roll along wobblingly, like a floppy tyre come loose from its wheel. He wears a black suit and a white shirt open at the collar. He keeps to the shaded side of the road. He seems to be in some distress—he must be sweating, in that suit. He is an unlikely apparition, on foot, on this leafy hillside. Rex is not surprised, however, for he has lived among people long enough to be accustomed by now to their frequently inexplicable ways. His sight is not what it was but his other senses are as keen as ever, his sense of smell in particular. He lifts his nose, which is the size and texture of a wet truffle, and sniffs the air, scanning for any hint of the man that a straying breeze might bring him. There is a tiny gland high up inside his muzzle, almost between his eyes, that can detect a single molecule of scent—and they boast of their opposable thumb! He is standing in the gateway at the end of the drive. Despite his age he cuts a commanding figure, with his square brow and thick-set shoulders. His tail has the elegant sweep of a frond of palm moving in a breeze. He strains his old eyes to make out the man's face but it remains a whitish blob. He produces one of his deep, far-carrying barks, which starts out in his belly and makes him give a little hop on his front paws. He turns his head to look back at the house. No door has opened, no one has appeared on the steps, not even a curtain twitches. Should he allow the stranger to enter, if he means to enter?

Which, as it turns out, he does. He arrives at the gate, gasping a little and dishevelled. Man and dog regard each other, then the man clicks his tongue and extends a hand and pats the dog's head, and the dog wags his tail. The stranger has a strong dark juicy smell, very pungent, a foreign smell, redolent of far away. 'Hello, Rex,' he says affably. Rex is astonished. How does the man know his name? He is smiling, too. 'Anyone home?' he asks, and shades his eyes with his hand and peers up the drive in the direction of the house. He has a bald pate ringed by a laurel-wreath of shiny black curls, an unhealthy-looking, bulbous face, white as a plate, and a nose like a broken little finger; his chubby, babyish hands seem pushed like corks into the ends of his fat arms. From the breast pocket of his suit he takes out a large white handkerchief and mops his brow and the pendulous bag of grey, froggy flesh under his chin. He steps past Rex on to the drive, and an ancient instinct urges the dog to sink his teeth into the fellow's ankle, but instead he sets off ambling in his wake, letting his hot tongue loll in the blissfully cool though dusty air.

Petra is upstairs in what is grandly called the morning room. It is a gloomy and inhospitable place and people rarely come up here, at morning or at any other time of day—the house has many such unused rooms—and she can work undisturbed. She has spread out her textbooks and medical dictionaries on the half-moon table with the spindly legs that stands against the wall opposite the windows. The table, which is old, has a wonderfully rich patina, and there are many deep and blackened scars in the surface of it, though the edges of them have been smoothed by age. How many others before her over the years have sat here like this, at this table, working, in the silence of a summer day? She pictures herself as someone looking on would see her, bent over her papers, pen in hand, like an engraving in an old book of a scholar at work on some legendary, abstruse concordance. Although she is right-handed she holds the pen as a left-hander does, her fist curled in on itself and the sharp knuckles white where the bones gleam under the stretched skin.

This is a marked day in the progress of her encyclopaedia of human morbidity, to which she has given the title *Florilegium Moribundus Humanae*—she is not sure if the Latin is correct but she is pleased with the sound of it—for she has just finished her entry on azotaemia, the last of the As, and tomorrow will make a start on the Bs, with bacillaemia, or possibly Babinski reflex, although strictly the latter is a symptom not a disease. She is writing in the quarto-sized blank manuscript book with the repeated fleur-de-lis design on the cover that her father brought home to her one year, from Florence, she thinks, it was, for her birthday. She writes with a steel pen, in lavender ink, with vigilance and concentration, always anxious not to make a blot. She likes the scratchy sound the nib makes on the heavy, cream-laid paper. To ensure the lines are straight she uses a ruler and a special implement with a toothed metal wheel to trace a ghostly track along which to write. She hears faintly, all the way from town, the Angelus bell. A trapped fly buzzes in a corner of the window behind her; the sound is like that of a tiny electric motor with an intermittent fault. She is not thinking of anything, especially not of Roddy Wagstaff, resting in his room after the rigours of his two-hour train journey. She is calm. Her mind floats like a hair on water. She writes along the ghostly dotted line: *an abnormal concentration of urea and other nitrogenous bodies in the blood—*

She had heard Rex barking down at the gate and at first paid no heed, but now something, some registering nerve between her shoulder-blades, alerts her that someone is approaching the house. She rises from the desk and goes to the window, still with the pen in her hand. She sees the man coming up the drive, with Rex at his heels. She draws back a pace, for fear of being seen herself. She hears the harsh sound of the man's tread on the gritted surface of the driveway. Watching him, she feels a sharp leap of misgiving, like the needle of mercury shooting up the barrel of a thermometer. She wonders who he can be, and how he got here, and what he might want. She does not like strangers coming to the house, especially like this, on foot, seemingly out of nowhere. It is her father being ill that has upset everything, and it is this that has brought this man now, too, she is sure of it. She is not sure what to do. Someone will answer his knock and let him in, but maybe he should be refused entry—maybe he should be sent on his way at once, without delay.

Abruptly she turns and flies from the room and across the landing and down the stairs two at a time, three at a time, and hauls open the heavy front door just as the man is lifting his hand to the knocker. He rears back in startlement, and Petra starts, too, so that they are both equally surprised, he at her and she at herself. There is the sense not of a door having opened but of a panel being slid aside between two worlds, and the outdoors seems to her unnaturally bright, as if lit from above not by the sun but by unseen giant lamps. She is breathing hard, and her cheeks are flushed. The man smiles. He says something she does not catch, his name, it must be. Rex, behind, puts out his head at the side of the man's knees and looks at her, questioning, uncertain. She moves back, jerking her arm out stiffly from her side in a curt invitation to the man to enter. He steps forward, stumbling a little on the raised stone threshold, and moves past her into the hall with his teetering, wincing gait—he is like a comically overweight ballet dancer whose shoes are too small and pinching him terribly. 'Do you mind if I sit?' he says, although he has already plumped himself down in the tall, forbidding black armchair with wings that stands beside the hall-stand; she has never known anyone to sit in it before. 'Pouf!' the man says, ballooning his cheeks. He takes out his handkerchief and mops his face again. His pasty skin gleams as if covered all over with a fine film of oil. His fat lower lip hangs loose, and she can see the tip of his tongue, pointed and greyly wet. 'Sorry,' he says, with, a desperate smile, panting harder to show her how out of breath he is. 'Hot.' He glances questioningly downwards—she is still holding the pen, poised as if to write, on air. She puts her hand quickly behind her back. She remembers the sound of the fly against the window-pane, its buzzing wings; to be trapped like that, she thinks, sealed off inexplicably from all that day and air and light outside, how terrible. 'Your name,' he says, and taps a finger to his forehead. 'I know I should know it.'

Rex stands in the doorway watching them with keen alertness, swishing his tail warily from side to side.

'Petra,' she says. Why should he have known her name?—how would he have known it?

'Petra. That's right.' He casts about him absently. Seated, he has sunk into himself, and seems to have no neck, and his head moves like a large, heavy ball set in a shallow socket.

'My father can't see anyone,' Petra says, more stridently than she had intended. 'I mean, he's not well.'

The man continues his vacant interrogation of the hall as if he had not heard her. 'I could do with a drink,' he says. 'Do you think there might be a drink? A glass of water would do.'

She looks to the open doorway, a tall box of light, where Rex still stands, with his tail still going, swish, swish. She is the only one, apart from the dog, who has seen this man, the only one who knows he is here. She could tell him to go now, could order him to leave, and no one in the house would be the wiser. If she shuts the door he will stay. But would he go, even if she told him to? From the ugly, throne-like chair he is looking up at her fatly from under his eyelashes, his small moist valve-like mouth twisted up to one side in a smile of friendly amusement.

Whoever, whatever, he claims to be, I, Hermes the messenger, I know who he is. *Et in Arcadia ille*— They told Thamouz the great god Pan is dead, but they were wrong. If he misbehaves, as I know he will, I shall box his ears, the scamp.

'Really thirsty,' he says, prompting. 'The road?—the dust?'

'Yes,' Petra answers, swaying a little where she stands, as if in a trance. 'The dust.'

So now there are three of us haunting the house, my father, me, and this rascal who has just arrived. This is a pretty pass. Yet I should not speak of this or that personage when speaking of the immortal gods—we are all one even in our separateness—and when I use the word 'father', say, or 'him', or, for that matter, 'me', I do so only for convenience. These denotations are so loose, in the context, so crude, as to be almost meaningless. Almost, but not quite, yes. They shed a certain light, feeble as it is. They are a kind of penumbra, one might say, surrounding and testifying to the presence of an ineffable entity. But what a darkling chasm there lies between that glimmer and the speck it would illuminate. Adam used to find himself groping through a similarly frustrating gulf of indefiniteness whenever he was called upon to step outside the safe confines of the grand consistory and address the more fanciful of his notions to a larger world. He always deplored the humble objects out of which his predecessors—so many of whom he helped to discredit— forged their metaphors, all those colliding billiard balls and rolling dice, the lifts going up and coming down, ships passing each other in the benighted night. Yet how else were they to speak that which cannot be spoken, at least not in the common tongue? He sought to cleave exclusively to numbers, figures, concrete symbols. He knew, of course, the peril of confusing the expression of something with the something itself, and even he sometimes went astray in the uncertain zone between the concept and the thing conceptualised; even he, like me, mistook sometimes the manifestation for the essence. Because for both of us this essence is essentially inessential, when it comes to the business of making manifest. For me, the gods; for him, the infinities. You see the fix we are in.

Take this fellow whom Petra, despite her misgivings, has let into the house. The name he is going under is Benny Grace. What he is doing here, or thinks to do, I cannot say, although I have my suspicions, oh, indeed,

I have. Should I fly down from the roof now—you remember the sad little effigy of me we chanced upon up there atop the Sky Room?—and give him an admonitory skelp of my serpented staff? With the likes of him, if he has a like, it is always well to get in early. I know him and his disruptive ways—how would I not? Look at him, squatting there in that grotesque chair, sunk in the puddle of himself with his fingers laced together in his lap and his fat knees lolling apart and that big, shapeless bag abulge between his thighs. Who does he think he is, who does he think he is pretending to be? Benny Grace, indeed—I shall give him Benny Grace. The dog is seated beside him, leaning a shoulder companionably against his leg. The girl stands with her hands clasped and gazes at the stranger helplessly. The day flags for a moment and all goes still. Benny Grace lifts his eyes to the ceiling, smiling his crooked little smile.

And upstairs, in the stillness of his darkened room, Adam on his bed has sensed the stranger's entry into the house as a faint, far-off tremor, a shimmer in the general atmosphere. He too heard Rex's alerting bark at the gate and then the commotion Petra made when she bounded down the stairs to fling open the front door. Now he is uneasy. Whoever it is that has been allowed entry here is no common caller. Adam has always entertained a lively sense of the numinous. Oh, yes, he has, unlikely though it might seem, for a man of his cast of mind. The gods that oversee his world are not divine, exactly, the demons not exactly devilish, yet gods they are and demons, as palpably present to him as the invisibles he has devoted his life to studying, the particles thronging in boundless space and the iron forces marshalling them. For all the famed subtlety of his speculative faculties, his is a simple faith. Since there are infinities, indeed, an infinity of infinities, as he has shown there to be, there must be eternal entities to inhabit them. Yes, he believes in us, and takes it that the hitherto unimagined realm beyond time that he discovered is where we live.

—Benny Grace! All at once it comes to him. That is who the newcomer must be. There is no doubt, he is certain of it. Benny—who else? I should have known, he thinks, I think. I should have known.

For Petra the life of the house, which is the only life she knows, is a process of endless, painstaking filling-in, as if a myriad-pieced jigsaw puzzle, or a vast cryptic crossword, had been thrust in front of her for her to solve. Now she must find the place in the puzzle to fit Benny Grace into, a blank that is exactly Benny-shaped. He tells her he has come to see her father—oh, but of course, why else does anyone ever come here?—but instead she thinks of her mother. Perhaps her mother needs to be protected against him: could that be it? He does not seem malign yet there is something about him that is distinctly unsettling. He reminds her of Mr Punch. Perhaps he will lay about her mother with a club. Petra does not like her mother but thinks that she must love her, for what else can this inarticulable tangle of pity, remorse and yearning be, if not love? Her mother presses them all down, all of them here in the house, even Pa, though he may not know it. She does not intend to, but she does, blowing aimlessly this way and that, like the wind over a cornfield. Perhaps Benny Grace will do something magical, not ply a cudgel but wave a wand, stilling all agitations, so that they will all, Pa, too, perhaps, they will all rise up, singly and in pairs, trembling with surprise and pleasure, in the calm, soft air.

She has taken Benny into the downstairs living room, which she feels is as far into the domestic interior as he should be allowed to penetrate, for now. The room is on a corner of the house and has two tall sash windows at right angles to each other, one looking across the gravelled semi-circle in front of the house and the other on to a dense and vaguely menacing confusion of rhododendron bushes with burnished leaves and lurking, arthritic limbs. The ceiling is high and smoked to a soft shade of wood-bine, and there is always a pleasantly tarry smell of turf from the fireplace, even now at the heart of summer when the fire has not been lit for months. The sofas and the armchairs are covered with faded chintz, the sofas sagging in their middles like the backs of elderly ponies. There are footstools the worse for wear, a brass coal bucket stands in the grate, and on the walls are hung native weapons, fearsome things, axes, assegais, knobkerries, and immensely long, slender spears adorned with feathers blackened by age, the leaf-shaped bronze blades of which have the shiny look of much-rubbed, ancient leather. Benny's presence makes her see these things anew, or even as if for the first time. She notices the silvery tarnish along the seams of the chintz where it is most worn, the rich deep shine in the dents in the coal bucket—why does that brassy shine make her think of Alexander the Great?—the mouse-coloured dust laid in neat lines like flocked trimming along the slender shafts of the spears.

'My father liked this room best,' she says. She does not know if it is true, or why she said it; it is she who likes it, her father does not bother about liking things, not things like rooms, anyway. 'It was—is—his favourite,' she says loudly, as if expecting to be contradicted, 'his favourite room, this one, in all the house.'

Benny nods, glancing about, seeming calmly pleased with all that his eye lights on. He has an air of waiting, in calm anticipation, for something of mild interest that he has been assured will take place in due course. He is pecu-liarly undemanding. He does not seem to mind that she has so little to say to him—he has not much to say to her, either—and all he has asked for is a drink, and although he has had to ask for it more than once he betrays not the slightest hint of impatience. It is Ivy Blount at last who ventures up from the kitchen bearing on a small brass tray a misted glass of water. The water, the surface of which trembles almost imperceptibly, is clouded and looks like recently melted ice—there is always air in the pipes here at Arden—but Benny drinks it off without hesitation and even smacks his lips. Ivy takes the empty glass on to her tray like a nurse receiving a specimen and goes out hur-riedly and shuts the door behind her with exaggerated care, making not a sound save for the tiniest click, as of a tongue. Benny again looks around the room, nodding to himself. The sun shining in at one of the windows makes a delicate and complicated cage of light that leans at an angle down from the sill. Petra fixes on one of the buttons in the front of Benny's white shirt; how strange a thing, she thinks, a button, waxy white like bone, with those two tiny gimlet holes punched side by side in the middle. She is sure Ivy is listening outside the door. It is a thing Ivy does. She reads people's letters, too. No doubt she is dying to know who Benny Grace is and what he has come here for. Duffy also is curious, it seems, for there he goes, sauntering casually past outside on the gravel, but not so casually that he does not manage to take a quick glance in through the window at the interloper. In fact, it is not Duffy but I, in Duffy's form—I think I may say I have by now perfected the cowman's defiant slouch. I must find any ruse I can to keep an eye on Benny, fat and full of himself in his shiny suit with the sweat-stains under the armpits, and his filmed-over soiled white skin and that little squiggle of a nose. He shall not disturb the house any more than I can help.

Petra starts at a brazen crash from the hall—Ivy in her agitation dropping the tray, of course—and she excuses herself in a mumble and walks swiftly from the room, trying not to seem to be running away, like timid Ivy. She hears herself breathing. Outside the door she catches a glimpse of Ivy's heels and her bent back as she ducks down the steps to the kitchen. The house around her has a hushed air, as if there are many ears listening for every slightest sound. Why has it been left to her to deal with this fellow? She still does not know who he is or what he is doing here, except what he said, that he has come to see her father. She follows Ivy down the stairway, hearing the hollow knocking her own feet make on the wooden steps; she feels like an actress who has forgotten her lines making a mortified exit through a trapdoor down from the stage. She thinks of her brother's wife and scowls inwardly.

Her brother is in the kitchen, sitting at the table tinkering with a radio set. He has taken off the back panel and is poking delicately in the innards with a long, slender screwdriver. His shirt sleeves are rolled. His forearms, each one as big as a small ham, are pink and palely furred. The radio is an ancient model with a cloth grille over the speaker and brown bakelite tuning knobs and a rectangular glass window with the names printed on it of places she has never heard of—Hilversum, for instance, where can Hilversum be? La calls it a wireless, even though, as Petra can plainly see, it is packed inside with wires, coils and coils of them, all different colours.

Ivy Blount is nowhere to be seen. She must have scuttled out by the back door.

Adam is frowning heavily in concentration, his upper lip hooked over the lower one like the tip of a little fat pink thumb, and a slick of hair hangs down across his forehead. He is good at fixing things. This is another reason for his sister to admire him, and to envy and resent him, too. When she comes down the steps he goes on working as if she were not there. She watches him for a moment; how deft he is, despite those big hands, their stubby fingers. He plies the screwdriver as if it were a stiletto. 'What's the matter with Ivy?' he asks without looking up. 'She ran through here as though she had seen a ghost.'

She tells him about the arrival of the stranger. 'He's come to see Pa,' she says. 'I didn't know what to say to him.'

He leans more intently forward, probing the blade of the screwdriver deeper among the coloured coils. 'What's his name?' She sees how the back of his neck has gone red as it always does when he is uncertain or upset. The stranger's coming is making everyone uneasy, first Ivy, now Adam; she is reassured by this, knowing she is not alone.

'I don't know,' she says. 'He told me but I didn't hear—he talks like Popeye.'

'—the sailor man.'

'What?'

'Popeye the sailor man. I yam what I yam.'

He laughs briefly into the back of the radio. She stands at his shoulder and gazes down at the nape of his neck where the redness has not faded yet. His hair at the nape gathers to a point in a little, coiled curl. He turns up his face to look at her. 'What does he want with Pa?' She bites her lip and does not answer. 'Did he say he knows him?' She does her shrug, jerking her left arm stiffly out from her side and raising her right shoulder and inclining her cheek to meet it. Adam slowly shakes his head. 'Didn't you ask him anything?' Still she will not answer, and only gazes back at him, dull and sullen. 'You're hopeless.' He turns away from her and takes up the back panel—also bakelite, is it?—and fits it into its slot in the rear of the set and begins to screw it home.

'What's wrong with it?' she asks.

'What?'

'That'—she points—'radio, wireless, whatever you call it—what's wrong with it?'

He puts aside the screwdriver and rises from the table, kneading a stiffened shoulder with one of those meaty hands. 'Honestly, Pete,' he says. But still he avoids her eye. It is plain he is as nervous as she is before the prospect of Benny Grace. But why should he be unnerved? He lives in the world as she does not; he should be used to unexpected occurrences, things going wrong, people turning up out of the blue.

He follows her up the steps and across the central hall into the living room. They find Benny Grace seated again, in one of the chintz-covered armchairs this time, serene as a figure of the Buddha, just as before, with his knees comfortably splayed and his hands in his lap with the fingers clasped; a small triangle of fish-pale belly shows through a gap in his shirt above the straining waistband of his trousers. As the pair approach he scrambles to his feet; he does not seem much higher standing than he did when seated. 'Grace,' he says to Adam, holding out a hand. 'Benny Grace.'

Adam frowns.

'My father is ill,' he says, '—did my sister tell you?' Petra notices how he speaks over-loudly too, as she did. 'Very ill, in fact.'

Benny nods; he is smiling, as if at some happy piece

of news. 'Yes, I know, I know.' He waits, still with his smile, his large round head cocked to one side—Adam thinks of a blackbird, plump and alert, its polished eye swivelling.

'He's in a coma,' he says. 'He had a stroke.'

'A stroke.' Benny with lips pursed waggles his head from side to side. 'That is too bad. That really is too bad.'

A silence follows. Adam is aware of Petra off to the side, breathlessly taking everything in. 'How did you get here?' he asks the little man. He also is aware of the volume at which he is speaking but cannot seem to lower it. Why are they all shouting like this at poor Benny?—it almost makes me feel sorry for him.

'Oh, that was easy,' Benny says easily. He, at least, speaks softly. His tone implies a lifetime of obstacles adroitly negotiated.

'I mean,' Adam persists, unable to stop, 'did you come by car?'

Benny shakes his head and shrugs. 'I don't drive,' he says. 'Never learned.'

Adam nods helplessly. He feels a sort of panic rising inside him; he is afraid that in a moment he will burst out in whinnies of hysterical laughter. He turns to Petra. 'Why don't you,' he fairly shouts at her, 'why don't you take Mr Grace up to see Pa?'

The girl frowns sideways at her brother's knees. 'What?' she breathes. Her left leg has begun to jiggle. In those old corduroy trousers and baggy blue shirt, thin and frail and almost bald, she looks like a prison inmate, or a refugee, the survivor of some terrible forced march.

Benny links his fingers together again in front of his belly and gazes at her, as if lovingly. 'Just a peek?' he says, cajoling. He is a sly old sprite. 'So I can say I saw him?'

They turn all three and make for the door, where there is a brief scrimmage as they find themselves inadvertently trying all three to get through it at the same time. From the hall Petra leads Benny Grace up the staircase. Light falls down from the glass roof like silent rain, indifferently, a thing absorbed in something else altogether. At the turn of the landing she falters a second and glances back at her brother, who has stopped in the doorway of the living room and stands there looking up at her. His face is blank, he gives no helping sign. She goes on, upwards, and the higher she goes the deeper her heart sinks. By her side, Benny Grace, goat-footed, pants softly as he climbs. What if Pa should wake up from his coma? What will he say to her, appearing before him suddenly with this stranger at her side? And what would she say to him? How would she account for herself?

Now here they are at the door to the stairs of the Sky Room. Petra knocks, and turns the knob. What air is this that flows down from on high, what spirits guard the way?

WHAT INDEED? Were I able I would rear up in my winding-sheets, my foul tubes wrenched from their sockets and spouting pap and piss, and slam that door shut in their faces. Ah, the sad braggadocio of the dying. It is not that I am afraid of Benny Grace; what I fear is disturbance. I am becalmed, and dread a suddenly filled sail. The history of Benny and me is long and intricate. When I peer into memory's steadily clouding crystal I see a great throng milling and elbowing and out of its midst Benny's fat face grinning at me, suggestive, sardonic, oleaginously eager. Has he come to harangue me in my last straits, to tell me I am going about dying in all the wrong way? I have known him, he has known me, for longer than I care to remember, though I will have to remember, I suppose, now that he has popped up like this. Indeed, I feel he has been with me all my life, which is hardly possible, since he is not as old as I am, and will remain so. Yes, Benny surely is of the immortals.

Suddenly I recall a nightmare I had when I was a

child, a very young child, it must have been, a baby, even, I think, still in my cradle, I have never forgotten it. How frightening it was, how fraught with significance, that I have retained such a distinct recollection of it all these years. Although I am not sure it can properly be called a nightmare, so brief it was and bare of incident. I am not certain it was a dream at all but rather a half-waking intimation of something I was too young then and now am too old and too far gone to interpret or understand. Anyway, in this nightmare, or dream, or reverie, whatever it was, I had been set down on a bare rock in the midst of an empty ocean. Yes, set down, for I had not been brought there by boat, or by any earth-bound, or sea-bound, means, but had alighted somehow out of the air, a fallen Icarus, it might be, my head in a spin and my wings doused of their fire, dripping and useless. The ocean all around me was of a mauvish shade, utterly still, without a surge or ripple—even where it ringed the rock on which I cowered the water's fringe showed not the slightest stirring—yet seemed to brim, full of itself to overflowing, and as if at any moment it might tilt wildly and upend, like a great polished disc pressed down upon violently at its edge. As far as I looked in every direction there was nothing to be seen, and no horizon, the featureless distances merging seamlessly into an equally featureless sky. No sound, no cry of bird or moan of wind. A vast void everywhere, and I terrified, clinging to my rock with both hands and barely holding the world from tipping on its end and letting everything slide off into the abyss of emptiness, including, especially including, me. What does it mean? It must mean something, or signify something, at least. Was I, a babe in swaddling, already dipping a toe into the waters of Lethe, paddling, even, in its shallows? Never too early to start dying.

I knew it was Benny. When I sensed the presence of an intruder in the house I knew it had to be him. I must have been expecting him, all along, without realising it.

From the top of the short stairs now the two of them advance creakingly into the gloom. To get a sight of them at all I have to swivel my eyes so violently to the side and downwards the sockets would hurt, if I could feel them. The pair seem phantoms, bearing down on me across the darkened room. I must not let them see me looking: they will think I am only feigning stupefaction, which in a way I must be, given that my brain is so busy. Probably I can see them better than they can see me, my eyes being by now so thoroughly accustomed to this damnable false night in which my wife has condemned me to live since I was laid low. Benny—look at him, my homunculus. He is speaking in a priestly murmur, his tonsured head inclined towards my daughter, who is inclining too; they might be monk and maiden in the confessional. I strain in vain to catch what he is saying to her, what mischief he might be pouring into her ear. *Mm mm mmm*. And here I lie, mumchance.

Petra goes to the middle window, the one that my bed faces, and lifts her arms and with a dancer's large dramatic gestures draws the heavy curtains open, leaning sideways first far to the left and then far to the right. How it pierces me now, the sight of a human being in movement. The daylight seems to hesitate a moment before entering. Dazzled, I shut my eyes tight, and on the inners of the lids the after-glare makes tumbling shapes, darker upon dark, like blobs of black dye bursting slowly in water already soiled. Yet I thrill to the unwonted glare, as I thrilled a moment ago to my daughter's dancerly swoopings. When the time comes, and it cannot be very long now, I want to die into the light, like an old tree feeding its last upon the radiance of the world. In these recent days—how many?—with the curtains pulled, I have felt myself to be in an enormous dark space where distant doors are closing slowly, one by one. I do not hear them close, but feel the alteration in the air, as of a succession of long, slow breaths being painfully drawn in. I always liked to think that death would be more or less a continuation of how things already are, a dimming, a contracting, a shrinkage so gradual that I would not register its coming to an end at last until the ending was done with. Perhaps that is Ursula's intention, keeping me in the dark so I will not notice the light failing. But I do not want to breathe my last in this room. Why did she banish me up here, of all places, site of my triumphs and so many more numerous failures? I want to be elsewhere. I want to die outdoors—I wonder if that can be arranged? Yes, on a pallet somewhere, on the grass, under trees, at the soft fall of dusk, that would be a boon, a final benison.

But what if at just that moment I were to begin to feel again, what if—no, no, that way there are things I do not wish to be confronted with. Let me die numbly, insensate, yet thinking still, if that were possible.

I feel—I feel!—by what must be a quaking of the floorboards Benny Grace approach the bed. Now in a show of hushed and reverent solicitude he stoops over me and peers into my face, and I am as a boy again pretending to be fast asleep as my suspicious mother bends over me in the light of a school-day morning. You see how Benny's coming has already reduced me to this childishness, these dreams and maundering fears dragged from out of the depths? Now, perhaps sensing how unsettled I am by his warmly breathing presence leaning over me like this, he snickers softly.

Should I open my eyes? Should I open my eyes.

'He hasn't changed,' he says over his shoulder to Petra at the window, where she remains, no doubt nervous of approaching too close to me, fearful of what she will have to look upon. I do not blame her: a catheter, for instance, even if only the suggestion of it, is not a pretty object for a daughter to have to contemplate, given what it is, and where it is placed. 'Still the black hair,' Benny says, 'the noble profile.' Again he gives his snuffly laugh. 'The original Adam.' This last he addresses as if to me, intimately, in a murmur; he must know I can hear him, or at least must suspect it. He turns aside and begins to pace, those hobbled feet of his making a goatish clatter on the wooden floor. 'Yes, years,' he says, from a little way off now, to Petra, continuing evidently an earlier train. 'The things I could tell you! The stories!'

I would laugh if I were capable of it. I am in a sort of

panic of amazement—Benny Grace here, at Arden, with his stories! And I flat out and speechless while he stands upright—Benny, of all people. I cannot credit it. I must have been wrong in what I said, or rather in what I thought, a minute ago; I must not have been expecting him, for if I had been, why would I be so surprised that he has come? But after all it was inevitable he would make an appearance at the end. Benny Grace, my shadow, my double, my incorrigible daemon. Yes, I would laugh.

I have never been any good in dealing with people. I dare say I am not alone in this sad predicament, but I feel acutely my incompetence in the matter of other folk. You know how it is. Say, you are walking down a not particularly crowded street. You spy, at quite a long way off still, out of the corner of your eye, out of the corner of your watchfulness, as it were, a stranger who, you can see, has in his turn become aware of you as you approach him. Even at that distance you both begin to make little adjustments, covert little feints and swerves, so as to avoid eventual collision, all the while pretending to be perfectly oblivious of each other. As often as not all your efforts of evasion fail, precisely because you have been making them, I imagine, and in the end one of you is compelled to sidestep clumsily to allow the other plunge past with a snarling smile. This is the way it is in general, with me, wherever I am, with whomever I happen to be. I am always, always on guard against coming smack up against one of my own kind. And when I am forced to enter on that agitated, long-distance dance of avoidance the broadest pavement becomes a tangled track, and I am as in an unsubdued jungle where the little apes howl and the birds of night scream and scatter. I do not doubt it could be otherwise. There is no reason not to stride forward smiling and clasp the approaching stranger manfully to one's breast in fellowship and affection. If I remember rightly it was the poet Goethe—entirely forgotten now but in his day there were those who would have ranked him above the sublime Kleist!—who urged that we should greet each other not as *monsieur*, sir, *mein Herr*, but as my fellow-sufferer, *Socî malorum, compagnon de misères*! Or was it Schopenhauer? Not to be able any longer to look anything up—ah! Well, no matter, you get the drift. For my part I would be happy to take this good advice provided I am allowed to send my greetings by semaphore.

I did not see Benny Grace coming, that was the trouble. It was in the far north that I first encountered him—or that he first encountered me, more like—which strikes me as odd, since I think of him as so much a creature of the south. An auditorium, a long, white room abuzz with people, and I in the front row, in a reserved seat, and a woman beside me agitatedly shuffling the text of a talk she was about to give, an ordeal the prospect of which terrified her, although she had undergone it many times before. Her name was Inge, or Ilsa, I wish I could remember which. Let me see: I shall settle for Inge. To open the colloquium there had been a reception—noise, laughter, champagne glasses of sticky white alcoholic syrup—and later on there would be dinner followed by decorous tangoing. One side of the room was a wall of glass looking out on a green slope dotted sparsely with spindly white birches. Were there deer? My memory insists on deer, peacefully at graze among the trees, fastidious long-legged creatures with beige-and-brown coats and stumpy tails that twitched comically. Weak northern sunlight, a delicate lacquering of bleached gold. It was midsummer then, too, the days endless up there in those latitudes. There had been rain, and there would be more, and the grass sparkled, as if with malice. I was aware of Benny first as a pair of hoof-like feet and two fat thighs clad in rusty black, inserting themselves with much squeezing and puffing into the place to my left. Then the globular head and moist, moon face, the smile, the wreathed dome—he was balding even then—and those whorled ears daintily pointed at their tips.

I cannot remember which city it was we were in, or which country, even. We had arrived that day, Inge and I, from elsewhere. Bellicose Sweden, I remember, was on the warpath again, mired in yet another expansionary struggle with her encircling neighbours, and travel throughout the region was hazardous and liable to delays, and I feared being stranded there, chafingly, in Somewhereborg or Somethingsund. Inge was a Swedish Finn, or Finnish Swede, I do not think I ever discovered which, for certain. Ash-blonde, tiny, very slim, child-sized, really, but an earnest savant famous in her field, which was, I recall, gauge theory—gauge was all the rage, at the time. I can see her still, little Inge, her tremulous hands and skinny legs and turned-in toes, can still smell her scrubbed skin and cigarette breath. She was forty and looked twenty, except first thing in the morning and late at night. Dorothy was not long dead and I was adrift in a daze of sorrow and remorse and would have clung to any spar in those dark, immense and turbulent waters. A sense of strangeness, of being generally estranged, comes over one in circumstances such as I was in, I am sure those who have suffered a similarly violent and sudden loss will know what I mean. Everything I did or saw, every surroundings I wandered woozily into, struck me as bizarre, wholly outlandish, and like an idiot child I had to be pulled along by the hand from one baffling spectacle to the next.

I really do wish I could remember more of Inge—I owe it to her, to remember. She took care of me, she who was so much in need of being cared for herself. It seems odd, that in my distress I should have sought out the likes of her and not the strong ones, those big mannish blue-stocking types in which my discipline abounds. Helpless myself, I cleaved to the helpless.

I was never a womaniser, not even then, in my wandering year of grief, despite all that was said of me. True, I was and am devoted to women, but not or not exclusively in the expectation of clambering on top of them and pumping away like a fireman at his hose, no, the fascination for me was that transformative moment when one of them would willingly divest herself of her clothes and everything became different on the instant. That was a phenomenon I could never get enough of; it was always a surprise, always left me breathless. How magical it was, how enchanting, when the head I had been talking to in the street, or on a bus, or in the midst of a roomful of people, suddenly, in a shadowed bedroom, unfurled from the neck down this pale, glimmering extension of itself, this body which, naked, was utterly other than what it had been when clothed. And not just the body, but the sensibility, too—a new person on the spot, candid, desirous, intimate, vulnerable. The prospect of the pure astonishment of holding this brand-new, cool-skinned creature in my arms, that was what held me there, in that glassed-in lecture hall, with the sickly taste of cloudberry cordial on my lips and an unyawned yawn making the hinges of my jaws ache, watching Inge, as if she were half blind, make her groping way to the lectern, still mangling her papers, and with a small round dark patch on the seat of her light summer dress where she had peed herself, just a little, in fright at the prospect of standing up and speaking to an audience.

This was in the early days of the great instauration, after we had exposed the relativity hoax and showed up Planck's constant for what it really is. The air was thick with relativists and old-style quantum mechanics plummeting from high places in despair; I trust they took the opportunity, as they travelled streetwards together, of putting their principles of relative motion and intrinsic spin values to the test. I was in the vanguard of the new science and already an eminent figure in what was, admittedly, at that time, a narrow and specialised sphere. My Brahma hypothesis, so-called—so-called by Benny, in the first place, as it happened—floored them all. In it I posited the celebrated chronotron, ugly name—Benny, again—for an exquisite concept, time's primal particle, the golden egg of Brahma from the broken yolk of which flowed all creation. Simplicity itself, that theory, once someone had dared to think it. To begin with I was laughed at, of course, always a sure promise of eventual triumph. It took them quite a while to get the point, but when they did, my, what a fuss. Looking back, I see myself borne aloft in triumph on the shoulders of a band of hot-eyed zealots, but a stiff and painted thing, like the effigy of a suffering saint carried in procession on a holy day, rattling a bit from being joggled overmuch, my mitre awry and my big toe shiny from the kisses of so many pious supplicants. I did not ask for their adulation. I was my solitary self when I took a flying kick and put my shiny big toe through their big Theory of Everything. The majority of them I despised. How they fawned and flattered when they saw at last the irrefragable rightness of what I had made. But then, did I not despise myself, also, myself and my work, my capitalised Work, of which I am supposed to be so vain? Oh, not that I think my achievement is less than anyone else's—in fact I think it is more than everyone else's, more than what any of my peers could have managed—only it is not enough for me. You take the point. The world is always ready to be amazed, but the self, that lynx-eyed monitor, sees all the subterfuges, all the cut corners, and is not deceived.

My peers? Did I say my peers? My peers are all dead.

I did not like the look of Benny Grace. He had a distinctly adhesive aspect. At dinner he again weaseled his way into the seat beside me. Inge should have been sitting there, but was in the ladies' room, crouched in a cubicle, sick and shaking after her public ordeal. However, not the most attentive lover could have been as irresistibly insinuating as Benny. Each time I chanced to look up from my plate those gleaming black eyes of his were fixed on me merrily, meaningly. Benny's mode is that of a conductor bending and swaying with hooped arms out-thrust in the effort of scooping up from his orchestra greater and still greater surges of magnificent noise. Beyond the plate-glass wall a breeze silvered the grass and set the birch leaves madly fluttering. How melancholy, this evening that refused to end but kept drawing itself out, thinner and thinner, in the pale, northern light. Benny was leaning forward and over the voices of the others at the table was introducing himself, a hand held out at the end of an arm that would not fully straighten, so plumply packed was it into its sleeve. 'I, of course,' he said, 'know who *you* are.'

Now he goes back to join my daughter at the window, overlooking the garden, and begins to explain to her my theory of infinities. Benny loves to explain. Petra is silent; she has heard it all before, but is too polite and well brought up not to give at least the impression of being entranced by novelty. I who now from this angle can no longer see her picture her instead, eyes lowered, arms tightly folded as if to prevent herself from flying apart in fragments, nodding and nodding like a child's mechanical toy. When she makes herself attend like this, such seemingly is the intensity of her concentration that she takes on the appearance of being thoroughly frightened, of being frozen in fright—of being, in a word, petrified.

All the same, it occurs to me that it is she of all the household who will suffer the least agitation at Benny's coming, I am not sure why—why I think it so, I mean, though I do, or hope so, anyway. That must be the reason the rest of them left it to her to bring Benny up here, to view the remains: they too must have seen that she is not the one to be overwhelmed by him. She is a dear girl, but troubled, troubled. Did I do wrong by making her my confidante, my familiar, my misused muse, when the whim took me? From the day she was born I favoured her over my son, that poor epigone—he was here earlier, blubbering at my bedside—yet now I think I was perhaps as unfair to her as I was to him, in singling her out as I did. Ursula used to assure me, in her kindly way, that by my attentions to the girl I gave her confidence, strength, tenacity of purpose, and perhaps I did foster in her a smidgen of these qualities, which, heaven knows, she is so much in need of. But I am not persuaded. I have done many wrongs, to many people, and I fear that if— But ha! is this where I embark on the famous deathbed confession? With not a soul to hear it, save the gods, who do not have it in their power to absolve me? Let us eschew the unbosoming and quietly proceed, unforgiven.

Over at the window Benny is telling Petra how her father as a young man at his sums succeeded in turning so-called reality on its head. 'What he did is not fully grasped or appreciated even yet,' he says, with large disdain—I picture him doing that circling motion he does with his right hand, winding the ratchet of his contempt. 'There is only a few of us that understand.' I am impressed by the trill of earnestness in his tone. He is putting it on for Petra's sake, to urge on her the glory of her pa's greatest days, the light of which glory, she is to understand, reflects on him, my mentor and my pal. Yet in those days of glory it was always Benny who was the one who was least impressed. When the rest of the academy were struggling with the disgraceful strangeness of this or that of my hypotheses, adjusting their frock coats about them and gravely tugging at their beards, Benny, sitting way up in the middle of the farthest row of the lecture hall, would lean back slowly and hook his thumbs in his belt and stick out his little round belly and smile. Oh, that shiny-faced smile. Whatever I did, whatever I achieved, Benny gave it to be understood that he had long since anticipated it. Nothing of mine was novel to him, and never enough. And he was always there, when I stepped down from the lectern and the scribbled-on blackboard, always there but always content to hang back while the others pressed forward in murmurous admiration or, as often as not, in consternation and outrage, even fury. Benny could wait. He had another gesture of the hand that I remember: he would hold it out before him, palm forward, one finger lifted, like that conductor again, commanding a pianissimo, tilting his head to one side with eyelids lightly shut and his lips pursed, the man whom nothing could surprise, nothing daunt, nothing confound. Even when I laid my ladder against the mighty Christmas tree that all the others before me had put up over ages and popped the fairy on the topmost spike, whereupon her little wand lit up in what before had been the outer dark an endless forest of firs, hung with all manner of baubles, a densely wooded region the existence of which no one hitherto, including myself, had suspected—even then Benny was there to tell me with gently patronising scorn how foolish I had been to imagine that anything could be completed, I of all people, who knew far better than anyone that in the welter of realities that I had posited everything endlessly extends and unravels, world upon world. And it is true, of course—how could there be any finish to what I and a few others, a very few others, started? Was it that I thought to be the last man? he would enquire, and gaze at me in head-shaking, compassionate reproof, smiling. And he was right—look at me now, the last of myself, no more than that.

Gulls, seagulls, their raucous noise, I hear them suddenly. They fly in all the way from the sea and nest in the disused chimneys of the house and rise up and wheel about the roof in great broken chains, their wingbeats crumpling the air, their voices raised in wild, lilting cries. I have always welcomed this annual pandemonium; it is one of the markers of my year. The young have a tendency to fall down the chimneys into the rooms here, dauntingly big brutes though they are, and more than once I have come upon one of them standing in front of a fireplace on its ridiculous grey legs, its plumage sooted and ruffled, a filmed eye skewed towards me in blank surmise. Other worlds, other worlds, where we are not, and yet are.

'You see,' Benny is saying to Petra in the self-swallowing gabble that is his explaining voice, 'you see, the infinities, the infinities that cropped up in everyone else's equations and made them null, and which cropped up in his, too, *he* saw as exactly what—'

Exactly what is it that keeps the two of them there at the window? Are they looking out at the gulls, craning to see them wheel and screech above the chimney-pots? Or is there someone in the garden, doing something interesting, that ruffian Duffy, perhaps, aware of being watched and pretending to work? But what would be the interest in that, for them? Perhaps they are not looking out at all, perhaps they are standing face to face, engrossed in each other, Benny on one side of the embrasure, leaning against the folded-back shutter, talking and jabbing a fat finger, and Petra on the other side staring at the front of his soiled shirt in that seemingly terror-stricken way of hers. God! not to know, not to be able to know the least of things! Doing, *doing*, is living, as my mother, my poor failed unhappy mother, among others, tried her best to din into me. I see it now, while all along I thought thinking was the thing.

'—an infinity of infinities,' Benny is saying, 'all crossing and breaking into each other, all here and invisible, a complex of worlds beyond what anyone before him had imagined ever was there—well, you can imagine the effect.' At last it seems they have remembered the man in the bed, but once again it is Benny alone who approaches in his creaky shoes and leans over me, and I hear him breathing down his crushed little nose, and feel another waft of his warm and sweetish breath against my face. 'Well,' he says again, so softly, almost a whisper, that it must be me once more he is addressing, 'well, you can imagine,' and again softly laughs.

Inge the gauge-theorist. Why did I think of her when thinking of him? Oh, yes, because I was with her that first time I met him—I believe it was the first time, that time—but also because poor shivering Inge was so much the opposite of the egregious Benny. Picture me there at that long white table, gazing out at the white birches, my nostrils flared in boredom and disdain, a fist set down before me on the tablecloth like a clenched crab, while Benny sought to woo me. Bereft and melancholy though I was, I was a handsome fellow in those days, no doubt of that. Whom did I resemble? Oppenheimer, say, J. Robert, who failed to build the bomb he boasted so much of, or Hilbert the geometer, who had a nice beard like mine —one of those cold and lofty doctors, anyway, whom the world takes as the very model of a bloodless man of science. Benny beside me is leaning forward in a conspiratorial crouch, murmuring blandishments and breathing into my water glass. He says we should get out of here and go to a place he knows down on the waterfront, a venerable tavern where Tycho Brahe is said to have stopped for a night on his way to Prague to take up the post of assistant to Johannes Kepler, the Emperor Rudolf's Imperial Mathematician, long ago, and where there are bear paws on the menu. We can sit on the terrace there and look across the water to the palely twinkling lights of distant Heligoland—or Hveen, is it?—and drink the speciality of the house, an aquavit with specks of gold dust, real gold dust, swirling in its depths. He has things to tell me, propositions to put. I do not deign to respond to these hot urgings of his. Aquavit, indeed—bear paws!

Nevertheless, it was the early hours though still not dark when I got back from town, panting, in wild disorder, with a split lip and a sleeve torn half-way out of my jacket. Where now was Benny, my bad companion, my cicerone into occasions of sin? Somewhere among the harbour dives he had abandoned me, or I had given him the slip. I did not want to go back to the hotel room where Inge would be under the bedclothes sobbing into her fist. In a state of fuddled euphoria and still breathing hard I wandered down to the lake—there was a lake— and watched a huge sun roll slowly along its shallow arc and tip the horizon in a splash of gold and promptly begin to ascend again. Behind me, in the lead-blue twilight, a flock of white birds dived and wheeled among the birches. Next day, if one may speak of separate nights and days up there at that time of year, I managed to get two places on a seaplane going south, and together Inge and I made our escape from Ultima Thule, seeing far below us two tiny armies all in white swarming towards each other over the tundra.

So is Benny my bad self, or one that I shed and should not have? Before him I had spent my life in hiding, head well down and the little eyes peering out. He tracked me to my lair then, too. It is not too much to say that everything I have done since that northern midsummer day when he flushed me out has been imbued with the dark wash of his presence. He—I say he when I think I mean I. I did great things, I scaled high peaks—such silken ropes, such gleaming grapnels!—and always he was there, scrambling behind me. That was then. I made a world—worlds!—and afterwards what was there left to do but wile away the day of rest, the interminable, idle Sunday that the remainder of my life has been. So why has he come?

III

WHAT? UM. Must have dropped off for a minute there. I am getting as dopily drowsy as my old Dad. Let me see, what has been happening in my absence? There is a sense in the house of people poking their heads warily above the parapets after an explosion that did not happen. That is the effect of Benny Grace's disruptive arrival. Yet why so much unease? See him now, quite content and peaceable, sunning himself in the sunken garden behind the conservatory. He is sitting on a stone step between two ornamental low stone pillars, with his jacket off and his shirt sleeves rolled. He has taken off his shoes and socks, too, to give his feet an airing, and at last we get a look at those goatish hoofs of his. In fact, disappointingly, they are more like a pig's trotters, blunt and pink with the toes all bunched together and the nails thick and tough as horn. His braces are bright blue. He is enjoying the heat of the sun on his bare pate. Through a gap between the straining buttons of his shirt he palps with idle fingers the folds of his belly, eyeing lazily, like the happy faun he is at heart, the sweltering bank of stirless trees that edges the garden. A hamadryad is a wood-nymph, also a poisonous snake in India, and an Abyssinian baboon. It takes a god to know a thing like that.

Preparations are under way for a late lunch, late because of Benny's coming, which has upset and delayed everything. Faintly behind him he hears the sound of plates and silverware being laid out, and now and then in the glass of the conservatory Ivy Blount's stark features materialise from the shadows as she makes another round of the table in there, for each time that she passes she comes forward and bends a hostile eye on Benny's fat, sloped back. As to this conservatory, it is really just another room of the house, the front wall of which was knocked out at some forgotten time in Arden's history and replaced by a large ugly extrusion of iron-framed glass. There must be hundreds of small panes in this structure, some of them original and bearing whorls and stipples from the oil on which the sheets of float-glass were poured out—oh, yes, my knowledge is not confined to flora and fauna, for among my many crafty attributes I am a maker and inventor and know the secrets of every trade and skill; I am, you might say, I might say, a Faust and Mephisto rolled into one. The metal frames fit ill and in the windy seasons let in vents of bitter cold, while at the start of summer the room swelters and only begins to be bearable in these last weeks of June when the sun is in the zenith and its rays do not strike directly through the glazing. The chicken is being cooked, and now and then Benny catches the smell of it; the savour of roasting flesh sets his saliva glands spurting. He has travelled far, he is hungry.

In the kitchen Ursula in her shapeless cardigan stands motionless. She has to lean forward and squint at an angle through the window above the sink to see Benny where he is sitting outside on the step. She knows who he must be. She recalls the first time Adam told her about him. Deep winter on Haggard Head and the two of them standing side by side in his study. They were not fighting, exactly. The sea far below the window was a bowl of steel shavings and the sky was steely too and there was no horizon visible. He was holding her wrist in the circle of a finger and thumb and squeezing so hard the small bones creaked and tears came into her eyes—how strong his hands were; they always reminded her of the metal claws in those fairground machines that children pay a penny to scrabble in for plastic toys or balls of bubble gum. It was his way to grab at her, distractedly, at the boy, too, young Adam, and give a pinch, a pull, a shove. She can see herself, a quarter of a century ago, standing there, and him holding on to her, and her biting her lip to keep from crying out. He did not mean to hurt, she did not think he did. Outside, the rain had begun to congeal into flakes of wet haphazard snow that spattered against the window-panes and dribbled down the glass like spit. No, he did not mean to hurt. How long had he known Benny Grace before he told her about him, him, and the woman? Oh, years, he said; years.

A loud and angry sizzle comes from the big black range where the chicken is roasting—the fat must have overflowed on to something. She has often considered becoming a vegetarian. Too late now. Too late for everything, now. She has the impression that her life is coming to an end, she feels it strongly. It is not that she imagines she is about to die, but that when Adam is gone, all that she was when he was alive will go with him, and that what of her will be left will be another person, one that she will not know and will have no interest in, and will not want to be. She has known of cases like this, people living on after the death of someone dear and becoming estranged from themselves. But for her there are the children to consider; she will have to take care of them, Adam no less than Petra. She thinks Adam's wife will leave him; she has that feeling and cannot rid herself of it. She imagines being here with them, her poor distraught daughter and her son come home to her, lost and helpless. Petra would grow increasingly crazed but perhaps more quietly, more secretively, while Adam would pass his days pottering about the house, mending things that do not need to be mended. And so the years will pass and the three of them will drift slowly into the future, sad survivors on their raft. That is what she sees, coming.

She sighs, still keeping her eye on Benny Grace. She only ever half believed that he was real. Until today she suspected he was Adam's invention, an alibi for his love affairs. That is why his turning up like this has so upset her. Though surely she should be glad to discover that he does exist and is not another one of Adam's elaborate inventions. His name, just the kind of absurd name that Adam would make up, always sounded to her like a jeer, a mocking reminder of her husband's deviousness, his cruel playfulness, his deceits. Was she expected to believe that Adam would consort with a creature such as he described Benny Grace to be, a mischief maker and a rogue? But there was that side to Adam, that compulsion to break things. Benny Grace, he said, was the part of himself he had suppressed in order to become what he became. Who was she to say it was not so?

She is aware of a presence at her back. Is it that ghostly antagonist she sensed in the sickroom, come to crowd and bully her again? No, it is her son, standing on the wooden step below the door into the hall. How does he move so quietly, being so large? It is as if he were made not of flesh and bone but some other stuff, heavy yet soft, too.

'Can you see him, from there?' he asks.

She does not reply, and he descends the last two steps and crosses the room and stands behind her and lays his hands lightly on her shoulders. The sunshine must be stronger now for Benny Grace has made a sun-hat for himself by tying a knot at each corner of his handkerchief, and is adjusting it to cover his bald patch. 'Your father used to do the same,' Ursula says, 'make a hat out of a hankie, like that. He was always cold, he said, yet he hated being in the sun.'

They contemplate in silence the fat man in his comical headgear. 'He looks like someone in a seaside postcard,' Adam says. If the fat man glanced sideways would he see them? Adam thinks of the child in the train. Benny is scratching exploratively under an armpit now.

'Do you know who he is?' Adam asks. Again she does

not answer. 'His name is Grace,' he says. 'He has come to see Pa. Pete took him up.'

She turns up her face and looks at him blankly. 'What? Where?'

'To see Pa. Upstairs, in the Sky Room.'

'Oh.'

She turns back to the window and the sunlit garden. A part of her is not here. Adam, still with his hands on her shoulders, gives her a grim little shake. Long ago, when he was a boy, one day he saw something glinting in the laurel hedge in front of the disused privy down behind the house, where the rats used to have their underground nests—they fascinated him, those rats, fat and furtive and quick and always somehow with an air of suppressed amusement—and reaching in among the leaves he pulled out an empty whiskey bottle, naggin-sized, and then saw the others, dozens of them, scores, drained to the last drop and pushed in neck-first among the dense, bristling foliage.

'Grace,' his mother says dreamily. 'Yes, Benny Grace, he's called.'

'You know him, then.'

'Oh, I know who he is.'

He supposes that when she is like this there must be a continual buzzing and muttering in her head, the confused noise of herself, that muffles the things that are being said to her. 'I think,' he says, loudening his voice, 'he'll be staying for lunch. I told Ivy to set an extra place. And Roddy Wagstaff is here too, you know that—you remember, he came down, earlier?'

She goes on gazing out of the window. 'A full house!' she murmurs. There is a wobble in her voice as if she might be about to laugh. 'Your father won't be pleased.'

Speaking of fathers, mine is waking up, at long last.

The two of them turn together as Ivy Blount comes in, carrying something. She enters not by the door at the top of the steps but through a dim and always damp-smelling corridor to the right of the range that leads directly into the conservatory—the house is honey-combed with hidden passages and connecting walkways. Ivy has exchanged her cut-off wellingtons for an old pair of cat-coloured carpet slippers that are absurdly too big for her. Ursula thinks she recognises them as her husband's. Why, she wonders with a flash of annoyance, has everyone taken to wearing his things, first Petra in his cast-off pyjamas and now Ivy Blount in his slippers? She wishes Ivy would lift her feet when she walks, she is sure she knows how much it grates on her to hear someone shuf-fling along in that sligging, slovenly way. And to think how well brought-up the woman is, a daughter of the gentry! What she is carrying turns out to be a faded red satin cushion with numerous rips and holes in it through which wads of cotton stuffing protrude. She sees Ursula peering. 'Rex was chewing it,' she says. She thinks how like a totem pole they look, standing there, the son close behind the mother and he a head taller than she. 'I think it's had it.'

Ursula clicks her tongue. 'Oh, that dog,' she says. 'He has been impossible since Adam's illness.'

Young Adam does not like the look of that cushion:

there is something gruesome about it, a suggestion of violence and blood. It reminds him of the chicken that Ivy brought in this morning. He recalls another fragment of last night's dream. He was high up, on a mountain top, no, in an aeroplane, or on a cloud, yes, a cloud, and flying over a forest, the canopy of trees below packed tight as broccoli and an enormous river meandering through like a dribble of melted tin, a thick-walled fortress on a hill, too, and a tower on fire. He steps from behind his mother and goes and sits down at the table where the wireless is, and takes up the screwdriver and once more unscrews the panel from the back of it.

'I doubt there will be enough stuff for lunch to feed them all,' Ivy says, and looks in vague helplessness at the ruined cushion she is still clutching, as if its destruction will add to the scarcity of the things there are to eat. 'Two extra, as well, Mr Wagstaff and that fellow out there in the garden.'

'Put on more potatoes, then!' Ursula snaps back at her, almost skittishly, and gives a kind of giggle.

Ivy looks at her.

It is not, Adam is thinking, that anyone in the house cares what anyone else does. Not that there is much doing, anyway—nothing gets done. He is sorry he came down, sorry he brought Helen into the midst of all this dithering and disorder. We should have waited, he tells himself savagely, until he was dead! The dusty valves and bundles of cable in the back of the wireless set all swim together in a blur before his eyes. He thought to fix this thing for his father but what good will it be?—his father will not be able to hear it, even if it can be got to work. His father is dying. He will soon be dead. They will never speak again, the two of them, his father will never have another opportunity not to call him by his name. Maybe, he thinks suddenly, he should join the army, become a soldier, go and fight in some foreign war, maybe that is what his dream is telling him. He tries to picture himself, in breastplate and bronze helmet, heaving a huge sword, the sweat in his eyes and a blood mist everywhere, horses screaming and the cries of the dying all around him. He throws down the screwdriver and rises strugglingly, almost stumbling, and the chair rears back, its legs shrieking on the flagged floor, and the two women turn, startled.

'Come on,' he says to his mother, going to her and taking her by the wrist, 'come and say something to this fellow.'

He bustles her out through the back door, which catches on the stone threshold and gives a rattling shudder, as it always does; how steadfast in your world are the humblest things, and yet how shamefully little notice you take of them. Ivy stares after the mother and son, pressing the scarlet cushion to her breast like a swollen, tattered heart. O humans!

Outside, Ursula lifts up a hand quickly against the light. 'What a glare!' she murmurs feebly. She is trying to free her other wrist from her son's grasp—his father's fingers, crushing her bones!—but he holds her all the more tightly and will not let go. He fairly drags her, tottering, across the paved yard to the little wicket gate that lets out into the garden. 'Ivy is getting worse, have you noticed?' she says gabblingly, playing for time, trying to hang back without seeming to. 'What is the matter with her, do you think?—I'm sure I don't know.' He does not answer. He feels her trembling, like a horse getting ready to bolt. He wants to shake her again, only harder this time. He wrenches open the wooden gate, and it also shudders on its hinges, as the back door did. They speak, the supposedly inanimate things, they have their voices and they speak, echoing and answering each other.

My father, moving heavily after his long sleep—yes, even the immortals are gross and lumpy at times—has joined me to watch what will come next. He knows Benny Grace for what he is, as do I. We have high hopes of him. We are a jealous and quarrelsome race, the race of gods, but oh my, we do delight in each other's adventures among men.

Benny has slipped into a doze, his chins sunk on his breast. When he hears the pair approaching behind him he starts awake and looks blearily in the wrong direction, towards the long stand of trees beyond the lawn. Adam lets go of his mother's wrist and pushes her in front of him. Benny, locating them at last, scrambles up, turning; he is still barefoot. One of his knees has gone stiff and he stoops and clutches at it, wincing and laughing. 'Oh! Ow!' he cries softly, ruefully laughing still. He straightens up, as much as he can ever straighten, and hobbles forward with both chubby hands extended. He is still wearing the handkerchief on his head. Ursula says nothing, but allows him to take one of her hands in his;

he holds it on his palm and pats it, like a baker patting a loaf. She glances down at his bare feet. He is telling her how eager he has been for them to meet, all these years, and that he cannot understand why they never did. She gazes at him glassily, watching his lips and moving her own in faltering imitation, smiling in a strained way and nodding; it is as if he were speaking in a foreign language of which she has only a smattering and must translate each word laboriously in her head as he utters it. My Dad, already wearying of all this, is muttering plaintively in my ear. He has the itch again and wants to know where his girl has got to. I try to ignore him. How glad I am that only I can see him, in the preposterous get-up he insists on as the father of the gods come to earth, the gold sandals, the ankle-length, cloud-white robe held by a clasp at one shoulder, the brass hair and wavy beard and lips as pink as a nereid's nipples. Honestly. Benny is lifting Ursula's hand to his pursed pink lips—oh, the cad!—but she tugs it back in dismay, and he must let go. He steps back, sketching an ironical little bow, and turns and sits down again on the step to put on his socks and his shoes, squatting forward with gasps and grunts. Ursula watches him, slipping her freed hand under its fellow at her waist. How harmless he seems, an obese putto. Adam meanwhile is—

All right all right all *right*! Keep your curls on, I shall look for her!

Why the old goat cannot go and find the girl himself I do not know. Or I do. It is a show of lordship, merely, he does it without thinking, and does it to all of us, to you as well, though you hardly know it, or have forgotten the effects. How I deplore him. I can almost hear it, my resentment, a mosquito whine, thin and furious. He is the very perfection of egoism—how would he not be, given who he is?—entirely self-absorbed yet wholly unselfconscious. Why do I jump to his whims as I do? Because I must. Because I am afraid of him. Because he would do to me what he did to his father Cronus, fling me headlong from Olympus to the lowest depths of the universe and leave me chained there for all eternity, lost to myself in the darkness under the world. Yes, yes. Zeus is not what you would call a loving father.

I am in the house. I would so much rather have stayed out there with Benny and Ursula and her suddenly wrought son. Now I shall not know what they do and will have to rely on hearsay. Only sometimes am I omniscient.

Here she is, look, the lady Helen, walking swiftly through the house, whistling. She wears a loose silk sleeveless dress, a type of shift, or tunic, girdled at the waist, light blue in colour, very familiar and characteristic, we know the original model well. Look how she moves, a swirl of Attic blue and gold. She has two, quite distinct, walks, one her own and the other that she must have learned when she was training to be an actress. In the learned one she moves with what seems a stately languor, each foot at each step placed carefully heel to toe in front of the other and the hips loosely swaying. A closer look, however, shows that there is nothing loose or languorous here, that on the contrary she is as tense as a tightrope artist aloft in a powdery criss-cross of spotlights, inching along with a fixed and lovely smile, not daring to look down. Her other walk, her own, is altogether different, is a kind of effortful yet exultant plunging, her head held forward and her thighs scissoring and her arms bent sharply at the elbows, so that it is not a tightrope she seems to be on now but a pair of skis, or even roller-skates, even the old, cumbersome kind, with thick leather straps and grinding metal wheels—do you remember them? I think it is the roller-skater my father prefers—among Olympus's lofty ladies there are none but tightrope walkers—since in this mode she appears so impetuous and self-forgetting, qualities he prizes highly, in a mortal girl.

She veers to the left and through a doorway and into a room where she comes upon Roddy Wagstaff, and stops whistling. Roddy is sitting on a straight-backed chair beside a pair of french doors, all alone, one knee crossed on the other, an elbow cupped in a palm and a lighted cigarette cocked at a quizzical angle in his lifted fingers; he looks as if he were sitting for his portrait. 'Sorry,' she says, not sounding so, 'were you meditating?'

Roddy does not rise, only puts on a chilly smile and inclines his head an inch, to the side first and then down; she almost expects to hear a click. 'Not at all,' he says. 'I was doing nothing.'

They do not know each other. They met only once before, that weekend a year ago when Roddy was first here at Arden, and then they hardly exchanged more than a neutral word or two. Roddy seems to her a figure from another time, interestingly outmoded. He is handsome, too, in a thinned-out, strained sort of way. He has the appearance of a painting that has been over-cleaned, brilliant and faded at the same time. He cannot really be interested in Petra, surely not.

'Nothing is what people mostly do, down here,' she says. It comes out sounding more sour, more petulant, than she intended. Roddy's look narrows to a keener interest.

We are in what is known as the music room, although there is no sign of an instrument of any kind, not even a piano, and it is a very long time since anyone has made music here. This is another corner room—for all that it is built in a simple square the house seems to boast more than its share of corners, have you noticed?—this time with two pairs of windows on two adjacent sides. The french doors open on to the lawn, a different stretch of it from where we were a moment ago, with other trees, and no figures to be seen. The walls are painted a pale shade of blue. There is a large and ugly sideboard and, between two of the windows, against the wall, a chaise-longue on which Helen now subsides and drapes herself in an effortless pose, drawing up her legs and setting one hand behind her head and dropping the other into her lap and raising her chin as if for something to be set balancing on it. The colour of her dress is very like the blue of the wall above her. She looks at Roddy along her handsome nose. Have I mentioned Helen's nose, the way it descends in a vertical line from her forehead, like the noses of so many of my female relatives? And have I said that she is short-sighted and will not wear spectacles because she is an actress and actresses do not wear specs? My besotted father sighs, leaning heavily at my shoulder. He dotes on that slight droop in her right—no, her left, is it?—eye, finding it a sign at once of languor and allure.

She and the young man speak of this and that, desultorily, with intervening silences in which they seem to trail their fingers, as if they were drifting in a skiff on a shining calm grey river. They are conscious of the summer day outside, its soft air and vapoury light. She mentions the play she is to be in, and tells him about her director, who is impossible. He nods; he knows the fellow, he says, and knows him for a fool. She notices his nails, bitten to the quick. The tremor in his hand makes the thin swift vertical trail of smoke from the tip of his cigarette waver as it rises. 'Oh, a fool,' he says, 'and a fraud along with it, everyone knows that.' To this she says nothing, only lowers her lashes and smiles. A breeze comes in from the garden and the curtain of white gauze before the open half of the french doors bellies into the room like a soundless exclamation and listlessly falls back. The scent of roasting bird penetrates here, too. A hollow rumbling noise comes up out of Roddy's innards—he too has travelled, he too is hungry—and he clears his throat and shifts quickly his position on the chair and recrosses his legs. 'And such a notion of himself,' he adds, widening his eyes.

Helen, I see, is wearing gold sandals, not unlike Dad's, with gold thongs crossed above the ankles. Her legs are pale, and her knees are bony and splotched a little with red—is this a flaw? My father will have none of it. He knows those knees.

She cannot think, she says, why the play is called after Amphitryon, since Amphitryon's wife Alcmene, her part, is surely the centre of it all. 'You could review it, when it opens,' she says. She smiles. 'I would expect nothing less than a glowing notice, of course.'

'Oh, of course,' he says, and looks away, somewhat quickly.

He rises and goes to the fireplace and crushes the stub of his cigarette into an ashtray on the mantelpiece. She sees the covert glance he gives to his reflection in the gilt-framed mirror on the wall in front of him.

'It could have been set here,' she says, with a broad and sweeping gesture of her arm, a swan flexing its white wing, 'here at this house, when it was first built.'

'Oh? But isn't it in Greece, in Thebes, or somewhere? I seem to remember—'

'The version we are doing all takes place round Vinegar Hill, at the time of the Rebellion.'

'Ah.' He frowns. He does not approve of the classics being tampered with, he says. 'The Greeks knew what they were doing, after all.'

'Oh, but it's not Greek,' she says before she can stop herself, and then to make it worse continues on. '—It was written only a hundred years ago, I think, or two, in Germany.'

He frowns again, more darkly this time. 'Ah, yes,' he says, mumbling, 'I forgot.' He walks to the french doors and stands in the open half, holding aside the gauze curtain, and contemplates the garden. She looks at his back, so straight and stiff. 'Sorry,' she says in a voice made small, pulling a face that he cannot see. He pretends not to have heard.

She sighs, and puts her feet to the floor—her toenails are painted a shell-pink shade, very fetching—and says that surely lunch must be ready by now.

She walks from the room, feeling the rope sag and sway under her feet, and what she takes to be Roddy's eyes on her is in fact my Dad shambling eagerly in her warm wake.

My FATHER DOES not like at all the prospect of this late-afternoon lunch, so late indeed it might be better called high tea—time is all out of kilter today, thanks to you know who. He complains that it will keep him from his girl, and it will. I cannot help that. There is a limit to how far I may interfere with the diurnal springs of their world. Holding back the dawn for an hour was child's play, mortal child's play, compared with the likely consequences of cancelling an entire lunchtime. How much and how often they eat fascinates and rather appals us, for whom a sip of ambrosia and a prophylactic pinch of moly taken every aeon or so suffice both to quell our peckishness and keep our peckers up. For them, though, everything is turned into an excuse for feeding, be it joy, grief, success, humiliating failure, even the deepest loss. In the weeks after Dorothy died old Adam, who was not old then, seemed to find himself six or seven times a day staring helplessly at a plate newly heaped. No sooner did he stand up and totter from the table than some kindly

194

soul would seize him by the wrist and lead him back again with smiling solicitude to the groaning board and hand him his knife and fork and refasten his bib and fill up his tankard for him to the foaming brim. Come, he was constantly being urged, come, you must eat something, it will comfort you and give you strength! What choice had he but to sob out his thanks and set to work on yet another helping of mutton stew, another homemade apple tart, another round of cadaverous camembert? And how they would beam, then, standing over him with their hands folded, nodding in encouragement and self-satisfaction. Compassion, he discovered, has a limited repertoire. Yet these kindnesses made him cry, as if he had not already sufficient cause for tears.

—But wait, what is this? Something has happened, in the garden, I bet, I knew it would, with me not there to invigilate. As I enter the conservatory hard, or soft, rather, necessarily, on the heels of Helen and my father and Roddy Wagstaff—what a procession we must make!—I detect at once a feverish atmosphere. There is not noise or agitation, on the contrary, all is subdued, yet it is plain we are in the midst of an aftermath. Benny Grace is there, standing beside the table with his fists thrust in the pockets of his jacket, looking over the place settings with a concentrated air, as if he were counting the spoons. Off in a corner of the glass gazebo young Adam is talking quietly to his sister, who gazes up at him intently, nodding the while, both of them glancing now and then in Benny's direction. What is it he is telling her? His expression is a giveaway, grave and at the same time almost smiling, as if there is behind it a suppressed hilarity that keeps threatening to break out. Where is Ursula? She said something to Benny after I left, I am sure of it, something inappropriate, perhaps outrageous. She has the inveterate drinker's weakness for blurting out baldly things that are at once consternating and lugubriously comic. Her husband used greatly to enjoy these rushes of inadvertent candour and accidental insult, though they mortify her, when she is able to remember them, that is, and what she said. I would not be surprised if she is even now cowering for shame in the disused washroom behind the scullery, administering to herself a steadying drop from one of her store of naggin bottles, full ones, that she keeps hidden there, my poor sad dithery darling.

Ivy Blount appears out of the dank passageway from the kitchen, bearing the roast chicken on a big tin dish. She has had to hold open the door with an out-turned elbow, and as she comes forward she releases the door and it swings to and snares one of the old grey carpet slippers she is wearing, and she has no choice but to step out of it, which she does, and blunders on, her feet, the bare and the shod, making an alternating slap and slither on the stone-tiled floor. Benny springs to help her but she bypasses him deftly, essaying a sort of caracole—she will not allow herself to look at him—and plonks the heavy dish down in the middle of the table. The others advance and all stand gazing upon the bird with expressions of doubt and misgiving. It is markedly shrivelled and its skin is of a brownish-yellow shade and seems to seethe slowly all over as the glistening coating of fat on it congeals. Rex the dog—where has he come from?—fetches Ivy's slipper from under the door and brings it to her in his mouth and deposits it softly at her feet and casts up at her a look of mild, sad reproof.

The humans distribute themselves to chairs willy-nilly, and Ivy returns to the kitchen to fetch the vegetables. From this shaded within, all that is without the high awning of glass, the trees, the sunlight, that broad strip of cerulean sky, seems a raucous carnival.

Petra finds herself in a chair beside Helen's and at once, without a word, she jumps up and crosses to another place, on Benny Grace's right hand; Benny swivels his head and gives her a conspiratorial smile, arching an eyebrow. Roddy Wagstaff has watched her manoeuvre with grim disdain; he has hardly spoken a word to her since he arrived. Helen reaches for her napkin and her fingertips brush the back of his hand; she does not look at him.

Ivy returns with a great brown wooden tray on which are platters of potatoes, carrots, peas, and a china bowl, unsettlingly suggestive of a chamber pot, with handles on either side, in which is sunk a steaming mess of boiled cabbage. She sets out the dishes and takes her place, to the right of Helen, where Petra was first, and begins to serve. The chair on the other side of her is empty. Meanwhile Adam sharpens the carving knife, wreathing blade and steel about each other at flashing speed, as if he were demonstrating a feat of swordsmanship.

Ursula appears in their midst so quietly, so greyly, that the others have hardly registered her presence before she has seated herself. She smiles about her in vague benevolence, her eyes lowered, looking at no one, and in particular not at Benny Grace, unless I imagine it. Oh, yes, there must have been an altercation on the lawn—I wonder what she said to him?

When Adam cuts into the chicken a sigh of steam escapes from the moist aperture between singed skin and moistly creamy flesh.

'Oh, cabbage, Ivy!' Ursula softly cries, in faintest protest, '—with chicken!'

Ivy ignores her and, still on her feet, brushes a strand of hair from her cheek and fixes her gaze above all their heads.

'I've invited Mr Duffy,' she announces loudly, and has to stop and swallow. '—I've invited Mr Duffy to lunch.'

A hanging silence follows, until Helen suddenly laughs, making a gulping noise, and puts up a hand quickly to cover her mouth.

Rex the dog is a keen observer of the ways of the human beings. He has been attached to this family all his life, or for as long as he has known himself to be alive, the past for him being a doubtful, shapeless place, peopled with shadows and rustling with uncertain intimations, indistinct spectres. These people are in his care. They are not difficult to manage. Obligingly he eats the food it pleases them to put before him, the mush and kibble and the odd ham bone when Ivy Blount remembers to save one for him; he has accustomed himself to this fare, though in his dreams he hunts down quick hot creatures and feasts on their smoking flesh. He has his duties, the guarding of the gate, the routing of itinerants and beggars, the vigilance against foxes, and he attends to them with scruple, despite his increasing years. Before old Adam was carried up to the Sky Room asleep—it was Duffy who did the carrying, by the way—and refused to wake up and come down again, it was Rex's task to take him for a walk each day, sometimes twice a day, if the weather was particularly fine, and for his sake even pretended to like nothing better than chasing a stick or a tennis ball when it was thrown for him. He is unpredictable, though, old Adam; he shouts, and more than once has aimed a kick. The girl Petra is to be wary of, too; she smells of blood. But they all need careful watching. They are not so much dangerous as limited, which is why, he supposes, they are in such need of his support, affection and praise. It pleases them to see him wag his tail when they come into a room, especially if they are alone—when there are more than one of them together they tend to ignore him. He does not mind. He can always make them take notice, especially the women, by barging his snout into their crotches, as it amuses him to do.

There is a thing the matter with them, though, with all of them. It is a great puzzle to him, this mysterious knowledge, unease, foreboding, whatever it is that afflicts them, and try though he may he has never managed to solve it. They are afraid of something, something that is always there though they pretend it is not. It is the same for all of them, the same huge terrible thing, except for the very young, though even in their eyes, too, he sometimes fancies he detects a momentary widening, a sudden, horrified dawning. He discerns this secret and awful awareness underneath everything they do. Even when they are happy there is a flaw in their happiness. Their laughter has a shrill note, so that they seem to be not only laughing but crying out as well, and when they weep, their sobs and lamentations are disproportionate, as though what is supposed to have upset them is just a pretext and their anguish springs really from this other frightful thing that they know and are trying to ignore. They have an air always of looking behind them—no, of not daring to look, afraid of having to see what is there, the ineluctable presence crowding at their heels. In recent days, since old Adam's falling asleep, the others seem more sharply conscious of their phantom follower; it seems to have stepped past and whirled about to confront them, almost as this fat stranger has done, just walked in and sat himself down at the table and looked them all in the eye as if he has every right to be here. Yes, the scandalous secret is out—but what can it be?

Does Rex detect the difference between Benny and me? I wonder. Or, rather, I should ask, does he detect the sameness? For in appearance we could hardly be more unalike, I being all spirit and Benny, in his present manifestation, all flesh, deplorably. The significant distinction lies far deeper than in the forms in which we choose to show ourselves. Sprites we both may be, but compared to Benny I am the incarnation of duty, stability and order. He is the boy who dismantles his father's gold half-hunter to find out how it works. In that arcane science of which old Adam is an adept there are two distinct types of magus. The first sees the world as all a boiling chaos and labours to impose on it a system, of his own devising, which shall marshal the disordered fragments and make of them a whole, while the second finds an ordered world and sets to tinkering in it to discover what principle holds all its rods and cogs in thrumming equilibrium. The latter most often will be plump and satisfied, the former as sleek as the sleekest prelate. There you have Benny, there you have me.

Yet surely Rex should know Benny for what he is. The animals are said always to recognise their panic lord and bow down before him. But what does recognising mean, in Rex's case, what does it, to coin a phrase, entail? Names and categories are of no more weight in his world than they are in ours—you humans are the relentless taxonomists. He crouches now sphinx-like on the stone flags just inside the door of the conservatory, front paws extended and his big square head lifted, alert and watchful. From here he has the widest possible view of the lunch table, although the light pouring through all those panes of glass is behind the lunchers so that seen from here they are cast somewhat into gloom, some of them faceless while the others, viewed in profile, appear as silhouettes. Being a quadruped, he is most familiar with the lower extremities of the bipeds. Legs are always far busier, down there in the half dark, than their owners realise. Benny, for instance, keeps crossing and uncrossing his, like a baby waggling its fingers. He sits happily asprawl, gripping his knife and fork expectantly in his dimpled fists, his plump thighs overflowing the defenceless chair on which he squats with an already mauled napkin draped over his paunch. He is addressing the table at large, telling over yet again the tale of his great friend and colleague Adam Godley's triumph on that day, which seems no longer ago than yesterday, when it came to him as a flash of lightning that in those dark infinities which had been disrupting his sums for so long there lay, in fact, his radiant solutions. No one is listening, not even Petra. Rather, all attention is focused breathlessly on the empty place at table which none dares look directly at, awaiting as it is the momentous coming of Duffy the cowman. I confess I am agog myself. What happy consequences have I set in train by my playful subterfuge of the morning? I experience a twinge of misgiving, however, when I suddenly recollect those shiny green shutters on the windows of Ivy's cottage. Do they presage something, sinister and insistent, like themselves?

'—that it should be possible to write equations across the many worlds, incorporating their infinities, see, and therefore all those other dimensions— What?'

Benny stops as if someone had said something to interrupt him though no one has. Helen turns to gaze at him and takes on the swollen-faced solemnity of one who is trying not to laugh. Ursula, sitting beside young Adam, peers gropingly into the sudden silence, wondering in alarm if she has said something that she should not have. Often nowadays she catches herself murmuring aloud things that she had thought she was only thinking, while sometimes when she does speak, or thinks she does, the person spoken to seems not to have heard. For instance, she is convinced that a moment ago she asked the Wagstaff fellow beside her to open the wine, but if so, he either did not hear or is ignoring her, for he is sitting with his elbows set delicately side by side on the table and his hands joined together under his chin as if he might be about to offer grace, and does not even glance at her. She shifts her attention to her son and watches as he carves the chicken in his irritatingly slow, methodical way, draping the slices of breast meat over the thighs to keep them warm while Duffy is awaited. Duffy, in the house, for lunch!—or did she only imagine Ivy saying she had invited him? No, she did not imagine it, for here he is.

Poor Duffy. He is a great anti-climax after all. He has put on his Sunday best, which is a much washed and faded slate-blue pinstriped suit the like of which I have not seen outside the Cyclades, where it seems every male infant is presented at birth with just such a piece of time-less apparel, to be donned ceremonially on his arriving at his majority and never taken off again before the grave and in many cases not even then. The shirt that Duffy wears is very white and open at the collar, and his boots are brown. He has pomaded his hair, with axle-grease, it would seem, and brushed it back fiercely from his fore-head, which gives him a slightly wild and staring aspect. He stops in the doorway and swallows, his Adam's apple bouncing. No one it seems knows what to say and Ivy cannot bring herself to look at him. Then Petra, of all people, rises from her seat and goes to him swiftly and takes him by the hand, yes, by the hand, which to the others, even to Ivy, and to their surprise, seems the most natural thing in the world, and leads him forward wordlessly to his place at the table. He nods his thanks, arranging the broad planes of his face into an unaccustomed and rudimentary smile. Ivy, still not looking at him, moves his napkin a fraction nearer to his plate, touching the cloth only with the tip of a middle finger, and clears her throat. He has a curious way of seating himself, in stages, as it were, putting his left hand to the table and leaning sideways, pressing the other hand to the front of his right thigh, and lowering himself gingerly on to the chair, which gives a frightened squeak. Perhaps he suffers from rheumatism, what his poor old mother before him used to call the old rheumatizz. Benny Grace is regarding him with frank and beaming interest. Helen picks up the corkscrew and hands it to Roddy Wagstaff. Meanwhile Petra goes back to her own place and sits, with eyes downcast, like a communicant returning from the altar.

'You're very welcome, Adrian,' Ursula says across the table, somewhat thick-tongued, carefully enunciating the words as if they had been glued together and must be prised apart, one by one. Adam is standing beside her with the carving knife upraised; she touches him lightly on the elbow. 'Mr Duffy,' she says softly, 'will take a drumstick, I'm sure.'

There is a general sense of dissipating tension. Duffy's coming, everyone sees, is not to fulfil the great things that were expected of it. Rex the dog, abruptly losing interest in everything, Duffy included, flops over on his side with a sigh and closes his eyes.

Young Adam is in a state of strange elation. It is as if he were suspended aloft, swaying above the room. He sees his hands as from a long way off, laying slices of meat on each plate as Ivy Blount holds it out to him, and when he speaks, his voice reverberates tinnily inside his head. He does not know what is the matter with him—is this happiness again, the same that he felt when he was driving to the station? Not really, but a sort of giddiness only. Yes, he feels giddy, looking down on the table from this height. His mother, beside him, bows her head over her wine glass and he looks at the pale parting in her greying hair and experiences for an instant a pang of what seems the purest sorrow. What is the matter with him, swinging wildly like this from one emotion to another?

Helen is talking to Roddy and smiling, and Petra is watching her across the table with narrowed eyes.

The carving done, Adam sits down to his plate, yet that teetering sensation persists. His mother on his right is speaking to him, fretting that there will not be enough meat to go round. He tells her to stop worrying, that no one minds. 'Duffy has his drumstick, look,' he say quietly, and makes himself smile, but she only gazes at him in that intently vacant way that she does, wide-eyed, with her head down and her chin tucked in. 'Don't worry,' he says again, more irritably now, more gruffly, 'everything is all right, I'm telling you.'

Is it? He feels acutely the absence of his dying father from this table where so often he noisily presided. But when was that father ever fully present, at this table or anywhere else in the life of the house? It is I who ask the question not young Adam, who is more forgiving than I am, than I would be, were I him. Ah, fathers and sons, fathers and sons. Not that I know so very much about the subject. I speak of my father as my father and of me as his son, but in truth these terms can be only figurative for us, who are not born and do not die, for birth and death are the sources, it seems, out of which mortal ones derive their sensations of love and loss. The old stories tell of us coupling and begetting, enduring and dying, but they are only stories. Like old Adam in the bosom of his family, we are not here sufficiently to be ever quite gone. Think, if you can, of a sea of eternal potential and of us as the shapes the waters make, surging and swaying; think of the air moulded by weather into transparent forms; think of ice; think of flame—so we are, at once eternal and evanescent.

Where were we? At the lunch table, among these people. All I am doing is passing the time here, flicking these polished playing cards into that upturned silk hat.

Adam looks round the table in a kind of wonderment, seeming now to be sunk in something and looking up, and all sways and shimmers. He feels as if he were being keel-hauled, in the air one minute, gasping for breath, and plunged in a green airlessness the next. How flat and featureless now everything seems up there, seen from down here, even the figures, the figures especially, his mother and his sister, his wife, the preposterous Benny Grace, too. He recalls Roddy Wagstaff passing under the shadow of the tree outside the railway station and seeming to fade for a second into the starkness of that gloom. How conceive of a reality sufficiently detailed, sufficiently incoherent, to accommodate all the things that are in the world? He lives in that reality yet cannot fully conceive of it. He stands aghast before the abundance of things, all of them separate, all of them unique. A single blade of grass is made of an unimaginable massing of tiny and still tinier particles—and how many blades of grass are there in this impossible world? This is the trick his father managed for himself, the trick he pulled off, making all the bits seem to cohere in a grand amalgam wrought by the mumbo-jumbo of mere numbers. Or so the son thinks.

He surfaces from this reverie with a jolt. The table has become animated, and there is a confusion of talk. Helen is telling Roddy Wagstaff about something—that play she is to be in, he supposes, she speaks of little else these days—her gold head thrust forward on its lovely column of neck. Her throat, Adam notices, is delicately flushed, with a rosy porcelain glow like that on the inner surface of a seashell. Roddy has pushed his chair back the better to face her, and sits sideways to the table with one bony knee crossed on the other and one arm folded and an index finger pressed to his chin at the side. He regards her unblinking and now and then nods, though his look is sceptical, with the shadow of a smirk. Adam feels for his wife the same rush of compassion that a moment ago he felt for his mother; why is Helen giving so much of her attention to this fellow, who surely despises her, as he despises, or so Adam believes, all of them here at the table? Petra too is still watching the pair of them, back and forth, back and forth, like a spectator engrossed in a tennis match; at intervals she darts forward to try to say something but is rebuffed by their refusal to notice her and subsides again, mute and rueful. Ivy Blount and Duffy the cowman sit side by side in an atmosphere all of their own, Ivy leaning forward over her plate and plying her knife and fork with concentrated intensity, as if they were a pair of knitting needles, while Duffy, his food ignored, glares unseeing at a salt cellar. They seem to be having an argument, and speak without looking at each other, in an undertone, in rapid bursts between brief intervals of fraught silence. But they are not arguing, not at all. They are, or my name is not Hermes, locked in negotiations towards the plighting of a mutual troth.

Suddenly Benny Grace's voice is heard above all others. 'Oh, no, he won't die,' he says, loud and emphatic, 'no, no,' and Rex the dog, still lying on his side, quickly lifts his large head from the floor and looks at him.

Adam's mother, on Adam's right, makes a low, choked sound that might almost be, Adam thinks, laughter. The table has fallen silent—this must be what is called a panic fright. Benny smiles at no one in particular and takes a drink of wine, his little black eyes sparkling merrily over the rim of his glass. His avowal has made all at the table uneasy. Nor is it clear to whom his assurance was addressed. Ivy Blount has lifted her head and is gazing at the little man, her lips parted and the jabbings of her busy knife and fork suspended. Duffy, frowning in the new-made silence, bends his attention to his plate, on which the single slice of chicken, which was all he got besides the scrawny drumstick, has begun to curl along the edges, while the cabbage has gone cold and acquired an unpleasant, whitish sheen. Is this Duffy noticing these niceties of detail, or I? Or is there a difference?

There is no doubt whom it is that Benny Grace was speaking of, whose demise he was denying, or at least the imminence of it. The very certitude of the denial, abrupt and seemingly uncalled for, is what has so unsettled the rest of the table. My kinsman Thanatos, son of Night, in his black robes, with sword unsheathed, has stepped into their midst out of the shadows where he has been biding all along. It is his sudden coming that wakened Rex the dog, who rises cautiously now and stands at point, nosing the tensened air. These are the moments that unsettle him most, when their moods change abruptly and seemingly for no reason. They were all talking, he knew that even in his sleep, and now they are quiet and sit very still, as if something had frightened them anew, that mysterious thing that always frightens them, all except the fat stranger, who seems concerned for nothing. Meanwhile outdoors, beyond the glass wall, the trees on the far side of the sunlit lawn stand like a line of people with their backs turned, gazing off indifferently at something else.

Not die, eh? So that is his little game, that is what he has been brought here to accomplish. Since when has he become the lord of life and death, Mr Benny so-called Grace?

Yet why am I vexed? What is it to me whether one of them dies or lives? They will all go, in the fullness, in the emptiness, of time. My sole task is to take over from the undertaker and escort them to the next life, whatever it be, different for each of them. Death they consider always caducous; the nonagenarian, bald and toothless as a babe, ignores the silt in his arteries, the amyloids in his brain, and imagines himself in no more than his late prime and good for at least another ninety rollicking years. We should let them have a taste of immortality, see how they like it. Soon enough they would come to us mewling and puking in their pain, beseeching us to finish them off. My father did once consider giving them the gift—ha ha—of eternal life. This was many years ago, oh, many years, in the time of Electryon king of Mycenae. Here is what happened. The old king's nephew Amphitryon—yes, the very same—and grandson of my brother Perseus the Gorgon-slayer, became enamoured of his cousin Alcmene, Electryon's daughter—yes, yes, I know, the bloodlines getting all tangled up, as usual. Amphitryon had fled to Thebes, having managed accidentally to kill his father-in-law in a bit of bungling on the battlefield —at least, he claimed he had not meant to run the old boy through—and Alcmene, a spirited girl, followed him there and married him, after vicissitudes too tedious to waste time picking over here. Alcmene was an exquisite creature, a golden girl, and needless to say my Dad took a shine to her, and employed what we know is one of his favourite wiles to get her into bed, to wit, he came to her at twilight in the very form and aspect of her husband. They passed a divine night together, pseudo-Amphitryon and his darling girl, and with the dawn my

Dad withdrew—I shall plod on, steadfastly ignoring the inevitable double entendres—when who should appear but Amphitryon himself, home unexpectedly from the wars. See how I am warming to my tale. The lady Alcmene was baffled, of course, to find her husband apparently popping up again in her chamber a minute after he had left and behaving as if their night of passion had not happened; nevertheless she gamely submitted to a further strenuous session on her already disordered bed—General Amphitryon had been away a frustratingly long time in Thessaly, hacking at his old adversaries there, and was no sooner in the door than he set to asserting his conjugal rights. The result of this double bout of fructifying romps was, in due course, a pair of twins, Iphicles, who was Amphitryon's son and therefore not much heard of again, and Heracles, whom my Dad was pleased to call his own.

A breather.

Heracles, this strapping lad, grew into a mighty man, the greatest of the great heroes of old, blah blah blah. Now, nothing that my father does is ever simple or straightforward, but the machinations by which he arranged for Heracles, who was brave but not the brightest, to carry out the plan to make mortals immortal were devious far above even his usual standards. Having first of all driven the poor fellow temporarily demented he next arranged for him to be instructed by the oracle at Delphi to put himself in fealty to Eurystheus king of Tiryns, who in turn was inspired to impose on the hero, for no apparent reason or discernible purpose, a series of tremendous and well-nigh impossible tasks. You will know of these famous Twelve Labours of Heracles, the killing of the many-headed Hydra, the capture of the Erymanthian Boar, the pinching of the girdle of Hippolyte queen of the Amazons, and all the rest; of the dozen of these tasks, however, eleven were no more than blinds behind which to pass off the twelfth, the supposed abduction of Cerberus, which feat was effected with the help of yours truly and my sister Athene, that headache, and which itself was yet another blind, for the intended elimination of Pluto himself, no less. This was my father's real intention, the true heart of his scheme, that Sis and I should escort Heracles to the gates of the underworld, where the barking of the guard dog would bring Pluto running to know who was the new arrival, whereon Heracles would bend his bow and loose an arrow into the dark god's heart and strike him dead. The death of death!—imagine! It was not to be, however. All of Olympus rose up in rebellion, or threatened to. Here was the time for solidarity, we said, the time to show old Zeus the limits of his powers. He had been throwing his weight about for long enough, cuckolding gods and men alike and swallowing his relatives whole. If he were free to destroy death he would be free to destroy us all. We would not stand for it, it was as simple as that. And thereby survived Pluto, the killer of men.

Why did Zeus think to put death to death? I have not enquired of him and never will; there are certain questions one does not pose to the father of the gods. However, this does not mean I may not speculate on the matter. Is it that he could not bear to think of his beloved girls—broidered with bulls and swans, powder'd with golden rain, as the silver poet puts it—writhing in agony on their deathbeds, who had writhed in his arms for joy? If so, why not just kill off all the males and let their better halves live for ever? No, it makes him out too kind, too caring. He wished them all, girls and boys alike, adults in their prime, oldsters and crones, all to know what we know, the torment of eternal life. Why must he have a reason? Call it cruelty, call it caprice, call it the revenge of heaven's lord on the creatures he had made. Or maybe he thought to make a new race of demigods, there is a thing to think of—not only living for ever but, my goodness, forever procreating, too, until the world is packed tight with them and they are forced to storm heaven for a new place to populate. Brr.

Anyway, there you have it, his dastardly plan was thwarted and, thanks to us, his extended family, men may go on dying in the good old way.

Rex the dog is growing drowsy again: his heavy head droops. The darkness that Benny Grace's words brought forth now gradually withdraws, and the others at the table pick up again uncertainly, like gleaners after their midday rest setting off again between the furrows. And I hover in the air above them, my chlamys spread as wide as it will go, in the attitude of Piero's Madonna della Misericordia, protecting my little band of mortal sinners. I am not all sneers and scathings, you see, I have my gentler side.

Petra seizes her chance and breaks the silence by asking of the table, in a loud voice, why it is that tumours are always compared to citrus fruits. 'As big as a lemon, they say,' she says, 'an orange, a grapefruit—why?' She looks about the table, fierce in her demand, but no one has an answer to offer her.

No two things the same, the equals sign a scandal; there you have the crux of it, the cross to which I was nailed from the start. Difference: the very term is redundant, a nonce-word coined to comfort and deceive. Oh, I told myself, I tell myself, that to say equal to is not to say identical with, but does it signify, does it placate? My equations spanned a multitude of universes yet they posited a single world of unity and ultimate order. Perhaps there is such a world, but if there is we do not live in it, and cannot know how things would be there. Even the self-identity of the object is no more than a matter of insisting it is so. Where then may one set down a foot and say, 'Here is solid ground'? As a child I was terrified at seeing the hands of a ticking clock turned back, thinking time itself would be reversed and all collapse into disorder, yet I was the very one who would break time's arrow and discard the slackened bow. Benny Grace used to mock me for my doubts and ditherings. What business is it of ours, he would scoffingly ask, echoing the schoolmen of old, what business is it of ours to save the phenomena? That was the difference—the difference!—between the two of us. I raged for certitude, he was the element of misrule. When I think of him now I hear again the music of the past, raucous and discordant but sweet, too, the sad sweet music of being young.

Whatever he may say to deny it, we did bring something to a close, we adepts of the temporal. After us, certain large possibilities were no longer possible. In our new beginning was an old end. I recall the atmosphere in the academies in those days, even in those early days of the revolution we had so fearlessly set going. Euphoria first, then the dawn of misgiving, then an increasing lassitude, an increasing jadedness. Arguments would still break out, squabbles rather than arguments, too overheated to be sustained, and ending always in impotence and savage frustration. There was a particular aspect people had when they turned and slunk away from these confrontations, hangdog, muzzled, the mouth drawn sideways in a snarl. A savour had gone out of things, the air was that much duller, the light that much dimmed. We could not comprehend it, at first, this darkening of the world that was our doing—it was, after all, the opposite of what we had intended. Somehow, extension brought not increase but dissipation. My final series of equations, a handful of exquisite and unimpeachable paradoxes, was the combination that unlocked the sealed chamber of time. The sigh of dead, dank air that wafted back in our faces from the yawning doorway out of what had been our only world was not the breath of new life, as we expected, but a last gasp. I still do not understand it. The hitherto unimagined realm that I revealed beyond the infinities was a new world for which no bristling caravels would set sail. We hung back from it, exhausted in advance by the mere fact of its suddenly being there. It was, in a word, too much for us. This is what we discovered, to our chagrin and shame: that we had enough, more than enough, already, in the bewildering diversities of our old and overabundant world. Let the gods live at peace in that far, new place.

What a pair we must have made, though, Benny and I, the overman in his overman's cape and tights flashing through the ether with his fat sidekick clinging on for dear life to his neck. Or was it the other way round, him flying and I clinging on, for dear life? For dear life is what I could never quite get the hang of. Others seem to manage it easily enough: they just do it, or have it done to them—perhaps that is the secret, not so much to live as be lived, let life itself do the work. Certainly that was how Benny seemed to carry it off. Fetching up breathless with emptied pockets and skinned knees after another one of our escapades together, I would look around and find him brushing the dust off his sleeve and humming unconcernedly to himself, as if we had been on nothing more adventurous than a Sunday-afternoon stroll. Did I have a taste for the low life before Benny came along and dragged me gaily into the gutter for a respite? I know I liked it, once I was there, paddling in the piss and spittle. Here, I told myself, is the real thing, the business itself, raw and coarse and vital, this is what it is to be alive. No gentle Inges or Ursulas down there, only drabs and cut-purses and the odd poor Gretchen searching forlornly for her Faust.

I should not exaggerate. I am at heart a timid soul and the scrapes that Benny got me into were no more than that, scrapes and japes and schoolboy pranks. He would turn up at odd times and in unexpected places, but if I was surprised, he never was. That was the uncanny thing, the way he would come bustling yet again into my life, in mid-sentence, as it were, and link his fat arm through mine and steer me aside from whatever I was doing and walk me off into a corner to propose in an earnest under-tone some new, preposterous wheeze. He always made it seem that he had been gone no more than a moment or two and now was back, doing up his flies or rolling his shirt sleeves, ready to get the ructions going again. Girls, of course, there were always girls, I marvelled at his way with them. What did they see in him, what was the secret of his roly-poly charm? He would wander off into a crowded bar, a hotel lobby, a conference hall, and come back five minutes later with a likely romp on either arm, the short one for him and the tall one for me. More often than not these encounters fetched up in disaster, or farce, or both—gin-tinted tears, smeared mascara, a definitively hitched-up black silk strap—but Benny was never daunted, would accept no rebuff, admit no failure.

He deplored my taste for Inge and her ilk, the dainty, damaged ones, but I felt no call to defend myself against his gibes once I met Madame Mac. Here I must pause, and confess to a slight constraint, a slight embarrassment.

That I took her at first for his mother is one thing, but that I am still uncertain that she was not—his mother, I mean—is surely quite another. He never said who she was, exactly, or specified the nature of their relation, and in the way of these things, after a certain interval it became impossible to ask. He referred to her only as Madame Mac or, sometimes, as 'my old lady', so there was no help there. Early on there seemed a clear disparity in age between them, and he could well have been her son, but as the years progressed and age coarsened his admittedly never youthful form the gap narrowed and with it my uncertainty widened.

He was not himself, not the self that I was accustomed to, when he was with her. His demeanour veered between a worried lover's fawning deference and a brusque irritability that to my ear bespoke the filial. I was first introduced to Madame Mac, if introduced is the word, in Rome, I believe it was. I was there to accept the Borgia Prize, founded in memory of gentle Cesare, peacemaker and patron of natural sciences and the arts. I remember well the hotel, one of those gloomy timeless palaces to be found in every capital city, the corridors humming with a vast silence, in all the rooms a worryingly fecal smell, and the unseen below-stairs staff audibly at their larks. In the muffled lounge, where it would always be afternoon, vague bodies were fidgeting over coffee cups and little cakes, and the tall windows were ablaze with an amazement of blue October sky. Had Benny and I arranged to meet or was it another of our chance stumblings across each other?—chance on my part, if not on his. Under one of the windows a woman was seated in an armchair before a low table; with the light behind her I could not make out her features, though I had the feeling that she was regarding me intently. She was leaning forward rather heavily, her skirt stretched tight over splayed knees, while the chair in which she was seated seemed to reach out its stubby wings on either side of her as if striving to draw her back into its brocaded embrace. The dress she wore was made of what seemed swathe upon swathe of multi-coloured stuff printed with a large design, roses or peonies or some such, and might have been a continuation of the figured covering of the armchair, so that she was camouflaged and appeared a congeries of disjointed parts, head, arms and hands, thick short legs. All this detail noted in hindsight, of course. At her back, in a corner of the window, an oleander bush tossed and tossed in the hot wind of a Roman autumn.

Benny when he arrived was all bustle and hand-rubbing. He was wearing his inveterate black suit and grubby white shirt. He complained of the chilly air-conditioning—it is never warm enough for Benny, we have that in common—and chafed his hands the harder. He seemed uninclined to sit, and due to the way my chair was facing I had to turn my head awkwardly to the side and upwards in order to meet his eye. Come to think of it, there was always an awkwardness in the stance I felt myself forced to adopt in his presence, I had always a crick in my neck when he is about. I noted a certain shiftiness in his manner on this occasion, a certain breathy excitedness. He said he would take a glass of wine but seemed to be concerned with something else. He was casting about the room as if at random, and now his glance came to rest on the woman by the window. Did they exchange a signal? Benny cleared his throat and mumbled something, then walked to where the woman was sitting and positioned himself beside her chair in the attitude, head back and one shoulder lifted, of a frock-coated gentleman posing for a daguerreotype, and directed back at me a summoning frown. I rose uncertainly and went to him. 'This,' he said gruffly, almost dismissively, 'is Madame Mac.'

She directed at me from her chair a calmly appraising gaze, and lifted a hand as if for me to kiss it, the back of it graciously arched and fingers limply dangling; I shook it. The thing had the cartilaginous smoothness and faint heat of a bird's claw. She was wearing something on her head, a close-fitting hat or a scarf tightly bound, which made me think of Lily Brik shouting the good news in that famous poster, or of one of Millet's cloched peasant women. I had the impression of bright festoons, bits of ribbon, silk streamers that shimmered and fluttered about her. Her face appeared wider than it was long, with a great carven jaw and an almost lipless mouth that seemed to stretch from ear to ear and managed to be at once froggy and almost noble. Her skin was greyish-pale and looked as dry as meal. Within the voluminous dress she wore there was the suggestion of hidden folds of unrestrained flesh. Foul-minded as I am I at once set to picturing Benny and her engaged in congress, like a pair of walruses thrashing and trumpeting in a boiling sea; perhaps that is why, the next moment, my mind introduced to me the possibility of a blood tie between them, so that I should never again be obliged to entertain such an image. Madame Mac's eyes were the thing that struck me most forcefully. They were glossy, slightly starting, not large but unnervingly piercing, and so intense they made the rest of her features, even that extraordinary mouth, fade behind their light. My memory of that first occasion insists her eyes were black, but later when I took the trouble to notice them they seemed a shade of deep violet—can eyes change colour, according to circumstance, the play of light, the mood of the moment? I must have sat down. I do not know what I said to her, or she to me. Did she have an accent? It did not strike me, if she had. Another mystery. At her shoulder, in the window, the oleander bush with its polished leaves shivered and shook, as if successive douses of water were being poured through it. Perhaps it was the contrast between the stillness of her broad grey flat face and the frantic movements of the bush behind it and the scraps of fluttering silk about her person, but what she reminded me of most strongly was an electric fan, with its warning tassel tied to the mesh, turning its bland, tilted head slowly from side to side, and the blades behind the mesh a motionless blur as they spun and spun and spun.

Benny launched on a rambling account of how he and I had first met, that chilly midsummer in the far north. There was an edge of dismissiveness to his tone, of heavy-breathing impatience, as if he were a pupil compelled to tell over a dull passage not fully memorised. Madame

Mac seemed not to be listening, seemed, indeed, oblivious of him. She was studying me still, letting her gaze, at once vague and penetrating, wander all over me with a feline impassiveness while, behind, the blades went on silently spinning. Held there, listening to Benny recite his ill-learned lesson and suffering Madame Mac's scrutiny, I had the uncomfortable sensation of being somehow lifted up and carried between them, like a satrap borne lullingly down an ever-narrowing defile towards the lair of the assassin. The waiter came with Benny's wine and Benny took the glass and sucked up a greedy gulp and stared off into space, no longer speaking. He seemed to require something of me, to be silently asking me for something, some understanding or tacit acceptance.

Later that same evening Madame Mac told me the story of her life, or parts of it, parts of the story, parts of her life. We were outside, on the hotel terrace, overlooking an expanse of floodlit historic rubble. Bats flitted here and there in the mauve twilight. I was chilled, and not quite sober, and could not concentrate very well on the knotted fabric of the tale she was elaborately weaving. At some time in the indeterminate past she had entered on a brief and, she emphasised, issueless union with the Honourable Mr MacSomebody, a wealthy invert with delicate lungs, ambassador Plenipotentiary of the Republic of Somewhere to the Holy See, owner of a succession of grand houses, on Capri, in Paris, in Manhattan and Sidi bel Abbès, who before his untimely and, she murmuringly attested, highly picturesque demise had enjoined her to employ the large inheritance she would have from him towards the betterment of mankind in general and in particular the encouragement of the physical sciences, in which the Ambassador had long maintained a keen amateur interest. I listened to this farrago in captivated bemusement, sipping at my sixth or seventh flute of sour prosecco and inhaling the stench of drains that Rome was sending up to us like the fumes from a votive offering. Madame Mac as she spoke bore into me mesmerisingly with those protuberant little shiny eyes of hers, swaying somewhat before me like a cobra poised on its rings. Perhaps it was all true, Mr Mac and his bad lungs, the minareted mansion in the Maghreb, the deathbed injunction, all of it. The world has many worlds, as who should know better than I, each one stranger, more various and for all I know more farcical than the last. Anything is possible. When she finished we both stood silent for some moments, looking into our glasses, then suddenly, with a sort of wobbling lurch, she leaned her large front against me and fumbled for my hand, which she found, and clutched tightly. The result of all this was that I lost my balance, and would have fallen down, taking her with me, if there had not been the pockmarked limestone parapet to support us. What if we had toppled off the balcony and plunged into the ruins below? What would Benny have thought, when we were found, bloodied and broken, spreadeagled hand in hand on a broken suggestum close by one of Vespasian's first erections?

It occurred to me that she might have been offering me money. Why else all this talk of the Hon. Mr Mac's love of science and his philanthropical bent and of the inheritance she had of him—why else the sudden impassioned intimacy, the desperate seizing upon my hand? Gently I disengaged from her, feeling like a young lady of genteel upbringing who has just been invited by a fat old madam to come for a try-out at the brothel. We turned and went back into the hotel, I embarrassed and she very thoughtful. And the next time I saw her, she was dying.

Was it the next time? Did I only encounter her twice? I do not remember. It was Benny, naturally, who took me to see her in that hospital in the mountains. High summer it was up there, the sound of cowbells impossibly close in the clean, thin air—I thought at first it was a recording that the hospital was piping into the rooms, instead of the usual soothing music. Madame Mac had been wandering back and forth across the continent for months, like a wounded animal searching for a place in which to die. Bald and bloated, she lay uncovered on the narrow white bed like something vegetable that had been thrown there, her eyes swivelling agitatedly and her fingers plucking at the sheet. Despite the circumstances she was tricked out as usual in her varicoloured bobs and bows. I tried not to see her large bare mottled knees. The Alpine sun shone in the window with gay indifference. At first I thought she did not know me but then she clutched my hand hotly in hers—again!—and started to tell me in a gabbled whisper about something that had happened a long time ago, even the drift of which I could not grasp. I pretended to understand, however, and tried to seem interested—oh, that sickly smile that smears itself over one's face on these occasions!—but Benny tugged at my arm and made a little moue of discouragement, and I stepped back, and Madame Mac let go my hand and of all things gave an exasperated sigh of laughter, as an aunt would sigh ruefully over a doted-upon but unmannerly nephew, and I felt clumsy and churlish, and snatched my arm away from Benny and walked out of the room. Whether or not I met her on more occasions than the ones I remember I do not know, but I do know that was to be the last I would see of her.

A little later on that occasion we found ourselves, Benny and I, standing on a deep, glassed-in balcony where wooden loungers were set out in a row, each with its folded red wool blanket and rubber pillow, while in front of us there sprawled a lavish view of jagged, snow-clad peaks that seemed to jostle each other rowdily in their eagerness to impress and charm. It was midday and staff and patients alike must have been at early lunch for not a soul was there save us two. Benny took the opportunity to smoke a clandestine cigarette, holding it corner-boy fashion in a cupped fist and stowing the ash in a pocket of his jacket. I have always envied smokers the little ritual they are allowed to indulge in twenty or thirty times a day, the lighting up, the long drag, the narrowed eye, the slow exhale. I tried to say something consoling to him but could think of nothing. Nor could I think why I had to be here—what was Madame Mac to me, or I to Madame Mac? Yet I had the impression of having been drawn despite myself into a kind of restive intimacy. Not only Benny had a filial aspect now, we both might have been a pair of grown-up brothers brought uneasily together at the bedside of a dying parent. Benny puffed and sighed, sighed and puffed, scanning the room as if in search of something that should be there but was unaccountably missing. Then he said a very strange thing, the import of which I did not understand, and still do not. 'There is no need for you to worry,' he said, frowning in the direction of my knees. 'Everything will be all right.' How portentous he made those simple words sound. I nodded, still saying nothing. Why was he reassuring me, when he was the one who would shortly be bereaved? I might have asked, but did not. My unwillingness had something to do with the place, I think, the elevation, and that unnervingly neat row of extended chairs, and the big window tilting over us, and those preposterously picturesque mountains sparkling in the unreal noonday light.

I never allowed Ursula to meet Benny or Madame Mac—I wonder why. She shied from the notion of them, from the very mention of them. I think she suspected something libidinous in my relations with them, as if they had inveigled me into a cabal the rules and rites of which were grounded in the flesh. I do not say she imagined orgies, with me inscribing runes and magic formulae in blood on Madame Mac's big bare bum while Benny Grace stood by with whip and manacles urging me on, no, nothing so coarse as that. Only she is something of a priestess of the pure, and in those two, or in the idea of them at least, she saw personified, I think, all the temptations of the base world and its steamy pleasures. But, after all, was she entirely wrong? She would save me from myself; that was her mission from the outset. She had the determination for it. Young though she was when we first met there was already something settled about her, something finished, a high fine gloss—finished, settled, polished, and yet wonderfully vulnerable, too. She had a certain dainty unsteadiness in the region of the knees that I found irresistible, a matter of disbalance not due to ungainliness but to the care and vigilance with which she picked her way over the world's treacherous terrain. That is how I see her in my mind, my dear sweet wife, stepping towards me delicately, frowning in concentration, eyes down and elbows lifted and her hands out flat on either side as if pressing on shelves of air for support, her knees brushing together and her heels a little splayed and her head lowered for me to see the parting in the centre of her hair, a perfect, snow-grey groove. Yet I wonder if I asked too much of her, or, worse, perhaps, too little. There is a primitive tribe that lives deep in the jungles of Borneo, or New Guinea, maybe, it does not matter which, a sturdy little people with pot bellies and blackened teeth who eat their ancestors and pickle the heads of their enemies, or the other way round, I forget. The female of the tribe wears a bone through her nose and distends her earlobes enormously by inserting hoops in them, while the male— surely I am making this up?—the male prosthetically extends his virile member by inserting it into a long, narrow shoot of bamboo, held erect before him at a sharp angle by means of a length of plaited cord tied to the tip, the tip of the bamboo, that is, and then looped back and tied in turn around his skull. At puberty these males undergo a ceremonial initiation in which each is presented not only with his bamboo stick and yard of string but also takes possession of a carved wood figurine, semi-abstract though suggestive of a fat little featureless woman, not unlike, I suppose, their little fat mothers. Very impressive, in their vernacular way, these totems, I have seen them in museums. When the boys receive them the dolls are already immensely old, handed down through succeeding generations, smoothed and polished by use and time. Their purpose is to be a lifelong comfort and companion, and also, most importantly, to act as a repository of all doubts, fears, violent urges, vengeful desires—to be an object of comfort and veneration, but also a whipping-boy, or a whipping-girl, as one might say. I wonder if Ursula has been something like this for me. It is a dark thought, and one I do not willingly entertain.

Children were a surprise to me, the second one no less than the first. Absurd to say so, I know, but it is true. Surely on both occasions that unignorably accumulating bulge in my wife's middle region should have cushioned me from the shock of the inevitable issue. But not a bit of it, the thing sent me stumbling in a daze, not once but twice. The most unnerving thing about these conjured creatures that were suddenly there, by a piece of biological sleight of hand, was their incontrovertible otherness. I know, I know, every other is other, necessarily. However, with Ursula, for instance, and even to an extent with Dorothy, the two human beings I have been closest to in my life, if I exclude my mother, which for the moment

I do—in my wives, I am saying, there was a passionate cleaving to me that gave at least the illusion of getting over that gap, the gap of otherness, an illusion that was far harder to effect when the object of one's baffled regard were these minute brand-new beings that were either uncannily quiet or at the slightest slight turned puce with rage. The boy I found particularly alarming, and not just because he was the first. He was like one of those babies in the cartoon films, chubby face plugged with a soother and bald save for a single question mark of hair, who suddenly reaches a brawny arm out of the cradle and delivers poor Sylvester the cat an uppercut that sets his eyeballs spinning and crowns him with a crooked halo of exploding stars. That was me, the same stunned reeling, the same goggling, cross-eyed stare. The girl was altogether different, lying there still and watchful, as though being born were a trick that had been pulled on her the aftermath of which she was certain would be even more violently mortifying than the event itself.

But she was my favourite. By the time she arrived the boy was a big fellow already, cautious, secretive, solitary. He was frightened of me, just as I was frightened of him. In the girl I could see from the start there was something wrong, something missing, a link to the world where the rest of us carry on with varying degrees of success the pretence of being at home. This, I should be ashamed to say, I found more gratifying than troubling. Here at last was a soul I could share with, one that was damaged, as damaged as I believed my own soul to be.

Did I, do I, love them? It is a simple question but

extremely ticklish. I shielded them from what dangers I could, did not stint or spoil, taught them such virtues as I knew and as I judged they would benefit from. I worried they would suffer falls, cut themselves, catch a cold, contract leprosy. I think it safe to say that in certain dire circumstances if called upon I would have given up my life to save theirs. But all that, it seems, was not enough: a further effort was required, no, not an effort but an effect, an affect, whatever to say—a state of being, let us call it, a stance in relation to the world, which is what they mean by love. When they speak of it, this love of theirs, they speak as of a kind of *grand mal* brought on catastrophically by a bacillus unknown to science but everywhere present in the air about us, like the tuberculosis spore, and to which all but the coldest constitutions are susceptible. For me, however, if I understand the concept, to love properly and in earnest one would have to do it anonymously, or at least in an undeclared fashion, so as not to seem to ask anything in return, since asking and getting are the antithesis of love—if, as I say, I have the concept aright, which from all I have said and all that has been said to me so far it appears I do not. It is very puzzling. Love, the kind that I mean, would require a superhuman capacity for sacrifice and self-denial, such as a saint possesses, or a god, and saints are monsters, as we know, and as for the gods—well. Perhaps that is my trouble, perhaps my standards are too high. Perhaps human love is simple, and therefore beyond me, due to my incurable complicating bent. That might be it, that might be the answer. But I do not think so.

And yet perhaps I do love, without knowing it; could such a thing be possible, an unwilled, and unconscious, loving? On occasion, when I think of this or that person, my wife, say, my son or daughter—let us leave my daughter-in-law out of this—my heart is filled, what we call the heart, with an involuntary surge of something, glutinous and hot, like grief, but a happy grief, and so strong that I stagger inwardly and my throat thickens and tears, yes, real tears, press into my eyes. This is not like me, I am not given to swoons and vapourings in the normal run of things. So maybe there is a vast, hidden reservoir of love within me and these wellings-up are the overflow of it, the splashes over the side of the cistern when something weighty is thrown in.

I always thought dying would be a great and saving confusion, like a drunkard's dreaming, but look at me, on my last legs or rather on no legs at all, yet in my mind as clear as a bell, though certainly, I grant you, not as sound. I am weakening; I mean my resolve is weakening. If things go on in this vein I shall end up sending for the priest to shrive me.

But Ursula, let us return to the topic of Ursula. I worry about her. I have not been fortunate in my wives— no, what am I saying? I mean my wives have not been fortunate in me. One I drove to drown herself, the other I drove to drink. This is not a good record, for a husband. I have not been fair to Ursula, have not given her the regard and respect that I should have, I know that. I treated my children as adults and my wife as a child. Is it that I was afraid of losing her, as I lost Dottie, and therefore must preserve her in a state of permanent girlhood? As if only grown-ups die. I do not know when she began to drink in earnest. After Petra was born, I suspect. The giddiness then, the temper fits, the morning lentors and the evening sobbings, which I took for the effects of post-partum trauma, I now think had a simpler cause. She is discreet, none more so; she is an artist of discretion. In this as in so much else she spares me pain, embarrass-ment, disturbance. And what do I give her in return?

My mind is tired, I cannot think any more, for now. When I got like this in the old days I would leap up and pace the floor, pace and pace, packed tight around myself and my distress like a panther, until equilibrium was re-established. How I loved the ordering of thought, the iron way of computation, the fixing of one term after another in the linked chain of reasoning. No such joy to be had elsewhere, or elsewhen, the quiet joy of a man alone, doing brain-work. Did Ursula envy my solitary calling, did she resent it? Did the children? Petra when she was little would creep into the room where I was working and sit on the floor curled up, hugging her knees, watching me as a cat does, blinking now and then, slowly. It was soothing, her being there, as the boy's presence would not have been. How unfair I was to him, unfairer than I was to Ursula, even, and now it is too late to make amends. Spilt milk, spilt milk—the dairy floor is awash and the dairyman and his missus are weeping buckets. And would I make amends, anyway, even if I had the time and means? There was a rhythm, somehow, to the girl, silent as she was, that seemed to beat in unison with something inside me. It was as if she were connected to me, as if I and not her mother had given birth to her and the vestigial umbilical cord was still unbroken. Yet Adam is the one who will care for Ursula when I am gone, I can be confident of that much. He is kind to her and always patient. He does not chide her, or try to persuade her to go the dry; far from it, for he is sweetly forbearing of her sad vice. I forbore too, but that was not the same: my forbearing, I suspect, was a form of indifference. Yes, he will be good to her, for her. Look at him now, following her into the kitchen with a stack of plates in his hands, being helpful and solicitous. How the sun strikes into this big stone room on days like this, shyly, one might say, at a sharp slant downwards through the big window behind the sink. Faint putrescent smell of gas from the stove as always, and three summer flies cruising lazily in circular formation under the light bulb above the table. She has a delightfully scurrying way, has Ursula, when she is excited, or upset, waddling a little on those knock-knees of hers. She favours shapeless soft wool dresses in shades of grey or lavender or mauve. In our early days together I used to call her my pigeon, and would chase her about the house, my tail-feathers all erect. How she would run from me, cooing frantically and laughing—'No no no no no *no*!'—until I caught up with her and held her under me, my panting bird. Ah, yes. Imagine me, as I imagine myself, striking my brow with clenched fist, again and again, thump, thump, without mercy, bemoaning over the lost years, the lost time. The opportunities not taken.

'—coming here like this,' she is saying, 'without a word of warning.' She pokes crossly at something in the sink, narrowing her eyes. She is short-sighted, like her daughter-in-law, and like her will not wear spectacles, out of vanity. 'And talking about your father dying.'

My son puts the lunch plates he has been carrying down on the draining-board in the sun. He has scraped all the scraps together on the top one, as his grandmother long ago taught him to do. Like me he wishes for an ordered world. I feel such a rush of tenderness for him suddenly. What is it in particular that has affected me? Something in his setting down of those plates, the disparity between this big, slow-moving man—my son!—and the dainty carrying out of the commonplace chore. When he and the girl were small I used to pray that I would live to see them grown; now I am thankful I shall not see them old.

'What he said is that he would not die,' Adam says, not looking at his mother.

He has a way, I have often noticed it, of going suddenly still, just stopping in whatever attitude he happens to be, as if he were playing that game we used to play as children, Statues, was it called? Ursula does it too; he must have got it from her. All these tics and traits that the genes pass on—why do they bother?

She lifts her head and looks at the sunlit window; I know that groping gaze. 'What?' she says.

Adam blinks himself out of his stillness and rolls his shoulders, animate again, giving himself a doggy sort of shake. Before he can speak Ivy Blount comes quickly in from the passageway by the stove, bearing more plates.

She has tied up her unruly hair with something at the back, but corkscrew tendrils have come loose and weave about her stark, pale face. The two stare at her, this mild Medusa, as if they do not know her. She halts, the crockery in her hands. Her look has a frantic cast. 'I have,' she says urgently to Ursula, or breathes, rather, '—I have to speak to you.'

Adam comes forward and takes the plates she is carrying, firmly freeing them from her grasp as if he were relieving her of a weapon, and sets them on the draining-board beside the stack of their fellows he already placed there. Dishes, sink, the sunlight in the window—how precious suddenly they seem, these perfectly common-place things.

I used to yearn so for Ursula that even when she was in my arms it was not enough, and I would clasp her to me more and more fiercely, octopus-armed, in an ecstasy of need, as if it might be possible to engorge her wholly, to press her in through my very pores. I would have made her be a part of me. If I could I would have had a notch cut in my already ageing side and a slip of her, my young rose, inserted there and lashed to me with twine. Tell me, tell me, was that not enough of love?

I wonder if my son is as abject in his desire of that lovely wife of his. Who could blame him, if he is?

When he leaves the kitchen now, padding soundlessly on those big feet of his, Ursula wishes she could go with him. She does not want to be left alone to deal with Ivy, for Ivy is clearly in a state. She seems to be quivering all over, like a struck tuning fork. What can be the matter?

The awful notion occurs that Ivy, impossible woman, is going to quit her place in the house. This is the catastrophe that Ursula has been dreading since she first came to Arden and took on Ivy to help her with the children and be a foil against Adam's fearsome mother. Her heart or some such organ has swollen up suddenly, suffocatingly, inside her breast, and her mouth has gone dry. How will she manage without Ivy? To be left here alone with a dying husband, a demented daughter—ah! She turns aside and walks quickly to the big bog-oak dresser—hideous thing that Granny Godley brought when she moved in with them, Adam and her, here at Arden, she has always hated it—and takes a white cup down from its hook. Ivy watches her, still with that shivering look of a retriever, moving only her eyes. Ursula comes back to the sink and fills the cup from the tap and drinks, opening her throat and pouring the water straight in, almost without swallowing; it tastes of tin. Through the window she sees the sunlight, the garden, the unresting mass of trees beyond the lawn; everything is so calm, so careless, and seems to mock her. She fills another cupful of water and drinks it off, the cold sharpness of the stuff hurting her throat and spilling into her stomach as heavy as lead. She feels a remote sort of pity for her body, as if it were something separate from her, some poor suffering thing clenched around its pain and dread. Is it whales that suck in tons of sea-water through their teeth to trap the plankton that they live on? I am like a whale, then, she thinks, with a sad, inward smile, only there is no sustenance, for me, to be sieved out of any of this.

'Mr Duffy,' Ivy says behind her, 'has spoken to me.' The words come up out of her like bubbles, trembling and plosive. 'Adrian, that is.'

Ursula frowns, but goes on looking out at the garden, giving herself time to think. So that is it, Ivy and the dreadful Duffy have been fighting. She feels a panicky urge to laugh. It is like something out of one of those old melodramas, the paterfamilias on his deathbed, the family gathered, and below stairs the servants squabbling. She thinks of that big blackened picture in the hall of the booted man in the black coat and high collar, reputed to be one of Ivy's ancestors. What was the story Ivy told her about him, something to do with the Ribbon Boys, a threatened lynching? She cannot remember; she cannot remember anything, these days.

'Spoken to you?' she says faintly, turning at last. 'About what?'

Ivy has done something to herself, has drawn herself up, or has been drawn up, somehow, like a doll on a string, with neck extended and eyes popping and arms dangling stiffly at her sides. Also her face is tinged with palest pink, like milk with a drop of wine in it; it might be from anger, or she might be blushing, it is hard to tell which. 'Well,' she says, and swallows, 'not spoken, exactly. That's to say—' She stops, helpless, and her face crumples, seems to crease down its middle, like the spine of a book that has been opened back too far—and are those tears that have sprung into her eyes, and has she clenched her fists, and does her lip tremble? Such distress! O Hecate of the triple way, is it all my fault, for taking on

Duffy's form and giving poor Ivy the notion that she was being significantly spoken to in that moment over the milk jug? If so, I shall have to speak to him, too, and put some mettle into him. I thought it was all fixed—what were they doing at the lunch table, if not fixing it? My name must not be Hermes after all. Oh dear, oh dear, how difficult are these matters of the heart, their hearts, I mean, I am an amateur in this arena. For now, I must manoeuvre Ivy out of here before there is more mischief done. She makes a sound, part a groan and part a grunt, and screwing the heel of a hand first into one moistened eye and then the other she turns away abruptly and hurries from the room.

Ursula blankly stands. She is not certain that what happened really happened, and that she did not imagine it. Latterly she has been having what seem to be hallucinations—she prefers to think of them as waking dreams—brief episodes of intensified reality, as if the flow of ordinary events had been compressed at a certain point and made to speed up and overheat. That is where the phantoms come from, those insubstantial revenants pushing past her, hindering her, haunting her days. She wonders, with a strange detachment, if she has damaged her mind, and if these lurid jumps and hurryings are among the first signs of its decay. Perhaps Ivy Blount was not here at all; perhaps for the past five minutes there has been no one here but herself, standing in this crooked box of sunlight imagining people talking to her, first her son, then Ivy. She stirs herself, and goes to the passage that leads out by the stove and walks through—dark-brown

dimness, a dank smell, the lino slightly bubbled underfoot—and comes into the conservatory, where the light is
so large and glaring that she falters. This, she thinks, this
is what her life is now, a listless, shadowed passing from
one hardly bearable patch of brightness to another. She
considers the big square table from which the last of
the lunch things have not yet been removed—where has
Ivy rushed off to?—crumpled napkins, smeared dessert
bowls, four empty wine bottles, three green and one clear,
the clear one looking self-conscious and a little shame-
faced in its nudity. At first she thinks there is no one here
but then she makes out the form of her daughter-in-law,
sitting, lying, almost, in a cane armchair in front of the
glass wall, smoking a cigarette and looking out into the
garden frowningly. The blue silk of her summer frock
reflects the light sharply in angled shapes; her legs are
crossed and one gold sandal dangles. She has not yet
noticed Ursula, and her face, unobserved, as she thinks,
appears almost featureless. Ursula leans forward to see
what is outside that the young woman is looking at so
intently. Benny Grace is out there, sitting as before on the
step above the sunken garden with his back to the house.
Roddy Wagstaff stands beside him, leaning negligently on
one of the stone pillars and gazing off into the trees across
the lawn. Whether they are together or have merely
drifted by chance into the same vicinity it is impossible to
tell. There is a blackbird on the grass, hurrying as if by
clockwork first this way and then that, the very one, as I
can attest, that young Adam at the window this morning
spotted flashing across in the dawn light. How all things

hang together, when one has the perspective from which to view them.

'I wish you would not smoke cigarettes in the house,' Ursula says mildly, and is gratified to see the start that Helen gives, the cane seat of the chair under her crackling in protest. 'It leaves the air so stuffy.'

Helen makes a series of small adjustments to her pose, leaning her head back and extending her legs in a show of languidness. She does not care to be chanced on unawares, especially by her mother-in-law. The slipper dangling from her toe falls off and makes an unexpectedly loud clatter on the flagged floor. 'You don't protest when he does it,' she says, gesturing with her cigarette towards the pair outside in the garden, 'Roddy what's-his-name.'

'Well,' Ursula answers, looking at her hands folded in front of her and measuring her words, 'he is a guest.'

Helen chuckles. 'How delicate you are. It's a wonder you can bear us at all.' As if he had heard his name spoken Roddy Wagstaff turns and peers vaguely over his shoulder, trying to see into the room through the opaque reflections on the glass panes. Helen shifts her weight again, and again the chair crackles, a milder outcry this time. 'Who is he,' she says, 'that other fellow?'

'Who?'

'Grace—isn't that what he's called?' She squints down the length of herself at the toes of her unsandalled foot and wriggles them; the polish on one of the nails is chipped, though she only put it on this morning. 'What does he want?'

'He wants Adam,' Ursula says sharply, and frowns.

Helen has turned her face and is gazing at her with interest sidewise from her chair. Ursula gives a small laugh, flustered. 'I mean my Adam—Adam's father, that is.'

'Wants him?'

'Oh, I don't know what I mean. He's just someone Adam knew.'

Helen finishes her cigarette and leans down to crush the stub of it in the big glass ashtray she has set on the floor beside her chair. The commotion in the cane-work every time she moves, like the sound of a flame sweeping up through a thorn bush, is setting Ursula's nerves on edge. She comes forward and bends to pick up the ashtray—three crushed butts, two of them lipsticked, standing at drunken angles in a parched puddle of ash— but Helen snatches it aside and glares at her. Such venom! She is wearing a large, ugly ring on the middle finger of her right hand: some kind of whitish metal set with a flat lozenge of polished black stone in which a curlicued initial *A* is carved. Ursula, still awkwardly at a tilt and seeking to save face, peers at it with exaggerated interest; the raised bezel brings to her mind an obscure and unpleasant suggestion of ulcers. 'That's new,' she says, straightening. 'How nice.'

Helen, sitting up and swinging her legs to the floor —one foot groping for its elusive sandal—glances disparagingly at the ring. 'Adam gave it to me.'

Ursula ventures a smile. 'So I see.'

'What?' Glaring again.

'*A* for Adam.'

'No,' with a shake of the head, quick, dismissive.

'*Amphitryon*. The title of the play I'm in. Or it could be *A* for Alcmene, my part. He said it was for luck but in the theatre you're never supposed to wish anyone luck.' Sitting on the edge of the chair she stretches herself, lifting her arms in an arch and leaning her lovely gold articulated head to one side and pressing her cheek, cat-like, into the hollow of her shoulder. Ursula catches a whiff of her sweat, sharp and hot; I can almost catch it myself, smell of civet and summer nights. Helen sighs. 'He's such a sap,' she says complacently, suppressing a yawn, 'your son.'

She rises and walks to the table and begins to gather the dessert bowls, stacking them with negligent haste and making them rattle. 'God,' she says and sighs again, more heavily, 'is there anything duller than a summer afternoon?'

'You mean, down here?' Ursula enquires gently.

'Anywhere.'

Ursula now comes forward to the table and begins to collect the napkins, thinking of snow. She glances out at Benny Grace where he sits on the step in a cobbler's slump and at the sight of him a shadow crosses her mind. 'They used to know each other very well,' she says, 'Adam's father and—Mr Grace.' Benny's name she pronounces with a sort of grimace in her voice.

Helen has picked up all the bowls and now is gathering the spoons. Her eyes are hooded, she seems far away. She takes the napkins that Ursula has heaped and puts them on top of the stacked plates. In single file, with Ursula leading, they carry the things out to the kitchen and I glide invisibly behind them along the passageway, still sniffing after Helen's feline scent. Who am I now? Where is my Dad? Enough, enough, I am one, and all— Proteus is not the only protean one amongst us. 'They were colleagues, in some way,' Ursula is saying over her shoulder. 'Only I think your father thought he was a fraud—I mean Adam's father—Adam. But then'—a shrug—'I suspect Adam thought—thinks—everyone a fraud, more or less. Even himself.' Helen puts the bowls into the sink and Ursula stands looking down at them, a jumble of shallow, grey-white discs against the greyer white of the porcelain. There is something faintly, comically, endearing about them. They remind her of— what?—circuses. A clown somewhere, a long time ago, spinning half a dozen plates on the tips of a dozen sticks, everything wobbling, the plates, the long slender sticks, the clown's extended arms. The recollection flickers, fades. Helen takes off the ugly ring and puts it on the window-sill and rinses her hands under the tap. Ursula watches her sidelong. Helen's hands are the least lovely part of her, boneless-seeming and slightly mottled, the fingers plump above the knuckles and tapered sharply at the tips as if each one were bound there tight with invisible thread. The sun has hardly moved in the window. Is there music playing somewhere? Once, when she was a girl, in some place, she cannot remember where exactly, a splendid park or the grounds of some grand house, Ursula reached up on tiptoe at a little moss-covered wall and saw into an enclosed garden, with masses of flowers and flowering fruit trees, exotic shrubs, climbing vines, all crowding there together in the sun, profligate and gay. Now in rosy retrospect this seems one of the sweetest moments of her life, replete with all the promise of the future, and she keeps it stowed jealously at the back of her memory, like a jewel box in a secret drawer. If she were to return there today she is sure she would not be able to see over the wall, it would have grown higher, somehow, or she would have become smaller, although she would know the garden was there, abundant and glorious as ever, waiting for others to come and glimpse it, and be happy.

'I hope,' she says in a rush, with a terrible feeling of falling over herself, 'I hope your play is a success—I hope—I hope you will have a great success in it.'

Helen is drying her hands on a tea-towel. Ursula regards her anxiously, pained and waiting—why, she asks herself, why must I blurt out things like this, like a fool?

'Do you?' Helen says tonelessly, and drops the towel on the draining-board; she is thinking of something else altogether.

Ursula sees anew how radiant she is, in that sky-blue dress and those gold sandals, with that tight-fitting gleaming helmet of hair.

My Dad is plucking at my sleeve.

'Yes, yes, I do,' Ursula says, feeling herself falling still, as in a dream. 'I wish you—I wish you everything.'

Helen turns abstractedly and walks from the room.

I can feel my father's burgeoning itch as together we rush after her from the kitchen into the music room and out by the french doors where she almost collides with her husband coming in from the lawn. She has never managed to accustom herself to these sudden loomings that he does. He is like, she thinks vexedly, a great large soft eager dog.

'Here you are!' he says breathlessly, grasping her by the upper arms and smiling into her face. 'I wanted to say—I wanted to tell you—'

'What—?'

She twists free of his hands and falls back a step.

'Well, just that I've decided—'

—*to leave you*, she finishes for him in her mind.

He does not know what he wants to tell her, what he wants to say. He is still all at sea, under that keel, sat at the end of that thrumming plank. He has a brimming sensation, as if he were himself a vessel that he has been given to carry, filled with some marvellous fluid not a drop of which must be allowed to spill.

'What?' she asks again, more brusquely. 'What have you decided?'

He frowns. How strange her look when she stepped away from him like that, drawing in her chin and glaring up at him, with stony unsurprise, like a child about to hear an announcement from the big world that the adults think momentous but in fact is only dull.

'I was going to say,' he says, treading over the flaw of doubt and rushing on, 'I thought we might—I don't know—I thought we might move down here, after—afterwards.' His forehead flushes. 'What do you think?'

'What do I think? Of moving, down here, to Arden?' She gives a sour laugh, a sort of snort, and looks past him quickly. It strikes her how like a lighted stage the sunlit garden seems, garish, innocent and faintly mad. 'I'm going for a walk,' she says.

Adam blinks. 'A walk?' This little scene between the two of them is already rankling in his mind, as if it were past already and he is recalling it.

'Yes, a walk—is that all right?'

'Of course, of course.' He laughs, his brow fairly on fire by now. 'Can I come with you?'

Although he does not move she has the impression of him dodging from side to side in the doorway so as not to let her pass.

'Your mother is drunk again,' she says. 'I think you had better look after her.'

For a second it seems he will put his hands on her arms again, more roughly this time. Despite his flustered smile and doggy eagerness she is a little frightened of him, so large and unnervingly blond, so sharp-eyed sometimes, as now. Points of stubble glitter on his cheeks and chin as if a pinch of reddish sand had been thrown in his face and stuck there. She imagines him hitting her, the jarring of fist on bone.

> *—oh, such a dream!*
> *We were upon some golden mountain top,*
> *The two of us, just we, and all around*
> *The air was blue, and endless, and so soft—*

You see how my Dad does it, putting all sorts of fancies in their heads to distract and confuse them? She begins to recall something from her dawn dream of love and then does not. But she will always remember this day, for as long, that is, as a mortal may remember anything.

Frowning now and suddenly helpless, her husband steps out of the way to let her pass. As she does, he tries eagerly to take her hand but she brushes him aside and is gone.

To make her way to the garden from the music room she must cross an enclosed, cobbled yard and go out by an iron gate. There is another yard beyond, where the chicken-runs are, and often the chickens escape and get in here through the gate because they like to peck among the cobbles, where there must be worms, or grubs, or something. Helen is nervous of these high-strung, baroque birds with their trembling wattles, the way they look at her with malevolent surmise and make that slow thoughtful gargling sound in their gullets. Their droppings are multicoloured, chalk-white and black—what do they eat?—olive-green and a shiny silk-green and a horrible glistening dark brown. She goes gingerly, careful of her sandals. The gate when she opens it resists her, dragging and shrieking on its rusty hinges.

The two she had observed from the conservatory are still where they had been, on the step above the sunken lawn, oddly consorting there, the one tall and sleek and the other fat and humped and bald. Benny Grace is eyeing her at an angle, and she sees that he is smiling to himself. He has taken off his shoes and socks again—is there something the matter with his feet? Roddy Wagstaff pointedly pretends not to notice her as she approaches. In her sandals she can feel the grass, it is moist and cool and tickles her toes deliciously. Because of the low level of this part of the lawn the sunlight shining down over the trees seems sharply bent, as if it were water and not air it is striking through. A stray wind, soft and lapsing, rustles through the trees and makes their leaves tinkle; the leaves are darkly polished on top and greeny-grey underneath. Summer seems an immense height, an eminence towering bluely over the day. See how all stops for a moment, here in this dappled grove, where now even the breeze is stilled. This respite is a gift of the god, your less than humble servant.

Helen is asking Roddy Wagstaff for a cigarette. He bends on her his finical smile and clicks open the slim, silver cigarette case with his thumb and offers it open flat on his palm. The still, bright air pales the flame of his lighter. They both ignore Benny Grace, squatting on the step at the level of their knees, squinting up at them, genial and quizzical. They smoke in silence for a little while, ignoring him—he might be a garden ornament, for all the notice they take of him—and then, together, without a word, they descend the steps and walk away along the lawn.

'That fellow,' Helen murmurs, '—who is he, do you know?'

Roddy shrugs. 'Mm. When you came along he was in the middle of telling me some rigmarole, about Greece, I think it was, about being up in the mountains there, doing something or other. I could make no sense of it. And that greasy little smile that he has!' He stops and lifts one foot and examines his shoe and frowns. 'How can the grass be damp? It hasn't rained for weeks.'

'No one seems to know who he is,' Helen is saying. They come to a vertical grassy bank—it must have been a ha-ha once—and pause to finish their cigarettes. When she looks back down the length of the lawn Benny Grace is still sitting where they left him, between the two stone pillars, a blurred homunculus, his bare feet glimmering whitely at the ends of his black trouser-legs, and she thinks of rats and drainpipes. 'He gives me the creeps,' she says softly, and makes herself shiver.

They turn and walk to the corner of the lawn where the bank becomes a ramp that they have to scramble up ungracefully—she thinks Roddy might offer her his hand but he does not—and find themselves on a weedy gravel path that meanders off beside another trail of trees. They are beech trees, someone told her; she likes to know the names of things, even things she does not care about. They have what seems to her a resentful aspect, brooding above her in the sunlight and slowly and haughtily moving their high heads from side to side in what little wind there is. It is pleasantly cool in their shade, though, and suddenly quiet, too, the air muffled by the great dark bundles of foliage. The white jet-stream of an aeroplane high up is unzipping the sky down its middle, swiftly, without a sound. She had not intended to go for a walk, that was only something she had said to get away from her husband, yet here she is, strolling along this path under trees in the middle of a summer afternoon, like one of those women in Chekhov, and with Roddy Wagstaff, too, who seems to her more like a character in a play than a real, living person.

What did he mean, Adam, about moving here—surely he is not serious? The things he thinks of, the notions he dreams up!

She always wanted to be an actress, from when she was a little girl and dressed up in her mother's clothes and mimed in front of the wardrobe mirror, preening and striking attitudes and stamping her foot. Later on she conceived of the stage as a place of self-improvement, of self-fulfilment, and still sees it as such. She is convinced that by an accumulation of influence the parts that she plays, even when the characters are petty or wicked, will gradually mould and transform her into someone else, someone grand and deep and serious. It is like putting on makeup, but makeup of a magically permanent kind, that she will not take off, only continue adding to, layer upon careful layer, until she has achieved her true look, her real face. She knows what people say of her, that she is hard-hearted, relentless, driven by ambition, and they are not wrong, she has to admit it, but what they do not know about—for of course she will tell no one, not even Adam, especially not Adam—is this notion she has cherished since she began, the notion of being destined to become something more than she is. This we must assume is the source of her interest in Roddy Wagstaff. He is like her, not quite achieved yet, not quite the full person that he will be, some day. He has no smell, that is a thing she has noticed. There are smells about him, yes, a smell of cigarette smoke, for instance, and of soap or cologne or something, of other things as well, but of Roddy himself, the flesh-and-blood man, she can detect not a trace, and this adds to her sense of him as hollow, a thing of potential more than actual presence. So there is a sort of affinity, after all, since this is what she is, too—pure potential, in a state of perpetual transformation, on the way steadily to becoming herself, her authentic self.

The tree-lined path without her noticing has taken them in a broad curve, and the garden is no longer in view, though she has a prickly sensation between her shoulder-blades, as if Benny Grace's eye is still on her, somehow. From here there is a view of the house she has not had before. At this angle the place looks crazier than ever, all slopes and recesses and peculiarly shaped windows; it is, she sees, more like a church than a house, but a church in some backward, primitive place where religion has decayed into a cult and the priests have had to allow the churchgoers to worship the old gods alongside the new one.

Roddy is worrying about his shoes again, and keeps stopping to peer at them, clicking his tongue in annoyance. They are narrow and sharp-toed, and a sickly shade of pale tan, like sucked toffee. He complains that the leather is bound to bubble up where the lawn has dampened it above the seams. 'They haven't seen grass since they were still part of a cow,' he says with a scowl. Helen laughs shortly and puts a hand quickly over her mouth— she is conscious of her raucous laugh: it always comes out before she can stop it and gives her an embarrassing shock. Roddy turns his head and stares at her, uncertain, faintly alarmed. He had not intended to be humorous. He does not care for jokes, does not understand them or what they are for.

The path ahead veers abruptly and leads into a dark little wood. This must be, Helen thinks, the wood she saw this morning from the bathroom window, the one she has never been able to find before, not that she has ever made such effort to find it. She does not hesitate but goes on without comment, and although Roddy falls back a step or two he soon strides forward again and catches her up, and they pass side by side under a sort of arch woven of brambles and ivy that is like a doorway into a church. Within the wood the day is suddenly different: it is dimmer, naturally, because of the shade, but it feels different, too, feels attentive, almost, watchful. There is a mushroomy smell, and the air that surely should be green, given all this greenery, instead has a bluish tinge, as if there had been a bonfire that had gone out and left its smoke thinly dispersed all around. When she makes a closer inspection, however, she sees there is not so much green, except high up where the leaves are, for down here it is mostly brown: wood-brown, thorn-brown, clay-brown. A bird breaks out of a bush and flies off rapidly, whistling shrilly. The path peters out and the ground becomes spongy underfoot, like a trampoline that has gone slack. She thinks of Hansel and Gretel—were they the babes in the wood or is that another story? They left a trail of breadcrumbs to find their way back through the forest but the birds ate them and they got lost. And then what happened? She tries to remember but cannot.

There was a witch, probably, there is always a witch, waiting in the wood.

Nature, though, how impassive it is, how indifferent. The trees, this lilac air, the leaning briars and the clinging vines, none of these register her and Roddy moving in their midst; even the moss on which she treads does not care that her foot crushes it. The cries of lost children would be lost on this place; even their blood would not stain the ground, or not for long, but would be absorbed like anything else, like dew, like rain. Yes, she marvels at how it all just goes on, not needing to notice anything or respond to anything. But then it comes to her that there is nothing going on, really, and that what these things are is not indifferent because that would mean they could be otherwise, that the trees could turn and look at them, that the creepers could reach out like hands and clutch at their ankles, that the briars could sweep down and lash them across their backs like scourges, and nothing like that ever happens. For nature, my dear, has no purpose, except perhaps that of not being us, I mean you.

Now they have reached the heart of the wood and here is a little—what should she call it?—a little bower, under a low, vaulted roof of ivy and brambles and sweet woodbine and other things all tangled together. 'Oh,' Roddy Wagstaff says, 'it must be the famous holy well,' and for some reason gives what seems an embarrassed laugh. A well? At first she sees no well but then she does. There is nothing built, no bricks or stones piled up, just the pool of water, brimming and still, like a polished dark metal disc set on the ground, with vivid wet green moss all around it. Now too she sees the rosaries, dozens of them, hanging among the ivy and the woodbine blossoms, and there are scraps of holy pictures propped between twigs or hanging from thorns, of the Virgin Mary and the Sacred Heart, and photographs of people as well, smudged and creased: a little girl in her First Communion dress with plaits, a toothless old woman squinting in sunlight, a cocky young fellow in an army uniform, holding his cap in his hand. Such a hush reigns here, at once tense and dreamy, as if some sound that had been expected long ago, some call or cry, had not come, and would not, now. All feels liquid under this densely matted canopy. The air is damply cool, and among the moss there are black rocks flecked with mica that gleam wetly, and something somewhere is making a steady, reverberant drip. In front of the well a place to sit has been provided, a narrow little bench with metal legs set crookedly in cement. It takes her a moment to recognise it as the seat from an old-fashioned school desk. Roddy is telling her how people from the farms and villages round about still come here to the well to pray—'There's even a May procession, I believe,' he says archly, with a smirk— and how her father-in-law had tried and failed to close off the right of way through the wood. She is hardly listening, watching the dust tumbling lazily in a narrow shaft of sunlight through the leaves.

They sit down on the narrow bench. She sees that despite the seeming stillness of its surface a little of the water is constantly spilling over from the well; it moves through the moss at her feet, a stealthy, swarming flow.

Where does it go to? The beam of sunlight is fading, like a sword blade being stealthily withdrawn, and yet somehow leaves the air faintly glowing in its wake. Roddy is offering her the flame of his lighter. She does not remember accepting a cigarette from him but there it is in her fingers, a slim white thing, untipped, the tobacco smelling of somewhere foreign. She pictures a crag, a crooked tree and golden, dusty distances, faint voices singing, hands linked in a ring, a round-dance on a summer day in a green glade. The heavy flab of smoke when she draws it in scratches the back of her throat. The feeling of being watched is so much stronger now.

'Your husband does not like me,' Roddy says, in a strange voice, not his own, and as if from a long way off. She watches the water brimming in the well.

'Why do you think that?' she asks.

'Because he is jealous.'

'Adam?' She laughs, then falters, shivers, and her voice falls to a whisper. 'Who is he jealous of?'

She does not look at him. Although he does not move he seems to draw himself closer to her, tensed and somehow as if suffering.

'How still the air is in this place,' he says. 'Do you not feel the presence of the god?'

'What god? What do you mean?'

She peers, squinting, into the foliage behind the well, fancying she sees a face there, then it is gone. She has finished her cigarette, though its perfumed, acrid aftertaste persists. Roddy's voice when he speaks is large yet makes a soft, a tremulous sound.

'You will remember this when all else fades, this moment, here, together, by this well. There will be certain days, and certain nights, you'll feel my presence near you, hear my voice. You'll think you have imagined it and yet, inside you, you will catch an answering cry. On April evenings, when the rain has ceased, your heart will shake, you'll weep for nothing, pine for what's not there. For you, this life will never be enough, there will forever be an emptiness, where once the god was all in all in you.'

She stirs, a start—was she asleep? She feels she might swoon and puts a hand on Roddy's arm, laughing a little in confusion and blurred dismay. 'Sorry,' she says, 'I thought—I was thinking—something from the—lines from the—'

He says her name, his mouth is by her cheek; she turns to speak again but he kisses full her open lips, his tongue burning on hers. Surprise floods through her, a sort of whoop, like laughter. Her eyes are open and so are his. Such a stare he has, as if straight into her soul! And his arms, two airy hoops that hold her fast. She tries to draw back, saying something into his mouth, his golden mouth. Something deep inside her stirs, a bud of something, stirring. At last he releases her and she gives a great gasp—'Oh!'—as one who has been drowning but is suddenly saved.

what other you is—

She leans back, at a loss, panting, her arms open, her lips still saying a silent Oh! He seems as surprised as she is, and blinks, and frowns, and touches his fingers to his lips as if to find a trace of her. She puts a hand to her hair, her cheek, her mouth.

'What do you think you're—what?'

'I don't know—' He shudders and takes out a handkerchief and wipes his lips. What is that medleyed music in the air, of pipe and tabor, bugle and flute, what voices chanting as the radiant cavalcade departs? 'I'm sorry.'

She rises from the seat and with a flowing movement, a dancer's sweep, leans down and slaps him smartly across the cheek. He draws back, stares, and his eyes narrow. He is only himself now, the god having abandoned him. The air is darkening. He makes to speak. A whiplash crack of thunder sounds directly overhead and seemingly at the level of the treetops.

Thunder? Yes!

Oh, Dad.

BENNY GRACE HEARS that thunderclap and smiles. It catches him stealing across the music room from outer door to inner. For such an ill-made thing he moves daintily when he must. Now he pauses, hearkening. All outside has gone breathlessly silent, from the shock of the god's great shout of anger. Presently our faithful blackbird will try out a splash of liquid notes in the dimmened and newly oppressive air, and then will come the first and faintest susurrus of rain, like the sound of a blind man's fingers reading braille. Where did the clouds appear from, how did they creep up all unnoticed? Benny knows a jealous deity ordained. He moves on, still smiling to himself. He is barefoot yet and carries his cracked shoes in his hands, each with a sweat-limp sock stuffed inside it under the tongue. One flap of his shirt has come out of the waistband of his trousers and not all his fly buttons are done up. Where is he going? Whithersoever his fancy takes him, so long as it is in the direction of me. The hushed air is his element.

Strange, how tentative we are when we come into their world, shy amongst the creatures we have made. Is it that we are worrying we might leave the order of things calamitously disturbed? Everything is to be put back exactly as it was before us, no stone left turned, no angle unaligned, all divots replaced. This is the rule the gods must obey. Did I say gods, did I say obey? Fine gods we are, that we must muster to a mortal must. But even our avatar, the triune lord of a later epiphany, forfeits the omnipotence you ascribe to him in the simple fact that the thing he cannot do is will himself out of existence, as one of the desert fathers, for the moment I do not recall which one, inconveniently pointed out and was promptly stoned to death—or crucified, was it?—for his impudence. It is all a matter of demarcation, the division of labour, one job one god. We too have our hierarchies, our choirs, thrones, all that. Seraphim. Cherubim.

What am I saying? I am mixing up the heavenly hosts.

My mind is going, going.

Benny Grace tiptoeing across the music room, his damp soles making unpleasant small smacking sounds on the parquet. His element, yes, this hush after thunder and before rain and the bird's sudden drench of song. It is so for all of us; this is where we seem to ourselves most really real, in these little lapses, these little creases in the fabric of our creation. For we do not come amongst you, not in the actual fact of being here, whatever I may claim to the contrary. To us your world is what the world in mirrors is to you. A burnished, crystalline place, sparkling and clear, with everything just as it is on this side, only reversed, and infinitely unreachable. A looking-glass world, indeed, and only that. Hence our melancholy, our mischievousness, too—oh, to put a fist to that blank pane and burst through to the other side! But all we would meet is mercury. Mercury! My other name, one of my other names.

Speaking of divots, I used to have a mission of replacing them. Well, not a mission, though I would get into a great rage at those who left them where they lay, wet and knobbled, like fresh-squeezed turds. This was when I lived on the side of that hill on Haggard Head, above the sea, and my garden, such as it was, abutted the seventh green—or do they say hole, the seventh hole?—of a public golf course, where anyone could hire a set of clubs at so much an hour and there were no green fees. The place was for the most part deserted, apart from the odd, solitary retiree stoically practising his swing in the dewy hour at dawn or eve, but on weekends and bank holidays feral youths would come by train and bus from the city's slums and hack up and down the course like so many wandering and malfunctioning windmills. I was never a golfer myself, need I say, but I had got into the habit of walking the links—links, that is another nice old specialised word, like divot—especially on those days when my mind seized up and I could not work, and increasingly there were many such. It pained me to see the fairways sliced and gouged. The torn-out sods, retrieved and turned right side up, now looked more like green scalps, or merkins, maybe. They made a satisfying squelch when I trod them back into the ground. What did I think I was doing, patching up this bit of the poor earth's epidermis? But I cherish the world, it is true, have I not made that clear already? Should have been a poet, perhaps, apostrophising skylarks and doting on daffodils. You will have noticed my way with words, supposedly rare in a man of my calling. Words are so friendly, so accommodating, so loosely adaptable, not like numbers, with their tiresome insistence on meaning only what they mean and nothing more. But what they have that words have not is rigour, and rigour was what seduced me from the start, the promise of one firm thing in an infirm world. It all seemed so simple, early on. I loved the process, the slow accumulating of many tiny parts into a vast and gorgeous gewgaw the joy of which was its utter inutility. What did it matter if some other, a mere technician, should extract from the middle of my mesh a bristling filament that fitted perfectly a slot in one of his infernal machines? Apply, apply away!—that was my cry. And apply they did, adapting my airy fancies to invent all sorts of surprising and useful gimcrackery, from the conversion of salt water into an endless source of energy to rocket ships that will fly the net of time. I was resented, of course; my kind always are. Benny used to warn me, but I never listened. Benny pretends to be a man of the people, though he is just like me, in his deepest heart. We are all alike, all we Olympians. We are supposed to be the celebrants of all that is vital and gay and light, and so we are but, oh, we are cold, cold.

I have left Benny stalled there in the middle of that room, with the evening light eclipsed and rain coming.

He is on his way to me, and in no hurry. Let him loiter, there is time enough, I am going nowhere, not yet. I feel suddenly a sad fondness for him, poor unlovely outcast creature, as I felt earlier for my son—I must be softening, here at the end. Benny is a solitary, we have that too in common.

He makes his way into the big central hallway. The aqueous light here is oyster-grey and glimmers on polished tiles and picture-glass. A leaning mirror gapes in mute amazement at all it sees. The rain is a steady, monotonous drumming now, as if the summer day had got a serious, grim new task, and the glass roof high above streams and shimmers, the glass panels darkened to a lambent shade of sea-green, and everything underneath it is adrizzle. He senses another creature nearby, and looks about him alertly. Rex the dog is crouching under an old striped sofa that stands against the wall beside a potted palm. He pants and shivers, big drops splashing off the end of his tongue, for he is terrified of thunder. Benny goes and squats down and talks to him, but the dog only bares his teeth and growls. 'All right, then,' Benny says indulgently, rising. 'All right.' He goes to the foot of the stairs and listens upwards, straining to hear; is it the sound of the rain or is someone speaking above, a feebly fretful drone that rises and falls? He ascends three steps of the staircase, stops, listens again. It is definitely a voice, murmurmurmur, a sigh, a softly plaining cry, murmur again. This is what Benny loves, what all the gods love, to eavesdrop on the secret lives of others. See him stealthily climbing there, face lifted eagerly and a dab of rain-light gleaming on his stub of nose, his fleshy fist mounting the banister-rail beside him in little hops, like a hunched and pallid toad. I could trip him up, wrap his trousers round his knees and send him tumbling arse over tip to bang his big fat head on those black-and-white tiles. But I will not.

He has to cross three sides of the landing before he finds where the voice is coming from. A door stands conveniently ajar. It is dim inside the room where the curtains are closed. She lies on a couch against the wall with a brown blanket pulled to her throat. Her arms are free of the blanket and she clutches something to her breast, a shapeless something, red and soft. Her son is seated beside her on a little chair and strokes her forehead with one of his huge hands, so gently, strokes and strokes. Ursula's eyes are closed. She murmurs a gabble of words, with frequent sighs, frequent moans. The rain rattles furiously against the unseen window, booms upon the glazed roof above. Benny presses himself to the wall, all eyes and ears. Is it not a quaint scene?—a moment out of Watteau, it might be, these figures about their ambiguous business, in uncertain light, as the day wanes. Let us leave them there, the three of them, for now, the languishing lady and attendant man, and the listener by the doorway, a meddling jester.

My heavens, what a downpour! Helen is drenched, to the very skin, her dress in big patches darkened to navy-blue and clinging to her knees, her thighs, her breasts. She arrives in a flurry, blinking the rain from her eyelashes and laughing, the kitchen door banging behind her. Even the band of her pants is shiver-makingly wet against her belly. 'Look at me!' she cries in happy dismay, and holds up her hands and flutters her fingers, sprinkling the flagstones with drops the size of pennies. Ivy Blount, who has been sitting at the table shelling peas, regards her for a moment without moving, her face reflecting the bedraggled young woman's undiminished light, for the rain has only made her more radiant, pinking her skin all over and turning her hair to polished wheat. She kicks off her muddied sandals and reaches behind her and with an effort undoes the top three buttons at the back of her dress—goodness, is she going to take it off? My father will faint if she does. But wait, Ivy is not alone. Who is it loitering there by the bog-oak dresser? Duffy, is that you? Aha, my bold spalpeen. He has a sheepish air and seems bemused. He does look like a man who has been accepted in a proposal he cannot remember having made. Ivy too is not herself: there is a hectic flush to her cheeks and her eyes are quick and bright. Have the words been spoken, has the deal been closed? I think so, I think I foresee strewn rose petals and the chanting of epithalamia. What a wily matchmaker I have proved, after all.

'I'll get a towel,' Ivy says.

She rises from the lyre-backed kitchen chair but hesitates a moment, looking hard into the bowl half full of sinisterly glistening peas, which is a way of not looking at Duffy, then turns and goes quickly from the room. Duffy too does not know where to look—I think he thought Helen might indeed be about to unsheathe herself from her wet dress, which I am sure would have called for another application of the smelling-salts. She crosses to the sink and leans forward and with her palms presses her hair hard against her skull, and a few squeezed drops spatter on the porcelain. The rain-light sinuates in the window, brightening, phosphorescent. Duffy averts his gaze from her invitingly elevated rump; he is something of a gentleman, after all, in his rough way. I have mocked him, usurped him, spuriously enthused him, yet I do not wish him ill. I hope that he will marry Ivy. I hope they will have a happy time of it, in the time that is left to them—though he is younger than his putative bride he is no spring chicken either, as his Ma would sourly say. Yes, I wish them happiness, in so far as mortals are capable of being happy. Duffy's life, like Ivy's, has not been easy, a long and joyless bachelorhood in that ugly house behind the hill, wriggling in restive impotence under the thumb of his jealous mother, who in her turn was beaten by her mother and abused by her father, who in their turn were similarly used by their respective sires and dams, and so on all the way back to Adam and Eve who no doubt mistreated their misbegotten brood, compelling them into an orgy of incest so that the race of men might flourish and fill all the earth. But Duffy's expectations are modest and so are Ivy's; they have that advantage as they set out on their adventure together, for the inevitable disappointments of married life will not hit them so hard as they would if they were young and starry-eyed. Have I mentioned that Duffy is illiterate? His mother—by the way, I thought we were to hear no more of that harridan?—did not hold with schooling, being little schooled herself. He hides his lack of letters by means of various stratagems, the devising of which took more effort than he would have expended in learning to read, but which are so subtle and convincing that even Ivy does not know his shaming secret. He is worrying already as to how he will manage to sign the marriage register. But it will be all right. I shall intercede with my stepmother Hera, whose bailiwick encompasses all matters conjugal, and have her arrange for Duffy to confide his secret to Ivy on the night before the wedding, and together they will spend a happy hour seated side by side at the oilcloth-covered table in Ivy's kitchen, their heads inclined and foreheads almost touching in the lamplight, while Ivy's tender hand guides Duffy's as he traces out laboriously, in pencil, over and over until he has them off pat, the magic letters of his name. More than the wedding itself, that little ceremony there under the lamp, all silent save for the soft scratching of graphite on paper, will mark the true beginning of their life together. Yes, yes, I have it all planned.

Helen turns from the sink and asks Duffy for a cigarette. 'I don't smoke,' she says, 'which is why I never buy them.'

Duffy's look turns leporine and he moves the tip of his tongue along his lower lip—is she making a joke?

'I only have roll-ups,' he says, showing her the tobacco tin from his pocket and quickly palming it again.

She shrugs. 'Roll me one, then.'

All the more alarmed by this he turns a quarter way away from her and remains motionless, staring at nothing. 'Oh, it's all right,' she says. 'Someone will give me a real one.'

He nods, relieved. She comes forward and stands by the table, leaning her hip against it and running the fingers of one hand back and forth on the wood as if the raised seams in its worn surface were the strings of a harp. 'What's keeping Ivy?' she murmurs. 'I really am soaked.' She seems unaware that the buttons of her dress at the back are still undone, affording Duffy a glimpse of a taut white elastic strap. The rain is ceasing and out in the garden the blackbird is piping again its heedless, piercing song. 'Damn,' she says without emphasis, and glances absently about the room. She has never slapped a man's face before and her insides are jangling still from the thrill of it. She feels as if it were she who had been delivered a tingling smack. Poor Roddy! She is amused, remembering how he reared back on the bench with almost a maidenly quiver, staring wide-eyed at her, a palm pressed to his cheek. She surprised herself by noticing his hands, pale and long and tapered, like her father-in-law's, their beauty marred only by those bitten nails. She was surprised too at how livid the mark was that she left on his cheek, how quickly it was spreading. She had not meant to hit him quite so hard—in fact, she had not meant to hit him at all, it had just happened, before she knew it. But what had he been thinking of, kissing her like that? She wonders if she should tell Adam. What would he do? Threaten to horsewhip Roddy, challenge him to a duel? She is sorry now she spoke of the play to Roddy, and regrets especially saying that he might review it. Not that it was entirely a joke, for the production would need all the notices it could get. Now, of course, if he does write something he will be certain to take his revenge on her; she is sure he is that sort, small-minded and vindictive. But then, she reminds herself, I did hit him, after all, and is all the more amused.

From the corner of her eye she can see Duffy begin to edge his way cautiously along the dresser in the direction of the back door. She wonders where Roddy is now. He fled the wood ahead of her, striding off furiously and still wiping at his mouth with his handkerchief, as if there was a foul taste that he could not get rid of. She hopes he is as wet as she is; not much hope for his slip-ons if he is.

Ivy comes back at last, bearing a huge white towel folded in her arms. She pauses for a beat, catching something in the atmosphere, and looks from Helen to Duffy and back again and narrows her eyes.

'Oh, you're an angel,' Helen says. She takes the towel and begins vigorously rubbing at her hair.

'Here, give me that,' Ivy says, not untenderly, and takes the towel back from her and makes her sit by the table.

Duffy, sidling, has almost reached the door, but pauses now to watch the two women, Helen voluptuously slumped with her hands limp in her lap and the back of her dress folded out at the top like a pair of small blue wings, and Ivy leaning over her, all bones and bird's-nest hair, with the white towel draped over her hands like the priest's communion stole at Mass, stroking slowly that helmet of damp, dark-gold hair. She says that when they are done she will prepare for Helen a nice hot cup of tea, but Helen, her voice muffled, says she would prefer a nice cold drink of something with gin in it. Ivy does not reply but only wields the towel more vigorously. Helen chuckles to herself in the warm tumult where she leans.

The rain has stopped and a weak sun is shining wetly in the window. Duffy moves to the door. Even when he lifts the latch Ivy does not turn her head to look at him. He steps out, and the door grates on the slate threshold. The scent of drenched grass assails him. Which would fetch the better price at auction, he is wondering, Ivy's house or his own?

Petra too got wet in the rain but was not drenched as Helen and Roddy Wagstaff were. She is afraid of thunder and ran back from the wood, her heart pounding, and did not stop until she reached the house, and she was crossing the lawn before the rain started up in earnest. How silent the house is, holding its breath, as if it too had got a fright. She stands in the hall to listen and hears beyond the noise of the rain the faint maunderings of her mother up in her room; it is a sound she is used to. Then from far off she hears the yard gate creak, and a moment later the back door rattles, and she knows that Helen or Roddy or both together have returned. She hopes they have suffered a good soaking, and that Helen will catch a cold followed rapidly by pneumonia, primary or atypical, pneumococcal, interstitial or lobular, she does not mind which variety it is, just so long as the attack is severe and accompanied by numerous and distressing and, if at all possible, fatal complications. Not to stray beyond the Ps, even pleurisy would do, the effusive form—*pain in the breast is common, of a cutting or stabbing nature, usually in the neighbourhood of the nipple*—and, for Roddy, at least a chronic pleurodynia of the intercostal nerves. That would teach the two of them.

On the landing she sees Benny Grace crouched and listening outside her mother's bedroom doorway, and through the part-way open door sees her mother inside, lying down, and Adam sitting by her. None of them notices her.

In her room she locks the door and kicks off her wet shoes and sits on the bed, hugging her knees, listening to the sound of the rain on the roof. The light is silver-grey and sad, and she would like to cry but cannot; she was never any good at crying. The rain on the window makes everything beyond the glass shimmer and swim, as if she were indeed seeing it all through tears, all those greys and watery greens and undulant browns. She wonders that she can be so calm. Everything is changed, her life is changed. Or, no, it cannot be changed, since what she thinks should be her life has not properly started yet. Roddy was to do that for her; Roddy was the one who was supposed to take her hand and lead her into the sunlit uplands of the future. It surprises her to realise, to admit at last, how high a hope she had of him. Everyone tried to warn her but she would not listen. Now she feels—she feels— She does not know what she feels.

She leaves the bed and goes to the door and opens it

cautiously and peers out. Benny Grace is gone, and the door of her mother's room is shut and her mother has stopped moaning. She flits across the landing on tiptoe —who does she think will see her, of whom is she afraid?—and opens the door and climbs the seven steps to the Sky Room. Someone has drawn the curtains again and she can hardly see. She gropes her way through the shadows until she finds the bed. She has to listen closely to hear her father breathing. She is getting used to the gloom and can see him now, or his outline, at least. How like a wax figure he seems, a life-sized waxen model of himself. Taking care not to displace any of the tubes or the feeding bottles dangling on their metal stand she crawls on to the bed and lies down by him on her side with her face up close to his. His profile is like a line of mountains, seen from afar, at nightfall. There is an unpleasantly sharp, ammoniac smell; she supposes it is from the jars that she knows are under the bed and that the other, unseen tubes lead down to, but behind that there is his own familiar smell, darkish, warm, a little musty. She puts her arm across his chest. He is so thin, hardly there at all, just a scant arrangement of bones under the blanket.

She is wondering how long Roddy and Helen have been lovers.

How strange the way the shadows all around her when she peers into them seem to move, billowing slowly, like smoke, like distant storm clouds. There is a thing dripping in her head, dripping, or ticking; it is often there, or maybe always there and she only notices it sometimes. She hears the cries of gulls, far off, then suddenly near, then far again.

Kiss me. Kiss *me*.

Oh. A sudden start. She opens her eyes—have they been closed? Did she fall asleep for a moment? She must have, for she has that feeling that she always has when she wakes up of stealthy things having been happening that she is not to know of. Not that anything has happened: she is still lying beside her silent father as before, here in the gloom of the sickroom. But something has changed—the rain has stopped, that is it. Such enormous silence, as if the two of them were lying deep at the bottom of a huge empty stone vault, stone, or metal, maybe, a huge rusty iron tank emptied of everything, even air. She lifts her arm from her father's chest and turns on to her back and gazes upwards at the uncertain ceiling. She thinks of her father facing blindly into another world, breathing other, even darker air. Why are the gulls no longer crying? Where have they gone to?

Kiss me.

In a little while she goes back to her room. Yes, the rain is over and the sky is clearing to a delicate, breakable blue. She stands by the window looking out on a rinsed and sparkling world. She can see rather than feel the chill that the rain has brought, for the air outside seems polished and shines thinly, and there is a new edge to everything, sharp as glass. Rex the dog is crossing the lawn; he stops, sniffs, lifts a leg, then after a moment of motionless gazing ambles on. The Salsol is parked on the gravel in front of the house, slewed at an angle. Duffy is walking along slowly by the box hedge, examining the hedge as if for damage; he has a furtive and a watchful mien. The limes along the drive are darker than everything else, as if night is gathered already among their foliage, waiting to be released into the air. These things seem to her set out just so, the countless pieces of a vast and mysteriously significant design. She looks downwards, inwards; how the light of evening pales her hands. Across the back of one of them there is a stippled scratch, like a chain of tiny rubies, where she caught herself on a briar. She did not really mean to spy on Helen and Roddy Wagstaff—how was she to know they would come to the wood? She had gone there, as she often does, to be alone and sit by the holy well and let her mind slow down and soothe itself. When she heard them approaching she hid among the woodbine and the ivy—why, since she did not even know who they would be?—like a child, she thinks, caught at something naughty. And indeed, like a child, she felt a secret, gloating thrill, crouched in her damp and odorous lair, crawled over by invisible mites, her nails digging into her palms and her face on fire. When the pair sat down on the bench before the well she was directly opposite Helen, who she thought would surely see her. As soon as they began to kiss she wriggled backwards through the undergrowth, not caring now if they heard her, but of course they did not: they were so busy, lost in each other. When the thunder crashed directly above her it almost sent her sprawling on her face, so loud it was, so near. And then she ran, stumbling.

She turns from the window. A sense of urgent anticipation is starting up inside her, familiar, guilty, hot. Has she locked the door? She makes sure that she has. From the door she goes to the wardrobe, opens it, kneels. There is a drawer, low down, at the back, hard to notice, an ideal hiding place, almost ideal. She draws it open cautiously, making not a sound, and slips her palms under what is inside and lifts it out and bears it to the bed and sets it down. Within its wrapping of thin tissue paper the green silk shines dimly, like a slab of jade half hidden under a dusting of snow. When she opens the paper she shivers as always at the terrible crackling noise it makes, like the noise of some precious, fragile thing being broken into pieces. She unfolds the kimono and lifts it by its wide, square sleeves. The seams release the faint perfume that she loves, soft and dry, like the scent of orange blossom or dried rose petals; she likes to think it is a lingering trace of the great lady for whom it was made, for it is an ancient piece, brought back from Japan by her father long ago. She undresses, and puts on the heavy garment over her nakedness; the silk lining is cold against her skin; it is always cold. She ties the broad belt of matt black silk and pauses a moment and bows her head, her eyes closed. The ritual has begun. With tiny, hampered steps she hurries to the door and makes sure yet again that it is locked. On her way back to the bed she touches in strict order with her fingertips these three things: the first stripe in the wallpaper to the right of the light switch, a framed photograph of her father on the mantelpiece above the closed-off fireplace, the back of a tortoise-shell hairbrush on the dressing-table.

From her pocket she brings out a ring made of heavy white metal—platinum, is it?—and set with a flat black stone in which an initial letter is carved. She slips it on to her wedding finger and admires it at arm's length.

Where do they see each other, where do they meet? Have they a room somewhere, a love nest? She pictures it, off a mean, cobbled street, up a dirty stairway at the end of a corridor smelling of cats. Lino on the floor, and the sagging bed shoved into a corner, two straight chairs and a stained table with an empty wine bottle and two glasses in the bottoms of which the purple lees of last week's wine have gone dry and turned to crystal. A meagre window with a yellow net curtain and a view of back yards and crooked dustbins. Two cigarettes smouldering in a tin ashtray, one smeared with lipstick. A cistern drips, a voice in the street calls out something. In the corner, in the shadows, his pale flanks moving, her stifled cries.

There is the sound of footsteps below the window, harshing on the gravel. She hides behind the curtain, then risks a quick glance down. Her brother and Roddy Wagstaff are walking towards the station-wagon. Roddy has his linen jacket draped over his shoulders. His hair, still damp, is combed flat across his high, narrow skull, and from this angle she can see that it is thinning on the crown—he will be bald before he is forty. He is carrying his suitcase. So he is not going to stay, after all. Why has he changed his mind—has something happened? Perhaps they saw her, he and Helen, when she was wriggling backwards through the brambles, and they are afraid she will tell what she saw. She supposes he hates her now, for

Roddy would hate anyone he has reason to fear. Does he at least feel ashamed, embarrassed? It is true, he never promised her anything. Does he talk about her when he is with Helen—do they lie in bed smoking and laugh at her for being childish, stupid? Adam takes Roddy's suitcase and puts it on the back seat of the Salsol, they get in, they drive away. Behind the passenger window Roddy is bending to light a cigarette; he does not look back at the house.

She could betray his secret, his and Helen's. She could tell her brother what she saw at the holy well, before the thunder came. What would he do? Would he break Roddy's neck, would he strangle Helen? No. He would be decent and stoical as always; he would bear his pain and forgive his wife, probably he would even forgive Roddy, too. She thinks of him as she saw him a moment ago, stumping over the gravel like a bow-legged sailor in those too-tight, ridiculous trousers he has been wearing all day, as if they were a penance, her big awkward blundering brother, and she knows that she will say nothing, will never let him know how he has been cheated.

She goes and takes the razor in its velvet case from behind the chest of drawers, where she keeps it hidden in the shallow gap there above the wainscot, and carries it to the window and sets it on the sill. The brushed black velvet seems to bend the light to itself from all directions and drink it in. She lifts the little brass catch. It pleases her how snugly the razor fits into its bed of scarlet satin. The ivory handle is cool and smooth, like cold cream made solid, and the round-headed blade is the colour of water. She takes the lovely thing and balances it lightly on her palm. There are raked shadows on the lawn, and birds, restless at the day's lapsing, whistle plaintively in the trees. She shrugs back the kimono's great loose sleeve. The underside of her arm is cicatriced all along its length, the crescents of healed skin brittle and shiny, like candle wax. She leans against the window-sill in a sort of anxious trance, all her flesh yearning for the kiss of the chill, steel blade. She draws in a breath, hissingly. When she cuts, the world suddenly has a centre, everything on the instant realigns itself and points to this edge, where the skin draws back its thin white lips and the first beads of blood make their shy début. She unties the belt and lets the kimono fall open and clasps her arm to her breast, and feels the ooze of blood against her skin; it is warm, and her own, and it comforts her. She waits a moment, then bares her other arm.

Ursula slowly wakes, rising from level to level, from dark to lesser dark, as if through successive shallowings of the sea. She feels herself heavy yet buoyant, a corpse somehow coming back to life. It always does her so much good, a little sleep at evening, disperses so many fogs and fumes in her head. For a minute or two she does not open her eyes, basking in the blanket's warmth, the pillow's softness. As soon as she does open them, she knows, the usual headache will start beating its unbearable drum at the back of her skull, but for now her mind drifts contentedly, weightless as a bubble, touching on random things and caroming off them lightly. She has so many matters to worry about but lately, she has noticed, her consciousness on first waking affords her a blank interval of grace before getting down to the grim business at hand.

Someone was here with her—her son—is he still—? Yes, she can sense him there, beside her.

She is fond of this room, where she and Adam shared so much of their lives together. He was always at his most manageable here, his most playful and forgiving, of himself as well as of her. She feels his absence, of course, feels it painfully, yet she has to confess to herself that this new solitude of the bedroom to which his illness has abandoned her is a surprising and a welcome luxury. Not that the room is in any way remarkable or particularly well appointed. It is large, indeed much too large, impossible to heat in winter and in summer forbiddingly stark, but all the same it has by day a reassuringly stolid aspect; it is like a room remembered from long ago, from the fixed antiquity of childhood, while at night, or in daytime with the curtains drawn, as now, it might be a great brown tent set down on the steppes of Muscovy or on the Arabian sands, ringed on all sides by a protecting vastness. She mocks herself for this fancy yet she clings to it, like a child clinging to a favourite toy. She does not regret moving the big double bed up to the Sky Room for Adam to lie in— to lie in in state, she almost thought—though its absence adds to the gauntness of the room. She felt he would want to be alone, as he always did when he was ill, hating to be fussed over. Even if the bed were still here she would not sleep in it, where she is sure the absence of her husband from it would pierce her all the more sharply. This old couch, or chaise-longue, really, is good enough for her, though it is hard and lumpy and when she lies down on it exudes a mildewy odour that she suspects is a vestige of all the bottoms that have sat on it over the many years since it was first carried in and set down here, at the behest of who knows what Blount ancestor.

She hears the late train going past on the up line.

Her moments of drowsy calm are coming to an end, and the needle of dread and doubt prepares to insert itself again. She remembers talking to young Adam before she fell asleep, remembers saying things, but not what things they were. She should not talk at all when she is in that state, though being in that state is what frees her tongue and lets her speak of all the things that concern and frighten and infuriate her. She must stop drinking, she must give it up altogether, for everyone's sake including her own. She thinks of the spectacle she might make of herself at the funeral, for instance, the drunken widow keening and caterwauling and trying to fling herself into the grave— She catches herself up. The funeral. The grave. The widow. How seamlessly she has accepted it all, the imminence of it, the inevitability. She opens her eyes at last and turns her head on the pillow to look at her son, to plead with him for something, some large gesture of exoneration, absolution, or perhaps only a word of solace. But with a jolt she sees that it is not her son who is there. It is Benny Grace. He has carried the chintz-covered stool from in front of her dressing-table and set it down beside the couch, and sits on it facing her in the pose of a Chinese sage, with his belly hanging over his belt and his fingers laced together in his lap. His shoes are by the stool, and his bare feet loll on their sides, turned inwards with the ankles almost flat against the floor, and she can see the calluses on his soles. He smiles at her in friendly fashion, and twiddles his toes. How long has he been here? 'I didn't want to wake you,' he says, as if she had asked the question aloud. 'You were having such a sleep.'

She struggles to sit up, the blanket getting into a tangle and sullenly resisting her. She is holding something —what is it?—a cushion? Yes, it is the old red satin cushion that Rex chewed up and Ivy rescued. How did it come to be here, and why is she clutching it to her so fiercely, as if it were a shield to protect her? 'My son,' she says, 'where did he—?'

'He had to go. His pal needed a lift to the station.'

'His pal?'

'The tall thin one. Wagstaff?'

'Has he gone? Oh dear. He was meant to stay.' What has happened now, what offence has been given, what umbrage taken? Yet she is glad that Roddy has gone. He did not even ask to visit Adam. She supposes it is the last that they will hear of him. 'He'll think me rude, not to see him off. He wants to write Adam's biography'—she laughs softly—'imagine!' He does not respond. She sighs, casting about her, fretful suddenly. Lying here like this, with this man watching every move she makes, is like being in one of those shameful social compromises that happen in dreams. She is wearing her dressing-gown, she notices; she does not remember putting it on. So many things these days get lost in the increasing confusion of her mind. She looks at Benny Grace again, his fatness, squatting there. What is she to do with him, what say to him? He has an unavoidable solidity, yet at the same time there is something fantastic about him. Yes, it is like being in a dream, so real it seems not a dream at all, and he is one of the figures looming in it. He gives no account of himself, that is what it is. He simply appeared amongst them, as if he knew them all and they must all know him. But no one knows him, except she, and what she knows of him is next to nothing, really. She throws the satin cushion on the floor and struggles again to sit up straight. She sets one hand on her thigh and folds the other over it, as her mother used to do when she was preparing to deal with something difficult.

'I'm sorry I spoke to you like that, in the garden, earlier,' she says. 'I was—harsh.'

He shrugs. 'Harsh is nothing. Harsh I'm used to.'

'Especially when'—she takes a deep breath—'especially when there is so much that I—that we—so much we must be grateful to you for.'

'Not me, Ursula,' he says softly, with a shake of the head, modest and smiling, 'you know that.'

'Well, you, and her.' Ursula, he called her—how dare he? 'Where is she, by the way?' He says nothing, only goes on smiling. 'Adam said she died but I did not know whether to believe him.' Still he will not answer. She intended to be direct, so as to shock him, but of course he is unshockable. She sighs again, irritably this time. He is just like Adam in that way he has of keeping silent and causing the other person to babble on and on, blurting out all sorts of fatuous and self-incriminating things. 'You mustn't think we weren't grateful for your—your kindness. And hers, I mean. Both of you.' All that awful money, years and years of it, just appearing in the bank every quarter without explanation, and Adam not saying a word so that she had to be silent too, no mention permitted, no acknowledgement, even though it was what they were living on, since Adam despite all his fame and his great reputation no longer earned anything, since he no longer worked. What did he think she would think? It had to be a woman, naturally.

The room seems to be swelling around her, as if it were indeed a tent, billowing and burgeoning as it fills up with more and more thickening, unbreathable air. The shadows seem deeper, too, a denser greyish-brown.

'He used to insist there are no great men,' she says, in a rapid murmur, 'only men who occasionally do a great thing.' She is not sure why she said it. Was she replying to something, a question, a contention? She cannot remember what he said last. She feels all the more irritated. What she wanted to do was ask him about the woman: is she, was she, beautiful, clever, worldly, all those things that she herself is not? 'I don't know why we're sitting in the gloom,' she says, with an unsteady, small laugh. 'Would you mind opening the curtains, Mr Grace?'

She looks after him as he pads across the room, his fat arms hooped and his big head bobbing. When he draws the curtains back she is surprised at how light the evening is. It will hardly get dark at all this night, for a few hours only. The thought for some reason makes her feel tired again.

He comes back and sits down on the stool. The light from the window makes a shining aureole all about him and sets a gleam on his bald pate. She draws the dressing-gown close about her. 'I don't know exactly why you've come,' she says tentatively, shrinking into herself. 'Is there something you want from us?' She feels small suddenly, small and crouched and wizened, as she knows she will be when she is old. Did they do something to Adam, this fellow and the woman between them, did they damage him, as she always suspected they did? But no, she thinks—whatever damage there was to do he would have done himself. Only the young can work, he always said, only they have the ruthlessness for it, the savagery. 'He always said,' she says, fingering the blanket, 'that by the age of thirty he had finished all he had to do, that he had given everything.' She looks at him pleadingly. 'Is it true?'

He shakes his head, impatiently, it seems, not answering her question but dismissing it. He has matters far more momentous to address. He leans forward, all confidential, and lays a hand on both of hers. She sees the scene as from above, the couch just so, the blanket covering her, the discarded cushion on the floor, red and swollen like a broken heart, and the fat man's head inclined, its monkish tonsure gleaming. From far off in the fields she hears the lowing of Duffy's cows; it must be the milking hour. The oval mirror in the wardrobe door seems a mouth wide open, getting ready to cry out. Something brushes against her, not a ghost but, as it were, the world itself, giving her a nudge.

'I spoke to him,' Benny Grace says. '—He spoke to me!'

Great consternation and commotion now, of course, voices calling from room to room, running footsteps in the hall, the telephone fairly dancing on its doilied table beside the potted palm, and Ursula's dressing-gown ballooning about her as she comes flying down the stairs like Hera herself alighting out of air intent on burning the daidala and claiming back her aberrant spouse. What shall I say? Yes, it is true, I felt something. First there was Petra, then the dog. The girl was upset, certainly I could feel that—no mistaking my daughter in her darker modes. How I wished I were able to reach out a hand to touch her, to offer her reassurance, as she cowered there on the bed beside me, trembling as she does. That young scoundrel Wagstaff must have said something hurtful to her, or else said nothing at all, which I imagine would have been more hurtful still. For this we shall give him cramps, side stitches, pinch him thick as honeycomb. Or will we? Perhaps not. We have not been kind to him, we have not been fair. He is not such a terrible fellow, after all, only disappointed, unsure, untried. Perhaps Ursula will let him write his book about me; that would be recompense. As well him as some other scribbler. Yes, he shall limn my life, in delicatest washes of blue and gold, and make a great success of it—this is my wish.

When Petra was gone the dog pawed open the door and came nosing through the shadows in search of me. What a racket his claws make on the floorboards when he is preparing his leap. As often as not he fails in the first and even second attempt, and slithers backwards off the bed, scrabbling and groaning, and collapses on the floor in a heap of fur and bones. Dogs are dim creatures, do not speak to me of their good sense—have you ever heard of a team of tomcats hauling a sled across the frozen wastes? Yet when he succeeded in getting aloft at last and flopped down beside me with a grunt and a sigh, I did feel his brute warmth. At first I did not recognise the feeling, I mean the feeling of feeling, and thought I was only imagining with an intenser acuity than heretofore. It would not have been the first such misapprehension I have suffered these past days. In my form of paresis, if I am using the term correctly— Petra would know—it is distressingly easy to mistake an imagined sensation for an actual one. This raises a number of interesting questions in the sphere of idealism, I mean philosophical idealism, and I would address them had I the time and wherewithal.

What was I saying? The general panic in the house, yes, and my experiences leading to it, and whether they were indeed experiences in the full and accepted sense.

So. The dog on the bed, his haunch against mine, its spreading warmth. This was more than my having felt Petra's trembling; this was a sensation in my very flesh, the suffusion in me of another creature's blood heat. Nothing had touched me like this in all the time I had lain here apparently dead to the world after being so curtly knocked off my pedestal. Yet my first impulse was panic, a sort of panic, or fluster, at least. How can I explain this curious and, as it surely seems, ungrateful, not to say churlish, response to the resurgence of feeling, faint as it was? When one is at death's door and waiting for it to be summarily opened, one does not care to be distracted by a tap on the shoulder from someone coming up casually at one's back in the street. It is no small thing to have got oneself properly aligned there, facing in the right direction, with one's exit or I should say entrance visa clutched in an already rigoring fist. I am not saying I was not glad at seeming to be recalled—being prepared to go is not the same as being eager to go—however faint the summons and however humble the summoner. It was just that everything had seemed prepared and ready, and now I would have to turn back, fizzing still with travel fever, and trudgingly retrace my steps at least some way along that weary road already travelled.

Did I speak to Benny, as he says I did? He came into the room, alone this time, and drew open the curtains again—I had been attending enraptured to the rain as it stopped, it is a sound I have always loved, the whispered ceasing of summer rain—and again leaned over me, surrounding us both in a breathy bubble of intimacy, and spoke my name. But did I really respond? I did want to say something, not to him in particular, but to someone, anyone, who would listen. I was upset, I was more than upset. It must have been the sound of the rain that had set me brooding bitterly on all that I will shortly lose, all that I shall be parted from, this frightful and exquisite world and everything in it, light, days, certain faces, the limpid air of summer, and rain itself, a thing I have never become accustomed to, this miracle of water falling out of the sky, a free and absurdly lavish, indiscriminate benison. *One last time among the living*: those were the words that formed themselves in my mind, and so perhaps in my mouth, also. One last sweet time among the living. I did not think it so much to ask, or would not have thought it so, if I did ask it—but did I?

I heard the sound of tyres on the gravel. It was Adam, returning from the station. How smoky the evenings become, even in midsummer; it is like the smoke of memory, drifting from afar. He passed under the wisteria, into the hall, stopped, stood to listen. No sound of anyone. He was still puzzling over Roddy's hasty departure, for which no explanation had been offered. The atmosphere in the car had been tense, and Roddy had smoked all the way, using the last of each cigarette to light the next one. He got on to the train with only seconds to spare, which was a relief for both of them. Climbing into the carriage he did not look back, but thrust his suitcase in ahead of him and sprang up on the step with one arm lifted behind him in a curiously abrupt gesture, whether of farewell or angry dismissal Adam could not tell. Nor when the train started and was going past did he even glance through the window from the seat where he had settled himself, but went on folding his jacket with a cross look, pouting his lower lip and frowning. Well, now he is gone, and there is an end of it. My biographer. He should change his name to Shakespeare.

In the kitchen Adam comes upon his wife on her hands and knees halfway under the sink. His step startles her and she rises up quickly and strikes the back of her head on the waste pipe, and swears. 'My ring is gone,' she says, sitting back on her heels and setting her hands on the tops of her thighs. 'I left it here, on the window-sill.' She turns up her glance to him. She has changed into a blouse and a blue skirt, and is barefoot. 'The one you gave me,' she says. She makes a feline smile. 'Will you hit me, if it's gone?'

He prepares a drink for them both, gin in a jug with lime juice and a big douse of soda water. It is what they call their gimlet. She is still on the floor, rubbing the back of her head pensively where she banged it on the pipe. He brings the tray of ice cubes to the sink and stands beside her and hacks at the ice with the point of a kitchen knife, his fingers sticking to the metal of the tray. 'It makes me shiver, the way it groans,' he says.

'What?'

'The ice—damn!'

She puts her hands to the edge of the sink and hauls herself to her feet. He shows her a bleeding thumb. 'Serves you right,' she says, and takes his hand and squints at the cut.

'Can't feel anything,' he says. 'It's numb, the ice numbed it.'

'Typical,' she murmurs, though neither of them quite knows what she means. He holds his wounded hand over the sink to let the blood drip there and puts his other arm around her waist and holds her close against him and kisses her. 'Mmm,' she says, drawing back her face, 'you smell of cigarettes.'

'It was Roddy, he smoked all the way to the station.'

She fingers a button on his shirt. 'He has no smell at all—have you noticed that?'

'Roddy? He smells like a priest.'

'What do priests smell of?'

'Ashes. Wax and ashes.'

Out in the hall the big clock there makes a laboured whirring and after a weighty pause lets fall a single, ponderous chime.

'Why did he run off like that?' Helen asks.

Adam shrugs. He is still holding her with an arm around her waist, like a waltzer waiting for the music to begin. 'He wasn't well, he said,' he says. 'Something about a stitch in his side. I didn't believe him.'

She leans back on his arm, arching her spine and rolling the font of her hips against his. 'He tried to kiss me,' she says, smiling. 'In fact, he did.'

'Where?' He is smiling too.

'You mean, where did he kiss me, or where were we when he did?' He does not answer. 'In that wood'—gesturing towards the door, the window—'by the well.'

'Did he say anything?'

'He made a sort of speech. Pure ham. It was very peculiar. I thought he—'

'What?'

Smilingly she shakes her head. 'Nothing.'

'So that's why he hurried off,' her husband says. 'Did you slap his face?'

'Yes,' she says, and softly laughs, 'as a matter of fact, I did. And then the rain started. He was very concerned for his shoes.'

'Poor Roddy.'

Now they both laugh, not quite cruelly, and he releases her and turns to the sink and scoops into the jug what ice cubes he managed to free before cutting himself—they are flecked with his blood—and she goes to the dresser and comes back with two tumblers, and he pours out their drinks, and they drink.

So you see, old Dad, she will not love you. We are too much for them; they prefer to settle for their own kind.

Petra sits by the window binding up her wounds. Although they sting and make her bite her lip she does not think of them as wounds but as the marks of passion, love scars, kisses. She is calm; a beautiful peace reigns in her heart. In the garden the blackbird hops on to a bough and pours out its song, and all the evening seems to stand back and listen dreamily. How pale the sky is at its edges, a barely blue, and higher up a swan-shaped cloud of purest white with a soiled edge sails sedately westwards. She has a sense of the air up there, the weightless enormity of it, thin and clear, arched over the world. She is proud of the skill with which she has learned to bandage herself. First she smears the cut with antiseptic cream to stem the blood, then puts on a patch of gauze and winds the linen bandage round and round. She makes a knot one-handed and pulls it tight with her teeth. Presently the first shy spot of crimson will appear as the blood seeps through the cloth, but soon it will stop spreading and as it dries will turn to a rich red-umber, like the paint in an old picture. She sees herself in a picture, she is its centre, its focus, a girl leaning at a window with everything attending her, the bird, the cloud, the hushed, still trees. The sting has turned to a steady throbbing now. She extends one arm along the window-sill and cradles the other in her lap. She has never got even a speck of blood on the kimono, in all the years; that is another thing to be proud of.

She hears her mother on the stairs, calling for her son, for Ivy Blount. She shuts her eyes and lays her forehead on her arm. Something is the matter, something has happened in the house. The heavy silk of the sleeve is cool and slightly rough, almost metallic, against her brow. Downstairs, Rex the dog begins to bark, loud, peremptory, with measured pauses. The telephone rings, and stops after two peals as someone snatches up the receiver. Two doors open, one is slammed shut again. More footfalls on the stairs, heavy this time. Her thoughts drift, calm as clouds.

My father is chafing to be gone. All is done with here, he says, but I think not, not quite, though it is true that to make a happy ending one must stop short of the end.

Petra lifts her heavy head; her eyelids too are heavy; she could sleep, now, but we shall not let her sleep. She rises, takes off the kimono, dresses, then folds the kimono and wraps it in its tissue paper and returns it to the drawer in the wardrobe. The razor is already in its place behind the chest of drawers. She stands a moment, looking carefully about the room. Everything has been put away, everything is in order. She loves herself, a little.

From the landing she looks down into the well of the hall. There are voices, but the speakers are not to be seen. She feels faint for a moment and seems to sway. What a weight her scarred arms are, and as if they were not hers, as if they were not arms at all but something else, thick lengths of liana, or the limbs of a tree. The throbbing of the razor cuts has abated but in the night it will return and keep her awake, and she will feel there is someone in bed with her, this throbbing other.

She sets off down the stairs. Before she reaches the bottom Helen appears. They stop, the girl on the stairs, the woman in the hall. It is not fair, Petra thinks, it is not fair.

'What's going on?' Helen asks. 'What has happened?' Petra descends the last few steps and holds out her hand. Helen stares, frowning. 'Ah—where did you find it?'

'In the kitchen. Here, have it.'

Helen takes the ring and turns it in her fingers, gazing at her sister-in-law, half smiling, with a quizzical light.

'Who is Z?' Petra asks.

'What?'

'Z—the initial carved on it.'

'No, no,' Helen says, 'it's an *A*, *A* for—for Adam.'

'It's not, it's *Z*. Hold it like that, look.'

They bend their heads together over the ring and Helen turns it first this way, then that. 'It seems an *A* to me,' she says doubtfully, 'but I suppose—'

Ah, crafty old Dad!

Now a little posse of people comes in from the direction of the front hall, talking. Adam and his mother lead, with Benny Grace and Ivy Blount and Duffy the cowman crowding at their heels. They have the excited air about them of a band of disciples hurrying towards Emmaus. Adam's colour in particular is high—he is tipsy on love and half a jug of gin gimlet—and he seems both eager and apprehensive. Helen makes to speak to him but it is to Petra that he turns. 'Come with me,' he says to her, sternly unsmiling, 'the rest of you stay here.' Petra asks no question, but follows meekly after him up the stairs.

'Where are they going?' Helen asks, petulantly; why will no one tell her what is happening? There is a tickle in her nostrils.

'It's your father,' Ursula says distractedly, not looking at her but gazing after her son and daughter as if they were being taken up in a cloud. 'I mean Adam—Adam's father. Adam.'

'What? Is he—?'

'Ssh.' This is Benny Grace. She turns and stares at him, but he only smiles, pressing a finger as if playfully to his plump and ruby lips. Ivy Blount too is gazing after the disappearing pair—they are shoulders and heads up there, then heads only, then gone—and clasps her hands before her breast. Duffy shuffles awkwardly.

'I wish someone would—' Helen begins, but has to stop, and remains a moment motionless, her mouth slackly open and her eyelids fluttering. 'Ah,' she says, 'ahh,' then sneezes, a snapping bark, and blinks in the surprise of it.

But look! What beast of burden, burdened beast, is this? Adam and his sister have reappeared at the top of the stairs—they suggest an elephant and its mahout—Petra leading him by what seems a set of reins and he bearing his father in his arms. Old Adam is wrapped in a blanket from his toes to his beard; his eyes are closed; he is not dead. The two embark on a careful descent, as if from somewhere immensely high—the packed trees, the shining river, the dust and blood of ancient battle—Petra still in the lead but turned watchfully sideways and Adam following with stiff and stately, pachydermous tread. Petra is carrying her father's feeding bottle and his waste jar, attached to him still by their rubber tubes. Rex the dog follows, waddling down the steps with his tongue out and his tail going from side to side like an untended rudder. Duffy advances a pace but stops irresolute, and Benny Grace with unsuspected agility darts past him and swarms up the steps to meet the descending pair.

'Careful!' Ursula calls, addressing at once her son, her daughter and Benny's back. She puts a hand to her mouth. 'Oh, please be careful.'

And Helen sneezes again.

When Dr Fortune arrives he finds the front door standing open wide and fears the worst. He is tired and out of sorts after a long day in the surgery—a couple of his elderly patients have been particularly trying of late—and he does not relish the prospect now of dealing with the Godleys. It was impossible to make out what Ursula was saying on the telephone, babbling something about grace—surely she has not taken to religion? She seemed to be insisting that her husband had come round, which he considers extremely unlikely, although of course one never knows with such cases, all of them tricky and each one tricky in its own way. But what if Godley has returned to consciousness? By all the indications he should have been dead days ago—indeed, he should not have survived the stroke at all, so severe it was. Could it be that a brain of Godley's type, exercised constantly throughout a lifetime, is tougher and more durable than the ordinary kind? That would be an interesting line of inquiry, and in his young days he might have taken it up, for he is not just a country quack and used to have a notion of himself as quite the man of science. How did it happen that he got so bogged down, and here, in the middle of nowhere? Sighing, he steps into the hall. His old black bag never feels so heavy as it does on occasions such as this.

If anyone ventures a word of criticism he will remind them all how strongly he advised against their taking the old man out of the hospital and returning him here.

He is well familiar with the house and advances through it confidently, though still with a somewhat quailing heart. Families are impossible when an illness strikes. As if they imagined Grandpa Gaffer and Granny Groat should live for ever. There is the faint sound of music coming from somewhere. He crosses the central hall, where for some reason the chequerboard floor tiles always give him the jitters, stops to tap the face of the big, oak-framed barometer there—the thing has not worked in years—then raps a knuckle on the door of the music room, where the voices are coming from, and, getting no response, pushes open the door and steps inside.

So strange and strangely quaint is the scene that greets him that in the first moment he thinks he is the dupe of an elaborately staged prank. Ivy Blount and Duffy the cowman stand each in one of the two tall windows, facing into the room, like figures in a pantomime, a faded Columbine and her rustic Harlequin, gilded both of them down their backs by the evening's tawny sunlight slanting through the glass. The dog is there, playing the sphinx again; when he sees the doctor he hardly stirs, except for his tail, which gives a languishing thump or two. The french doors are opened, the gauze curtains drawn aside, and a sofa has been brought right up to the doorway, and on it Adam Godley reclines full length, wrapped in a red blanket to his chin, though his pyjamaed arms are free and draped along his chest. His drip stand is by him and the tubes are still in his nose, his waste jar is pushed under the sofa, where it gleams. His eyes are open, and he gazes into the garden, yearningly. His wife is perched awkwardly by his side, and is holding one of his hands and stroking it. One of his feet is visible too, long and slender and pale, like a prehistoric artefact, and this in turn is being stroked by his son, who kneels cumbersomely by the end of the sofa, in a pose that seems designed to illustrate filial subjection, filial love. Hand and foot, hand and foot, as ever. Petra is the most striking figure of this tableau, standing off to the side with her arms folded around herself, each of her hands clutching an opposite flank, and gazing at her father with a look of—of what? Sorrow, anger, pain, all of these, and more? Although her sleeves are buttoned at the wrists the doctor sees at once by her pallor and the leaden shadows under her eyes that she has been cutting herself again. Poor child, poor child. He notices the bandage on young Adam's thumb; surely he too has not, surely—?

'Oh, Ferdy,' Ursula says, seeing him. She smiles, and blushes. 'I—we—'

The doctor says nothing; what is there for him to say? He makes a gesture, helpless and accepting. He looks at the figure on the sofa, waited on hand and foot, as he would wish. As well end here, he thinks, as anywhere.

On the mantelpiece there stands an old-fashioned wireless set, its green eye pulsing. From there it issues ancient music of pipes and plucked strings, tiny and far, as from another world.

Those shiny green shutters, I see them again.

And where is Benny Grace? The last anyone saw of him he had a finger to his lips, saying *Ssh*. Benny has gone, has stepped back into that old rackety machine to be winched up into the flies. Shortly the contraption will return for my father, who would be gone, now that he has given up his girl. See how he strides, as strong as ever was? It is always this way, when he lets them go. Debilitating business, being in love; it puts a hundred thousand years on him, the fond old fool. Well, Father, and what now?

They shall be happy, all of them. Ursula will drink no more, she and her son will go down and ceremonially empty the laurel hedge of its burden of bottles and the rats will come out and frolic like lambs. Adam and Helen will move here to Arden to live, Adam will delve and till as his originary namesake did, while Helen will wear a bonnet and carry a pail, like Marie Antoinette at the Petit Hameau. Petra will put away the razor and wound herself no more. Will Roddy come back and make amends to her? Perhaps that is a little too much to decree—we shall find someone else for her to love and be loved by in the short time left to her. Ivy Blount and Duffy we have already accounted for. What else? Adam, of course. What gift shall we give him? A hitherto unsuspected letter will turn up, a final note written by Dorothy his dead wife, exonerating him of any blame for her sad end. Will that do?

He gazes into the twilit garden. Thick, tawny sunlight creeps along the grass, drawing spiked shadows in its wake. The trees tremble, talking of night. The birds, the clouds, the far, pale sky. This is the mortal world. It is a world where nothing is lost, where all is accounted for while yet the mystery of things is preserved; a world where they may live, however briefly, however tenuously, in the failing evening of the self, solitary and at the same time together somehow here in this place, dying as they may be and yet fixed for ever in a luminous, unending instant.

Wait, who is this? Helen, of course. She rises from the armchair by the fireplace where she was sitting all unnoticed and comes forward now, smiling. Light swells in the windows, the evening's last effulgence. The doctor expects to be spoken to but Helen seems to pass through him, somehow, a golden breath. Beyond him she stops, starts, as at a touch—it is my father, bidding her farewell, his hand on her cheek. He nods to me. I fly to Helen's husband, where he kneels, and breathe a word into his ear. What have I to tell him? Why, that his wife is, as in our antique way we quaintly put it, with child. He hastens to his feet and turns. Helen looks back, and sees his look. She presses a hand to her womb.

'Oh!'